DESPERATE HOUSEWIVES OF OLYMPUS

SARANNA DEWYLDE

Corvus Lotus

Published in the United States of America by

Saranna DeWylde © 2012, 2015, 2023

Cover Art by Dee J Holmes

ISBN-13 : 978-1-948001-33-5 (ebook)

978-1-948001-31-1 (print)

CHAPTER
ONE

HERA

A new goddess had moved in to the empty temple on Ambrosia Lane. She was thin, hollow-eyed and leggy. Just like a mortal runway model. Hera's only consolation was the goddess's breasts were like those of an overweight prepubescent boy—two sickly fried eggs sagging from thumbtacks.

Hera looked down at her own generous swells and sighed. *She* liked them. She'd been told they were magnificent. Too bad Zeus didn't think so. He'd fed her some line about how for every beautiful woman, somewhere, there was a man who was tired of her. A little hurtful, she supposed, but she'd told him the last vestal virgin she'd turned into a man had a better package than he did. Maybe not the best route to go when trying to play kiss and make up.

A sharp sound on the marble floor behind her caught her attention and she paused before popping another champagne grape in her mouth. Hera turned her head all the way around on her shoulders like Athena's beloved owl.

"Don't even think about it," she snapped at her god-husband.

Zeus looked like a goat that had been caught chewing on dirty underwear. Randy old bastard.

"I wasn't..." he trailed off, nodding his golden head.

Of course, he so obviously *was*. Why he bothered to deny it was beyond her. That only added fuel to the fire, as if he believed her to be so stupid she couldn't figure out what he was up to. It wasn't like she'd been married to him for the last eon or anything. She almost snorted out loud. Gods could be so...*god-like*. Hera growled under her breath in frustration.

His tanned and well-muscled arms were loaded up with an obscene gift basket filled with Bissinger's fig truffles, blackberry caramels, Tentation apples, several bars of Mo's Bacon Milk Chocolate and a bottle of ambrosia wine. That was only what Hera could see. She didn't know why he'd bother to take the new goddess food because it was obvious she didn't eat and—oh, *hell no*. Were those the last of her champagne grapes?

He was a dead man.

Hera accepted the fact her husband was a lecherous, lying, cheating, fondling bastard. She'd made herself right with it millennia ago, but the part where he was doing it right in front of her and using the last of her champagne grapes to do it? It wasn't to be borne. Her grapes were the line in the sand. She'd had enough of him taking what was supposed to belong solely to her and giving it away with both hands.

He could just see how he liked it. She'd been faithful to him their whole marriage. Vestal virgins didn't count, because well, that's what they were for. To be fair, she didn't hold them against Zeus either.

She wasn't sure where she'd find a man to measure up to her golden god of a husband, but when she did, Zeus better grab his ass with both hands and hang on tight because he was in for the surprise of his eternity.

Hera smiled, the expression almost cracking her face. "You know what? Go ahead and welcome the new goddess to the block, but so help me I shall smite you both if you give her my grapes. She can have your 'mighty thunderbolt' as many ways as she can stand it, but not my grapes, got it?"

"Hera, I was just being neighborly." He said this as if she'd accused him of something.

"And so you are, but the fact remains my grapes are still wrapped in hideous pink cellophane." Hera twisted her head back around the correct way and stood. She impressed herself by gliding over to him, regally if she did say so herself, and zapping the grapes out of his basket. His mouth dropped open, but he promptly snapped it shut. It didn't do for gods to be running around agape. "Well, go on. What are you waiting for?" Hera arched a perfectly shaped brow in question.

"You're not angry?" Zeus watched her like he would a hungry lion and inched away from her the same as he would any ravaging beast.

Yes, as if that would save him. Nothing could save him now, not all of the careful maneuvering, his lies, or his damned charm.

Nothing.

"Why would I be angry?" she asked as if she really had no clue why he would have such an idea. "You always say I should trust you more. I'm ever a dutiful wife." Hera almost choked on the drivel she'd spewed—and if he believed that, she had a bridge she wanted to sell him.

Zeus narrowed his eyes and took a ginger step toward the door. She widened her smile and was aware that rather than looking like a sweet, doting wife, she looked like a vulpine hyena. He took another step before darting out of the door as if Cerberus were nipping at his heels, welcome basket in hand.

The new goddess could take him with her compliments, but that didn't mean Hera was done with him. "Thalia?" she called out to the muse of comedy.

A wispy presence swirled around her like a silk shawl and manifested in the form of a slight woman. "Yes, Hera?"

"Your father has made me very angry for the last time. I should like some inspiration, please." Of the most ironic sort, she hoped. Contrary to popular belief, Hera took no issue with Zeus's children. She adored most of them, all but Hercules. He was as pompous as his father. He'd tried to seduce her once and that had ended badly. In reality, if she'd taken issue with all of *his* issue, there would be a scant number of creatures she didn't despise. Yes, creatures. Not people, men or gods, *creatures*.

Pervert.

"Hera." Her voice was whisper light like a Tibetan bell. "You don't need inspiration, the ploy is as old as time. Hades has been lonely since Persephone high-tailed it back to her mama." Thalia winked at her and disappeared.

Her husband's brother was as dark as Zeus was golden; Hades was the eternal bad boy. His hair still fell over his brow in the surly way of young men with a grudge against the world, his eyes were blue flame, but she knew they could be dark pools like melted chocolate when he felt tender things. Hera had seen them look like that liquid seduction only twice and more recently it was when he looked at Persephone—the spoiled child of a spoiled goddess who held her breath when she didn't get her way. He'd looked at her like that once, a long time ago when the worlds were young. Like an idiot, she'd chosen Zeus instead. She thought of his eyes again, when they'd been filled with chocolate promises. There was only one thing Hera liked better than chocolate and that was yanking her husband around by his short and curlies.

Would she wear the white Grecian dress or the white Grecian—*BORING*. She hated absolutely everything in her closet. Even her crown was plain. How did a body manage to get saddled with a plain piece of headgear when it was supposed to proclaim to all the universe she was Queen of Gods?

Hera tore it out of her coif and flung it across the pink marbled floor where it clattered all the way out of the door and off the balcony to drift into the ether. Now, she had to buy a new one, couldn't be running around crownless, could she? Hera felt practically naked without it. She maybe should have saved the disgusted flinging for after she'd gotten a new one.

First, to Jean Pierre's. She needed to have her hair done, a massage, and perhaps even a peel before she unveiled her new look and implemented her plan for total Olympus domination. Yes, she rather liked the sound of that. Why stop with cuckolding a god when she could dethrone him and throw his cheating ass in Tartarus where the new object of her affections would be his jailer?

CHAPTER
TWO

ABSTINENCE

Abstinence peered out of the window of her new temple and sighed, her breath marking the glass. She'd heard things about this Zeus character who was currently striding up her front walk as bold as if he'd been invited. It had almost been a deal breaker with her new digs, but she figured she didn't have to open the door. She didn't need Hera smiting her for something she hadn't done. She was Abstinence; she wasn't going to have carnal relations with Zeus or any man.

His arms were laden with other gifts she couldn't partake of either: chocolate, wine, ambrosia fruits... She'd think he'd have done his research before he came over and started trying to get in her toga. Perhaps the other goddesses had made it too easy for him and this was what constituted effort on his part?

Color her flattered with the bullshit crayon. She didn't need this today. Or any other day, really. It was bad enough walking around hungry, thirsty, sleepy, and horny all at once without having to deal with a creature that not only wanted to relieve her of all of her discomfort in one sitting, but was capable of doing so.

This was why he didn't have to try.

Well, Abstinence was something different. If she gave in to his seduction, she wouldn't be Abstinence any longer. She'd be dead. And while that in itself wasn't so horrible a fate, her duties would fall to her sister in her stead. Her beautiful, lush sister who gloried in her excesses, never leaving any dish untasted, any magnificence unexamined, or any dare untested. She had children that needed their mother, a devoted husband who still made love to her with the same fervor he had when they'd first married twenty years ago. No, the mantle of Abstinence fell to her and she would bear it with pride. No matter how heavy it became or how wide the shoulders were of the man who stood before her.

Sweet bleeding Hades on fire. What was that in his pants? That couldn't be what she thought it was. It just couldn't. She wasn't sure what else it could be—a pet toga snake? He wasn't wearing a toga. Damn it. He had been when he'd started up the walk. Now he was wearing CK jeans and a cashmere sweater. Men didn't wear cashmere, did they? Wow. Her eyes were wide and she knew her mouth was hanging open, but she couldn't fathom that beast. She'd never seen one like it when she'd been mortal. No wonder he was such a man-whore. He probably had to be or that thing would eat him alive.

It was a simple matter. She wouldn't open the door, like she'd told herself earlier. Then she was moving back to her own plane and her run down shoddy temple. This was what she got for trying something new. She definitely should have abstained from that as well. Making friends?

Having other goddesses to talk to? Abstinence didn't need this grief.

She'd talk to the realtor in the morning and get the blue fuck out of Dodge. Or maybe that's where she would move *to*. Dodge City, Kansas. Yep. She could buy a nice little tract home, have a garden. Even though she wouldn't eat whatever she grew, it would give her something to do. And she could give it to the homeless. That was self-sacrificing. Legend had it that if she sacrificed, *abstained* for long enough, she could free her family line from the curse that demanded one of them serve as Abstinence. That certainly wouldn't happen if she opened the door and let tall, blond and hot inside.

He rung the bell without letting go of his package and Abstinence had to wonder if it was *his package* ringing the bell. Goddess, she had to get her mind back to business and not on him. Otherwise she'd fail her first test and then her sister or one of her nieces would be stuck with this shit-ass gig.

Over her dead body, no pun intended.

When she didn't answer the door, he simply teleported inside. Yeah, that wasn't creepy at all.

"Hi, I'm the welcoming committee," he said with a lopsided grin.

"I gathered." She crossed her arms over her chest.

"Did you? Then why didn't you let me in?" Zeus asked boldly.

"Because I know better?"

"Do you, now? And who may I thank for your education?" He raised a golden brow.

"Yourself, of course."

"How's that?" He put the basket down on her foyer.

"Your exploits are legendary."

"My exploits?" he parroted while he picked through the welcome basket he'd brought her and emptied it on her foyer table.

"Ah, classic signs of deflection. Repeat the question to give the brain time to work to come up with a good lie. Really, you immortals aren't so different from humans."

"Now I'm insulted." He obviously wasn't. Zeus was still going about his task as if she hadn't already told him she'd be interested when purple harpies flew out of his ass.

"Then why are you still standing here?"

"I see sweet words and gifts are not the way to get between those bony little thighs." Still unfazed, but now he almost seemed more interested.

Wait, what? No. She was not! "Bony?" She stomped her foot. "I'm *slender*. Not bony, thank you very much."

"Nope, I do believe you're bony," he replied with unabashed glee. "But that's not necessarily a bad thing. I like to mix it up a bit. Can't have steak for dinner every night, can I? I think you'd be like crab."

"Excuse me?" She blinked like a night animal that had been struck in the face with a searchlight. Had he just compared her to seafood? At least it wasn't tuna. Then there was the STD comparison and she didn't care for that at all.

"Yeah, there's not much meat to them and you have to work like a dog for what you do get, but when it's finally on your tongue, it's so tender and delectable you can't get enough."

"It's obvious that you think that was a compliment, but the image I get is me with my legs broken apart so you can suck the marrow from inside."

"And what sweet marrow it would be, between those legs."

Abstinence found herself with her back up against the wall and his strong hands kneading up her thigh. She shoved at his chest to put some space between them.

"Tell me, oh King of Gods, does this sort of garbage actually get you laid?" It must work because he kept doing it, but his behavior bordered on needing to watch a No Means No PSA. She couldn't believe he'd spoken to her to crudely.

He spluttered and looked like he was going to choke on his own tongue and he stepped back.

That was much better. "Hey, just because I'm Abstinence doesn't mean I'm a dumbass, okay? I wouldn't have gone home with you *before* I was a goddess. Does that tell you anything?"

He recovered quickly. "Yeah, that you don't know a good thing when you see it."

She rolled her eyes. Abstinence knew a good thing when she saw it and Zeus wasn't it. She even doubted he was a good lover because he was so selfish in all of the other aspects of his existence. There was no reason for her to expect he'd be any different in bed. Unless of course, it was a vanity thing. Even then, she could imagine him getting distracted by a dresser mirror so he'd be watching himself instead of his partner. The story of Narcissus came to mind and wondered what would happen if the gods turned that sort of judgment on themselves.

"Did you have any other reason for violating the sanctuary of my temple or was it simply to get a piece of the new meat?" Abstinence hoped he got to the point, she could say no and then he could leave—all nice and tidy.

"I brought you a gift." This was said as if it would somehow entice her.

"Meant to get in my pants." She rolled her eyes again.

By the time this visit was over she imagined her head would feel like a pinball machine from the frequency with which his male petard inspired her to roll her eyes.

"That's always an option, but no, it wasn't only to give you a mustache ride. We do have quite a sense of community here on Olympus. It's a good place for immortals to raise their children or to live a quiet life, insulated from the mortal world. Although, we have made the move to modern technology. The wife does love her gadgets. Anyway, think of Olympus as the ultimate gated community." He looked very proud of himself.

"So far, I find security to be lacking." Abstinence looked pointedly at the door and then back at him. She wondered if they had some version of Brinks or ADT to keep out unwanted gods who thought it was okay to teleport wherever they chose.

She had this horrible imagery in her head of being in the john and having him teleport in on her in the middle of the deed. Which was stupid, because Abstinence didn't eat, so she didn't need those sort of facilities. Therefore, he wouldn't be catching her mid-deed. She rather imagined it was like the nightmare where she thought she'd gone to school naked.

"Oh, that." He had the good grace to look a tiny bit bashful. "Honestly, I thought you simply didn't hear my knock. If I promise not to do it again, will you forgive me?" Zeus smiled and his dimples gave him a boyish look that was almost impossible to resist.

So that was how he did it—how he inspired everything with an X chromosome to fall over ready to submit to his will. (She'd heard the stories about his legendary conquests that really couldn't be described as XX or XY.)

She found herself smiling back at him, even though

she'd been convinced only moments before she'd rather gargle broken glass than give the libertine that much. He was good. Too good and way out of her league. He'd have her on her back in a month. Too bad she couldn't invoke herself, for herself.

Perhaps that wasn't such a bad idea after all.

Abstinence smiled again. "I suppose I could forgive you this time." What had just come out of her mouth? Get the hell out would have more appropriate than this smarmy flirting. Was she possessed?

"How about a little sip of ambrosia wine?" The cork was out of the bottle and he held two crystal glasses in his hands. "My apology," he said by way of explanation.

"I'm afraid I must abstain."

"You will be abstaining. See, I offered you a full glass. If you decline and only have a sip, you've still abstained, but indulged at the same time. Very epicurean." He promised all of this like a car salesman trying to get her to sign on the bottom line before she read the contract too closely. Yet, he was still somehow likable.

The scary part of it was that his reasoning did make a certain sense. She wondered if she weren't on Mt. Olympus at all, but lunching in Hell with the Devil. Abstinence took a small sip of the wine and when it touched her tongue, it was like dipping the edge of a papyrus in water. It was absorbed so quickly through her tongue and burst in bright energy through her body. She wanted more.

But that was her curse. She always wanted more of everything. More taste, more touch, more scent, more, more, always more. Abstinence would have taken another drink when he plucked the glass from her thin fingers.

"Wouldn't want you to glut instead of abstaining. Never

let it be said I led you from the path of righteousness." He smirked.

"No, never that." Her eyes rolled of their own volition and she was starting to get dizzy.

"I've never met a woman as unimpressed as you seem to be. Or is it all an act simply to make me desire you more?" Zeus asked.

"I don't want to be desired." Liar. "I'm new, so it's like finding a new restaurant. After you get bad customer service a few times you'll be back to your old favorites in no time."

"Why is sex always likened to food? Have an answer for me next time I visit and I won't seduce you." Zeus grinned and disappeared.

How rude. He disappeared before she could retort. Not that she cared. She had nothing to say to the god. Poor Hera. How did she deal with him? Abstinence still saw things through mortal eyes and felt them with a mortal heart.

If her husband had ever treated her like Zeus treated Hera, it would have shattered her heart time and time again. The sex couldn't be *that* good, could it? Or maybe Hera wasn't even sleeping with him anymore. Was there such a thing as the immortal clap?

THREE

PERSEPHONE

Oh. My. Gods. If she had to listen to her mother blasting White Snake's *Here I Go Again* just one more time, Persephone was going to smother the goddess in her sleep. It made it impossible for her to angst out to *Resurrection* by His Infernal Majesty. Ville Vallo's vocals made her think of Hades in all of his dark, tortured and misunderstood beauty.

She'd been devastated when he released her from the curse that demanded she spend the winter months with him in the underworld. He'd said he was letting her go because he loved her enough to want her to be happy. Persephone remembered his hands in her hair, the hard slash of his mouth crashing into hers and that moment with his fingers between her thighs when the universe had stopped still while galaxies exploded for her. She'd been so afraid of him at first; his broad shoulders, his eyes with their curious flames, the strength that thrummed through him like the pulse of eternity. She'd been sure his hands on her would have been like the Kraken trying to hold a butterfly, but his touch had been tender, considerate. He'd waited for her to say yes to all the things he wanted from her, but she'd been too afraid.

Persephone remembered those nights in his four poster bed, dragons and gargoyles intertwined; carved in stark relief. She remembered the solid length of his body and how he'd held her so gently against him, even with his cock hard against her belly. Still, he'd not rushed her to give him anything she hadn't been ready for.

Now, she wished he had. She wished she'd spread her thighs for him and loved him as a grown goddess should. He'd still be hers and she'd be in his arms, in his house and she would be his forever instead of rotting topside with her over-protective yet somehow still self-indulgent mother, Demeter.

Demeter who demanded her daughter's purity, demanded her devotion and commanded every aspect of every breath she'd ever drawn. That wasn't love. If she'd loved her, she would have seen how happy she'd been with Hades. Sure, maybe it had been a little bit of Stockholm Syndrome at first, but that wasn't something one could build eternity on. Persephone *wanted* Hades. She wanted his hands, his mouth, his body and his soul.

Where Demeter got off handing down her edicts like she was in charge of something besides Spring, Persephone didn't know. She couldn't even sustain her own relationships without being needy and grasping. Everyone left her, even her human devotees eventually moved on when they realized she did nothing but take. Zeus had kicked her to the curb pretty early on for that kind of behavior.

She cranked the volume on her iPod. "Goddess, Mother! The 80's are dead. Let them rest in peace." Persephone slammed her door so hard the entire temple shook. Her mother never even acknowledged the door slam anymore. It used to piss her off proper. And that made Persephone even angrier. She had no way to vent her frustrations, or engage in normal youthful rebellion. Oh no, she couldn't do that because then her mother would get her thong in a knot and plunge the world into eternal winter.

It was bullshit.

Maybe Zeus would help her. He was technically her father. Not in the Odin All-Father way, (though, from the rumors, he took that title way too seriously as well) but in the biological way.

Yes, technically that made Hades her uncle, but it didn't work that way with gods and goddesses. They were all related in one way or another anyway, this one or that one leaping from Zeus' head, or his foot... she wondered if any of his children had ever been spawned from a hemorrhoid. They'd come from every other part imaginable; his tears, his fingernails. That would be something to worry about: having another mouth to feed every time wind was broken, as Eros was fond of saying.

Eros, the God of Love, was also on the list of unsavory company as far as her mother was concerned, but that didn't stop her from sneaking out to the garden to talk with him every night. Yes, he was handsome, but contrary to her mother's beliefs, not everything male would try to get into her chastity belt. (Her mother would have a stroke if she knew Persephone had figured out how to get the damn thing off and had been sans belt for sometime.)

Granted, he read her poetry of the most salacious sort, but he used the poems to amplify the magic of his arrows. She gave a satisfied smirk when she imagined the look on her mother's face if she discovered that Persephone not only knew what the word fellatio meant, but that she could rhyme it with six other words that meant the same thing.

She frowned. Persephone was more than millennia old and she still had to hide things from her mother like she was some kind of mortal school girl hiding her cigarettes under the bed. Although, Persephone wasn't permitted to go through a rebellious stage like every other creature in the universe, no. Because if she did, her mother threw the kind of fit that could end human existence and while the gods were loathe to admit it, they needed the mortals and if not their belief, the energy from the stories they told about them to keep them alive.

Persephone had been tempted on more than one occasion to ask Eros to shoot someone for her mother so Demeter would have someone else's life to meddle in besides hers. But she wouldn't wish that fate on anyone.

He was bringing her an untraceable cell phone tonight for her help with this latest poem and she was going to call Hades. She wouldn't blame dark god if he never wanted to speak to her again, but Persephone had to try. She refused to go the rest of eternity without him.

CHAPTER
FOUR

NYX

Nyx was looking forward to her afternoon at Jean Pierre's with Hera. It had been an age since they'd taken a girl's day and went shopping or had their hair done. A quick pomegranate salad here or a coffee there, no time to get to the meat of what was going on in either of their lives.

She pulled the blanket of night around her and sighed. There was a new goddess on Olympus and no doubt Zeus had already tried to dip his thunderbolt into her cumulous places. Why Hera didn't divorce him, she'd never know. It's not like she wouldn't be Queen of the Gods any longer. That title was hers until she croaked or chose to pass it on.

Unless she had hatched some evil plan to make him pay and Nyx could definitely be on board for that. In fact, she'd captain that ship with certain glee. Zeus had been dicks-macking the goddesses of Olympus for long enough. It was time for him to pay the piper.

Nyx teleported to Jean Pierre's and was surprised to see

Hera was already there. The pretty goddess already had a white towel wrapped around her hair and the Frenchman behind her in the tight leather pants was cooing happily. One dark tendril hung from the towel and Nyx looked at her questioningly. Hera was a redhead—or she had been until this recent visit to Jean Pierre.

"What did you do?" Nyx asked with a giggle.

"Something crazy, sugarbabe."

"How crazy?" Nyx bit her lip.

Hera grinned and whipped the towel from her head. Her signature waist-length red locks had been cut to her shoulder blades and they were as black as the night Nyx draped over the mortal world until the last two inches of her ends. Those were royal purple. Hera made a kissy face and suddenly, her lips matched her ends.

"*Non!* You promised!" Jean Pierre cried.

"But I like it," Hera wheedled.

His gaze slid to Nyx. "Only if *you* make it up to me."

"Me? She's the one wearing the purple," Nyx pointed to Hera.

He narrowed his eyes with contempt and Nyx shrugged. "What is it you want?"

"I will color no more hair today. But I could be persuaded to take color off."

"Oh no. Not a chance, JP."

He cringed. "Now, it is a must. No one ever calls me JP. You know better, Nyx."

"Ugh," she groaned. "How is it you always get your way? We're goddesses and you're... you."

"Because I *am* me, *mon cherie*. And I am French." Jean Pierre eyed her hair with a satisfied expression.

"If this goes bad, I blame you." Nyx looked to Hera. "I can't believe you started without me."

"I'm sorry, I knew if I didn't do it I'd lose my nerve. Now I *have* to wear something besides the toga, or my hair won't look right." Hera leaned back as one of Jean Pierre's assistants began massaging her hands and dropped a warm towel on her face.

The good thing about immortal make-up, it tended to be water and steam proof. It was really more the experience of having the facial than any of the post-treatment benefits.

Nyx couldn't believe she was going to let Jean Pierre take the color off of her hair. She'd feel positively naked. Her tresses hadn't been without Midnight Number One since 1920. Without it, her hair was silver. Not gray or blue steel like what some older mortal women were saddled with, but pure silver. Like moonlight, her lovers had told her.

Nyx still thought it made her look old.

As the warmth began to spray over her hair and slip down the drain; the armor of color with it, Nyx tried to relax. "The things I do for you, hooker," she grumbled.

"But you love me."

"Of course I do. Though, I will love you considerably less if you don't open that sexy purple mouth and tell me all about whatever devious devices you've got up your sleeve."

"I'm going to fuck the Cerberus loving hell out of Hades."

"You are NOT. Are you? Oh my gods." Nyx giggled. "That will serve blondie right. He's treated you like refried Minotaur crap for long enough. He's lucky if that's all you do."

Good. She was happy to see her friend taking a stand against her cock-led husband. Nyx's first husband, Nod had been a right bastard too and Nyx had sent him packing without a second thought. He'd pleaded with her to come back right up until the day he died. Nyx had cared for him in his end days because she'd never stopped loving him and he'd given her two beautiful sons, but she'd held firm. It warmed her heart sometimes to see her sons smile his smile, or laugh the way Nod had before he'd turned into such a cock, but it made her even happier to know at their cores, they were nothing like him.

"Jean Pierre, I must swear you to secrecy," Hera said earnestly.

"I will tell them nothing!" he swore vehemently.

And he wouldn't. Hera would erase it from his memory as soon as they left. She'd known Jean Pierre for a long time, but she wasn't stupid.

"Well, you know I'm going to do Hades like he's *never* been done before. But I'm a kingmaker, Nyx. I made Zeus who he is and I can unmake him too. Forget alimony, he can rot in Tartarus while Hades wears his crown."

Oh, this was more serious than she thought. "You can't just...you know...leave him? Why do you have to do the whole bloody insurrection thing?"

"You won't support me?" Hera asked in a quiet, disbelieving tone.

"Don't be a dumbass. Of course I'll support you. It's just, if you don't do this very carefully heads will roll, Hera. One of them will be yours. Remember the last time someone tried a little bite of mutiny cake? Zeus is paranoid as a meth head when it comes to his rule."

"I know. That's why everything will be done under the cover of night. In your realm, where he can't look unless you allow him."

"Oh, that's going to go over like a steaming pile of Cyclops shit. He comes to me and demands to see, what do I tell him? Uh, hell no?"

"Yes."

"No."

"Why not?" Her recently waxed and shaped brows came together over her bright eyes in consternation.

"Hello? Am I the *only* one who remembers Prometheus?" Being chained to a rock and having an eagle rip out her still-beating heart from her chest every day for eternity didn't look like it would fit anywhere in her schedule. She hoped to be a grandma one day.

"No, of course not. He can't do that to me, though. I'm the Queen," Hera said in a haughty tone. "He can't do it to you, either. You're technically a titan."

"Technically, but you know what happens when he gets a little bitch in his kitty. There will be smiting and what turned out to be a simple matter between an unfaithful husband and his paragon of a wife will turn in to Armageddon."

"Not if it's handled with a bit of finesse."

"Does Hades even *want* to rule the gods?"

Hera sat straight up as if the possibility he may not want the throne had never occurred to her and Nyx was three bricks shy of a load for even bringing it up. "Why wouldn't he?" She blinked like a velociraptor contemplating which small mammal to eat first.

"Maybe he's accepted his lot in the universe and has found some peace," Nyx said, showing the wisdom that came with her great age.

"And maybe little green pigs with wings are going to crawl out of my ass and sing *Fly Me to the Moon*," Hera snorted.

"They might." Nyx nodded sagely. She'd been around the block a couple more times than Hera had, but Nyx was as old as dirt. Literally. She'd seen a few things and liked to think she knew a little bit about godly nature. Mortals she'd never understand, they were taught the same lessons over and over again, but never seemed to learn anything until it was too late. Gods were different. Or perhaps she was a bit myopic when it came to the whole thing. Still, she didn't see Hades as burning to take the reins of leadership from Zeus. He probably could have done it himself if he'd wanted it; he didn't need to wait on Hera to come down and offer it to him like a virgin sacrifice.

Nyx knew better than to say anything else. Hera was the kind of creature who learned by doing, not telling. Hades would have to tell her straight out that he didn't want it before Hera would believe it even to be possible. She'd plotted her course of action, drawn up her battle plan and nothing would get in her way once she started marching. Even Hades. Before it was all said and done, Hera would get what she wanted. She'd have Hades agreeing to dress in a glitter tutu and dance to Swan Lake if it would get her off his back. She was cool like that. Hera had even nagged Zeus into a few things. It had taken a century of picking at him like a scab, but eventually, he'd caved. Nyx wondered why she hadn't done that with the cheating, but she didn't ask. Hera and Zeus' relationship belonged to them alone and they were the ones who had live within the confines they'd set for themselves. Not anyone else. So it really wasn't anyone else's business unless Hera made it such. That was something else Nyx had learned in her long existence, not to poke her nose into things that were best left alone. She also wondered when, if ever, Hera was going to learn that lesson. She just knew this was going to end badly.

"Puh-lease, girlfriend. He's sitting down there all dark and broody thinking about the unfairness of it all. And I'm going to make it all better. There's nothing a good piece of Hera can't fix."

"Whoa. I can't believe you went there." Nyx wasn't used to this Hera who said whatever happened to drop from her brain to the tip of her tongue. Usually, she had to nag and prod to get to the crux of whatever was on her friend's mind. Maybe this was good for Hera—maybe not so healthy for Nyx, she thought as she considered Prometheus' plight again.

Hera slapped a hand to her mouth and stifled a laugh. "I can't believe I did either. See, the new hair is already doing its job. After this, we're going shopping. I want something with leather and a corset."

"Don't forget the hooker boots. Although, they are super tough to get off if *you're* trying to um... get off, if you get my meaning." Nyx winked.

Hera squeaked with laughter and allowed the assistant to begin working on her pedicure. "How would you know this, St. Nyx? I thought your wild days were centuries behind you."

"Perish the thought, sister. I am more likely to have a one night stand than a relationship at this point. Who needs entanglements and grief? Certainly not me."

"Who was the last one?"

Nyx gave her a sardonic look.

"Come on. Tell. I told you my plans for world domination. I thought this was a give and take relationship?" Hera sing-songed and shifted in her chair.

"Fine. It wasn't a god though," she warned.

"Whatever. A mortal. Fine. Spill." She motioned impatiently with her hand that Nyx should get to the telling sooner rather than later.

"I didn't say it was mortal. I said it wasn't a god."

"Then what?" she began, waiting for Nyx to fill in her story.

"Athena."

Hera squeaked again.

"Stop that, you sound like an orgasmic chicken."

"But *Athena*?"

"What's wrong with her?" Nyx narrowed her eyes.

"Aside from the fact it's a *her*? Nothing."

"Oh, you mean to tell me that after millennia of existence, you've never..." Nyx was incredulous.

"No." Hera blushed.

"Why not?"

"No one—," she shrugged and broke off.

"You should have Athena over. She's really very sweet and has the good grace not to be weird in the morning."

"Zeus always asked me if I would with one of his mortal lovers, but I was always too jealous of them to try and he stopped asking."

"Yeah, well, he was a dick to already be putting it to them and *then* ask the wife to join. No class." Nyx shook her head.

"Absolutely none," Jean Pierre interrupted. "He doesn't even have the courtesy to give a reach around when he comes in for my *signature* massage."

Hera and Nyx both burst into laughter.

FIVE

DEMETER

D emeter had a secret.
Like all secrets, it gnawed mercilessly at her
gut, trying to get out. A trapped rat, willing to
chew through anything to get free. It was stronger than
most because it was a secret fueled by hatred so deep and
pure, it was acid.

Demeter *hated* her daughter.

She hadn't thrown the bitch goddess of doom fit and
plunged the world into unending winter because Hades
had stolen her daughter. No. It was because Hades had
taken *Demeter's* life. As the earth goddess, Demeter had a
life cycle. She wasn't simply unchanging and enduring; a
forever being like the rest of them. Even though she'd
hidden it well.

When Persephone fell in love, Demeter's life would
enter the long, cold winter before oblivion. From that love,
Persephone would grow ripe and bear the fruit of life and
when that life took its first breath, Demeter would die and

Persephone would become the Goddess of Fertility and Spring in her place.

During Persephone's time with Hades, Demeter had grown sick and weak; her body failing though her will was strong. She'd know the second the first tender shoots of love had thrust out of the soil of her daughter's innocent heart.

Getting rid of mortal seed was easy, so Demeter had only ever had relations with her priests. Or so she'd thought. Zeus had wanted her for as long as she could remember—wanted her all the more because she'd said no. He'd disguised himself as an initiate and had pleasured her well. It wasn't until her thighs were wrapped around his waist and he was spilling his god-seed inside of her that she recognized him for who he was.

Her murderer.

Some would say Demeter had been given enough; she should take joy in the cycle of life and be glad her daughter would know a love of her own, motherhood. Demeter would have to disagree. She'd never wanted a child, didn't take joy in the small, chubby fingers entwined with hers, the exultation in watching her run with glee through the endless fields of flowers in Elysium and laugh when the sprites danced on the end of her nose. Those first toddling steps behind her hadn't moved Demeter to anything akin to motherly pride, but rage.

Rage at knowing after those steps she'd grow tall and strong, soften into feminine curves and her baby heart would be a woman's that yearned for things as a woman does. When she reached out to take them, Demeter would die. She'd kept Persephone weak—dependant—as long as she could. Demeter had kept her afraid of men, afraid of what happened between men and women.

Yet, the bastard had gentled her.

Hades, the dark and violent Master of the Dead who struck fear into the hearts of mortals and gods alike had treated her virgin daughter softly, carefully. What turned her stomach the most was that he had loved her—thoroughly. Centuries he'd waited for Persephone's heart to melt for him and his patience had paid off. When she'd been ready to submit to him, that was when Demeter knew she had to do something.

Demeter had prayed every night to the powers greater than herself, although she knew not what those were, that Hades would kill her. She'd been on her knees fervently hoping against hope he'd only taken her in some plot to twist his brother around to his will and when Zeus didn't comply, Persephone's death would be his punishment.

That was too easy for Fate. It would have wrapped up all of her angst in one neat little package and tossed it out of her extended existence. No, of all the stupid cow-eyed girls to soften the Lord of the Underworld, it had been her whey-faced daughter and her golden hair.

Demeter hated her. Every breath she took was one that she'd stolen from Demeter. When the girl had been sobbing in her arms after her ordeal, Demeter had comforted her. She'd petted her hair and stroked her back while Persephone wailed into her lap until her voice had failed her and the well of her tears had run dry. In that moment, she'd known peace such as she hadn't felt since before Persephone had been born.

Demeter wondered if her own mother had felt such hatred for her and if she had, she'd decided she couldn't blame her. It was all a big act, the overprotective mother shielding her little girl from the lusty ways of gods and men. She stared across the yard at the one god who might possibly be able to figure out her secret if he looked close enough.

Eros, the God of Love.

He could see what love lay in the hearts of beings and if he looked into her heart, all he would see was the dark blanket of the love Demeter had for herself.

He'd been coming every night to read poetry in secret to Persephone. But secrets were relative. Eros was sadly mistaken if he thought anything happened in her temple she didn't know about, but she didn't want to antagonize him just yet for fear he might decide to take a good long look in the depths of her heart. He'd find it black as Tartarus and just as cold.

Eros wasn't at all what one would expect from the God of Love. He was shy and reserved, quiet. He was a measure twice, cut once sort of person and that was a quality Demeter respected. She also knew he was a virgin, so she had little fear he was bent on seducing Persephone. That was the bitch of it when one could see into the depths of a person's heart; all of the dark little secrets are shoved into the light of day and melt through the veneer of affection like a splash of boiling grease on styrofoam.

It would make sense he wanted to be around Persephone, Demeter had kept her heart pure like brand new white linen sheets. Anything she felt for Hades was pure too. It would be pink and clean with the sweetness like that of a crisp apple. Yes, while he read her poetry, he wouldn't seek to despoil her. After all, she was the only one of them who wasn't rotten in some way. Aphrodite had told her long ago that Eros had learned at a young age not to look too closely unless he really wanted to see.

And he'd seen more in these long centuries than any of them. Eros was a reserved and quietly stoic creature.

Demeter didn't think that made him weak though. She knew the power of Love was strong. It could drive anyone to great heights of self-sacrifice or equally dark depths of depravity. She wouldn't make the mistake of underestimating him.

"Eros," she greeted. "What brings you to my temple this morning?" Demeter made a show of bringing the snap dragons on the walk to vibrant life.

"I've come to ask your permission to take Persephone to Elysium for a picnic tomorrow," he asked earnestly.

It was a double-fisted punch to her gut. Had she been wrong? No, no, she soothed herself. Eros wouldn't ask her permission if he had some nefarious intent. He'd been reading her poetry, but never had he sought to come in through Persephone's window, or tried to touch her, or steal a kiss. This was the manifestation of his comfort with her—their honest friendship. Demeter was sure that while Persephone may have been the only one he found to be unspoiled; he'd want to keep her that way. Even if it meant not having her himself. It made sense.

No one had ever asked her permission to take Persephone anywhere, not after she'd unleashed the wolves of winter on the world when Hades had taken her. Yes, Love was strong and bold indeed, even when it spoke quietly. It could be a good distraction for the rest of Olympus to see Persephone out with a god.

A smile curved her lips and she schooled her emotions to keep them from blaring in Eros' face. He couldn't help but look if she shoved them under his nose, could he? "That's kind of you to invite her, Eros. Have you already asked her?"

"No, Demeter. I wouldn't do that without asking your

permission first. I know you've both been through a great deal," he said respectfully.

She was tempted to snort. He wouldn't do *that*, but he'd creep into her garden at night to read love poetry to her? His sense of morality was interesting. "You may ask her. I think it would be good for her." Demeter watched him carefully. "I can trust you with her, can't I?"

"Of course." He looked at his feet for a moment. "She's got a purity that's been lost to the world. I wouldn't do anything to change that."

Demeter smiled again. "I know you wouldn't, Eros. That's why you may go. I trust you."

He looked at her for a hard moment and she could feel his eyes boring into her—blazing into her dark places. "Demeter, you don't trust any man or god. But I think I'm as close as any will ever be to that status."

"You're right," she admitted and patted his arm in a calculated move to make herself appear more nurturing. It would have been useless to lie and would have only spurred him to look deeper. Demeter needed to avoid that as long as she could. She knew eventually something would catch his eye, draw his singular attention, but hopefully, all of her planning would have come to fruition by then so it wouldn't matter what he saw. Neither he nor anyone else would be able to stop her.

His amber eyes suddenly blazed to a golden flame—a fire lit by power of prophecy. Panic grabbed hold of her with deadly jaws.

"There will come a day, Demeter, when you will have to love, forsaking all else. Trust or perish." She didn't speak and as the flame died out of his eyes, he shook off the vision. "I apologize. Touch tends to bring visions, so I usually avoid skin to skin contact."

"No, forgive me. I didn't know." Demeter could have palmed her forehead as Persephone was so fond of doing. How did she not know that? Knowledge was power and to let something so important escape her net... She had to bite down on her lip to keep from growling in frustration.

A sudden awareness spiked through her. It was something she hadn't felt in centuries—carnal desire. Images flashed through her mind; conjured by his words. *Skin to skin.* Vignettes washed over her, she and Eros; bodies slick and hot writhing against each other under the noonday sun in the garden—his hair and skin golden and glowing, him taking her from behind in the hot tub, his mouth sucking her fingers as he took pieces of fresh pomegranate from her hands and knowing his lips would work against her clit the same way. She was bombarded by sensation too. Demeter could feel her nails digging into his back, and the smooth muscle there rippling with his exertion as he drilled into her. The heat of his mouth on her breasts, her belly, her neck... All of that quiet intensity inside of him focused solely on her.

She'd always thought of him as a godling, even when he'd grown tall and his shoulders wide. He'd been a boy, a child, the same as her Persephone. She'd changed his swaddling. But there was no longer any trace of that innocence or youth. Where once he'd been baby round, he was a male full-grown; all hard planes and defined muscle. Demeter had seen Aphrodite in the sullen pout to his lips, his large amber eyes, but that had hardened into something else too. There was nothing feminine at all in the full set of his mouth or those eyes that bored into her more intimately than his cock ever could.

Her gaze was drawn down his body to where his traditional style of toga barely brushed the tops of his well-formed thighs. His sandals were laced up to his knees and again, on any other male, she would have found this to be feminine, but on Eros, it only accentuated the very masculine lines of his musculature.

Demeter almost gasped when she saw evidence of his desire for her as well. The hard length of him was outlined against the filmy material and it was then she knew everything she'd seen in her vision had been real.

She wanted to touch him again, but more than a motherly pat on his arm. Why hadn't she noticed how golden and warm he was before? Demeter was both dismayed and thankful at the same time. Even if he was willing, this wasn't something she could do. If she let herself get distracted now, all of her hard work would be for nothing. As it was, she had to hope he didn't decide to delve deeper inside of her because of his reaction.

Her channel clenched when she thought of Eros delving deep in to anything. Sour twinges of guilt were like ice on her spine. He was here for Persephone, and that suited her purposes. Or at least it had until she'd become aware of his cock.

He seemed blissfully unaware of the cause of her reaction and inspected her intently. "Demeter? Are you unwell?"

"I'm tired. I used too much of my power on my garden today. I was tired of waiting for the strawberries. I adore them with cream," she babbled.

Cream. How trite such an obvious word would make her clench again, but it did. Demeter imagined all manner of creamy things, number one being his seed on her lips and breasts. Kissing her after, tasting himself on her and wanting more.

"Let me help you inside." He reached out to touch her,

but fell short of the mark. He manifested a pair of black leather gloves and then took her arm.

His touch—even blocked by the leather—thrummed with sexual energy. It coursed through her blood and made her ache for things she hadn't wanted or needed. Demeter realized to her horror she was in danger of fainting.

She was hot everywhere, she couldn't breathe, her skin was being torn with a thousand thorns and was hit in the face with another realization. This heat wasn't only the attraction to Eros, her body was going through The Change. Her death was certainly imminent.

Double damn Persephone. Damn her.

Who was it she loved? It wasn't Eros and it couldn't be Hades. So who was it? She clenched her teeth against her new predicament, as if gnashing her own teeth to bits would help anything.

She swayed like a willow tree in the wind as she surrendered to her rage. Eros caught her as she fell. He hauled her up into his arms and as he did, his fingers brushed the edges of her breast. Her nipples tightened painfully, every inch of her wanting more of his touch. She couldn't help but wonder at what it would feel like if he was touching her with his own flesh. *Skin to skin.*

The rage bubbled again. She didn't want to be thinking of him, of sex. Demeter had to come up with a way to save her own life, not how to get the God of Love between her thighs.

He carried her with ease up the white temple steps and into her bedroom. "Demeter, this is more than using too much power on strawberries. In fact, you should be able to bring endless droves of strawberries to bloom with a kiss and a promise. What's going on?"

Don't look, she pleaded silently. Don't look to see

what's inside. She decided to hide her duplicity with the truth. Demeter knew he wouldn't betray her by telling anyone and he'd see the bright shine of the truth on her words so he wouldn't look any deeper.

"My time is almost up." She didn't look up at him when she replied.

"What are you talking about?" He demanded and eased her gently onto her bed, but he didn't let go of her. She found herself held against his chest as if she were something precious. The mendacity of the reality was like ash on her tongue.

"I have a life cycle. As will Persephone. I'm aging, this form is degrading and I'll die."

"Does anyone else know?"

"No," she confessed.

"But you drink ambrosia," he said as if that would negate all the facts in front of him.

"Yes, I do. It doesn't change the fact that when my time is up, I'll be dust. Just like the mortals."

"Have you told Persephone?"

"No, and I forbid you to tell her. She's been through enough."

"Maybe she can help you, Demeter. My vision was clear you would have to trust or die. This doesn't have to be the end for you," he said in a measured tone.

"I think I'd rather die," she replied.

So much honesty in one day made her stomach turn.

Suddenly, she felt awkward and old there in his arms. Like he was holding an old woman's hand because there was no one else to do it.

"Go on, I'm fine. Why don't you read some more poetry to Persephone? I'm sure she'd enjoy the company. There's pomegranate cookies and lemonade in the kitchen. Leave an old goddess alone."

He froze; she could feel the tension in his body. Demeter slapped at his arm. "I may be ancient, but I'm not stupid. Did you really think I didn't know you were creeping through my hedges? I'm not angry either, so off with you." She shooed him away.

Eros moved to do as she bid, but he pulled the green silk sheet up over her. "You're not that much older than I am, Demeter. Only a few centuries. Maybe you feel it because you're dying, but if you see a line there, it's only because you drew it."

She found she had nothing to say to that, not even when the tickle of butterflies in her stomach jumped as she realized he had been as affected as she'd been by their contact. Demeter watched him leave her bedroom and for the first time, she felt regret instead of rage. If only things were different. Demeter could have called him back; she could have had his mouth on her, his hands—all of the things she'd seen and knew she wanted unequivocally.

But they weren't different and never would be. No matter what she wanted. Yes, if things were different, she could have loved her daughter. She could have been happy to bring bright life into the universe. She could have taken joy in her daughter's beauty, her kindness, and basked in the love that was a mother's by primal right. Demeter could have been warm inside and the power she used for green and growing things would have wrapped the world abundant life—the way things had been before Zeus had taken what he wanted.

She could have been in Eros' arms, enjoying the act of the divine and the pleasure all of her visions promised. Demeter sighed, her mind unwilling to be still or quiet. During the most intense images, the one where she'd felt everything to the marrow of her bones, there was light too. It was as if her heart had been given the wings of an eagle to soar through endless sea of the skies, but she knew they weren't eagle wings. They were those fashioned by Daedalus—doomed to melt when they came too close to the sun. When he was touching her, making her come with his hands and mouth, his body slamming into hers, he'd whispered: "I love you."

For all that Demeter had learned in her long existence, she knew with those words lay the path to destruction. Even if things were different.

CHAPTER
SIX

HERA

era was going straight to Tartarus—just like her mother had always warned her would happen. The titan had told her if she didn't slow down, she'd go straight to Tartarus in an urn. Now, she was going, but it wasn't in the threatened urn. It was in a purple velvet corset and leather pants tight enough to double as a contraceptive device.

She looked damned good if she did say so herself.

Purple was her new favorite color. Everything was going to be purple from now on. No more white. White everywhere for millennia. Vomit. She'd had enough. Hera wanted bright, rich color and what better proclaimed her royalty than purple? She even had a new amethyst crown set in platinum. Hera was damned tired of gold too. It was boring.

The black gates of Tartarus loomed before her; hopeless and forbidding. They shot up out of the barren and desolate ground to reach high into the swirling blue-black depths of the underworld sky like dead briars in a long forgotten and rotted garden. Ebony roses bloomed along the bars, but Hera knew better than to touch them. They were poisonous, even to a goddess.

It was then she saw technology had even inserted itself down here amongst the ruined. There was a video screen and a keypad off to the left. Hera pushed the call button.

"Fuck off." It was mumbled, so she couldn't tell if it was Hades or not.

That wasn't the welcome she'd expected. Perhaps she should have worn the white Grecian for her first visit—just to ease him in to things. She knew he'd been suffering, but Hera realized she may not have grasped the depth of his pain.

"Don't be a dick, Hades."

"My apologies, Hera. I didn't realize it was you," he said affably in a smooth baritone. "But I'm afraid I still have to ask you to *kindly* fuck off. Whatever Zeus wants, I'm not interested."

"I'm not here for Zeus." She realized he didn't have the video screen on. Why install one if he wasn't going to use it?

He didn't say anything else but the doors swung open and she stepped inside, careful to side-step the latest steaming pile Cerberus had so graciously left as a welcome mat. Gods, if she'd stepped in that thing, it would go up to her knee. Not in these boots, hell no.

That was when she heard it: the thundering of paws as large as she was as they crashed into the ground. Hera quickly drew herself up into her goddess form and braced for the three-headed mutt as it slammed into her, all three heads trying to lick her at once.

She zapped him with a bolt of energy that was not terribly unlike Zeus' thunderbolts. The hellhound paused and sat. He waited patiently for his treat and the affection he knew would be forthcoming from her hand.

Hera scratched behind all of his ears twice before giving him a silent command to take her to Hades. She shrank back down to a mortal form and climbed up on his back and he bounded toward the dark iron castle in the distance.

She'd have to remember to come see him more often. He got lonely, being the only one of his kind. Even with the three heads. Although, the Norse pantheon used to come for house parties and bring the Fenrir occasionally and they got along well.

Before Hades had freed Persephone.

What was the world coming to when the God of the Underworld went altruistic? Next thing a body knew, Zeus would be dressing up like the jolly fat man and handing out presents every Solstice. Hera shuddered.

No, steps had to be taken.

When they arrived at the iron castle, Hera was once again amazed at how darkly beautiful it was—it was like something out of a fairy tale. The Grimm brothers had it right the first time; with its jutting spires and wrought-iron parapets, arches covered with gargoyles and dragons.

She breathed a sigh as she took in the sight before she started up the stairs. This wasn't the first instance she'd wondered if she'd chosen the wrong brother. Hera smoothed her hands down her corset and realized they were clammy. This would never do. She was grabbing her fate by the balls and she'd be damned if she'd do it with sweaty palms.

An unseen servant opened the door for her and quiet rustling of the dead guided her to a sitting area. It overlooked a molten and bubbling lake of red and gold lava. Dark curtains had been pulled aside to reveal a door out onto the balcony.

Hera saw Hades' boots before the rest of him. He was reclined on an overstuffed black velvet lounger; his booted feet propped on a stone gargoyle that looked none too pleased at the indignity of being a footrest. It growled when it saw her.

Her eyes traveled up the length of him, dressed to the nines as a Victorian English gentleman. His riding pants were gray gorgon skin and they clung to him in a fashion that made her feel hot, even though the frigid underworld wind blasted over her exposed skin. His jacket was royal blue velvet and it made his shoulders appear impossibly broad. He held a bottle of Pomegranate Stolichnaya in his hands and he brought the bottle to the generous curve of his sensuous lips as the brisk wind blew his hair down into his eyes.

HE APPRAISED HER COLDLY, his irises burning with a light blue flame. Sweetest Elysium, how had Persephone been able to say no to him? Hera wanted to throw herself on her back right now; she felt like a turtle that'd been flipped by a semi and run over twice.

"What do you want, most honored wife of my bastard brother?" he drawled.

His voice slid down her spine like a caress and slipped between her thighs. If only the power of his voice could touch her in ways her husband hadn't with his hands in centuries, what could the rest of him do? She shivered with anticipation.

Hera decided she might be out of her depth. Why

hadn't she noticed this about him before? She'd been too wrapped up in her own sorrow to notice. Damn Zeus, damn him twice for making her eternity miserable.

She reached out to take the vodka from his grasp and her fingers brushed his; the contact sent jolts of pleasure straight to her cleft. Hera could imagine those hands doing all sorts of deliciously wicked things to her. How lame would it be if she answered that she only wanted him? Would he see it as a bold move, or would he mock her? Zeus didn't want her anymore, so she wondered for a moment if maybe Hades wouldn't either. Hera could hear Nyx in the back of her head telling her not to be stupid, he was a male. Of course he wanted her. She needed this liquid fortification as much as he thought he did.

"Your efforts to save me are misguided, sweetness."

Hera paused; trying her damndest not to think about the way that simple endearment set her blood ablaze. "I'm not trying to save you, Hades. I know better." Her eyes met his over the rim of the bottle and she took a drink, laving at the last drops on the lip of the container before handing it back to him.

He laughed: a bitter sound. "Ah, come down to party with the sinners and the lost? Abandon hope all ye who enter here?" He mocked her and brought the bottle to his lips again. Hera couldn't help but remember her own lips had been there but a moment before.

"Something like that. Is there room for one more at your misery table? I'm tired of eating bitter ashes alone," she confessed.

Hades stood and handed the bottle back to her. "No, Hera. I won't let you slum down here in the dark. There are those down here who would hurt you. After all, you damned many of them. Have a good cry and run back up to Olympus and my sanctimonious brother."

He still didn't understand. "Who would hurt me, Hades? Won't you protect what's yours?" She couldn't believe she'd said it, the look on his face said he couldn't either. The shadows gathered around him and that made her even hotter for him. He was so powerful, so strong, but broken too, just like her.

"Mine? What fresh insanity is this? You told me no millennia ago, beautiful Hera. You wanted a crown of gold instead of a crown of thorns. What I can give you hasn't changed, except where once I would have loved you, all that's left is the endless dark."

"Give me your darkness, Hades. All of it. Hard and fast. Spill it inside me and make me yours," she said breathlessly.

He yanked her against him, slamming her into the broad and immovable wall of his chest. "What has my brother done now you would punish him so?"

She pushed her hands inside his jacket and up the planes of his back and shoulders. "Nothing he hasn't done before. I made him the King of the Gods, Hades. He doesn't deserve the title any longer. I want to take that away and give it to you."

"I'll be far worse than Zeus, lovely Hera. Whereas he gnaws at your heart one bite at a time, I'll rip it out of your chest. My own heart is nothing but soot and ash. There will be no love from me. Nothing but me fucking you in the dark."

She knew his words were meant to shake her, meant to make her fear, but they didn't. She only wanted him more. Hera boldly propped her leg on the chaise behind them and she drew his hand past the laces of her leather leggings and into her wet heat.

"At least it'll only hurt once."

He pushed three fingers inside of her slick channel. "It'll hurt more than once. Because when your heart is gone, the shadows burn. They're just as hungry and needing as a heart ever was." His other hand cupped her face, a gesture at odds with his words and the violent thrusts of his fingers inside of her.

"I don't care, Hades. Do you want me to beg?" She turned her face in to his caress and stroked her tongue down the length of his forefinger. Pleasure shot through her when he closed his eyes against the lust she'd wrought in him. "How long has it been for you? How long did you deny yourself for Persephone?"

"Centuries," he growled. Hades pushed another finger inside and she was stretched as fully as she'd ever been. When she thought she couldn't stand any more, his thumb brushed her clitoris, he was in control again. "What if I said yes, that I wanted you to beg me? Beg for my unclean touch; the Master of the Dead to violate you in ways that will live in your nightmares, but make you come so hard you need it as much as you fear it."

Her slit tightened at the promise, but she eased away from the pleasure of his hands and slid down to her knees. Anything to make Zeus pay had become anything to get Hades to comply. She didn't just want him now for the act of betraying her husband—she wanted him because her body sang with ecstasy at the slightest brush of skin on skin. She wanted him because he could give her all the things Zeus wouldn't.

Hades had always burned with a single-minded intensity. He may not ever love her, but if he was fucking her, it would be only her. She looked up at him—met his gaze unflinchingly.

"Then I would beg, Master of the Dead and Lord of the Underworld. Violate me in any way you've ever dreamed, make me suffer for denying you, only touch me." She unlaced the corset to give him an unobstructed view of her heavy breasts.

"Take it off," he demanded.

She complied, bared herself to his gaze.

"And what of my brother, your husband?"

"What of him?" Hera lifted her chin in defiance.

"Will I be getting his leavings? When I sink into your heat, make you scream, will you be full of his seed?" Hades asked coldly.

He truly didn't know. This knowledge that she would share with him made her look away. She could look him in the face and demand to be his lover, but she was ashamed to admit her husband didn't want her any longer. "Zeus hasn't touched me. Not since before you took Persephone."

At his silence, a heavy weight fell over her and she realized with a dawning horror he didn't want her either. Hera eased to her feet and clutched the edges of her corset together. She wouldn't shatter here, not where he could see her. She'd said things; begged him to... and he didn't want her. "I shouldn't have come."

Hades wouldn't let her turn away; he caught her wrist behind her back and held her against him again. "No, you shouldn't have come here, but it's not because I don't want you."

"Then why else?" she demanded.

He tangled his other hand in her hair, twisted her newly colored locks between his fingers.

"I'm not stupid, Hades. I know if Persephone comes back to you, it's over."

"See, that's where you're wrong again," he whispered against her ear.

"Don't…" she tried to twist away from him again. Hera would never believe he wouldn't take that golden beauty back in a second if she wanted him.

He released her and shoved something into her hands. "No, Persephone will never have power over me again." Hades laughed bitterly.

Hera looked down at what she held. It was a box, simple. Nothing special about the carving, just a wooden box. Hades twisted the key in the lock for her and the lid popped open. Inside was a small, black thing. It was charred and somehow desolate, lying in the box as if it were a coffin.

"What is this?" she whispered.

"It's my heart."

CHAPTER
SEVEN

ABSTINENCE

Before Abstinence had been become Abstinence, her name had been Merry. Yet, she hadn't been at all joyous. She'd always known it was her lot in life to become this goddess of Have Not. She'd accepted it the same way an adult accepts the pain of a needle when they need the medicine inside to get well. She'd borne the trepidation, the certainty it was going to suck, but forged ahead anyway.

On her thirtieth birthday, she'd ascended, having never known what it was like to be in love, the taste of chocolate frosting on graham crackers with a milk chaser, or what it was like to feel a good cashmere sweater against her skin.

She'd inured herself to hunger, cold, and most importantly, luxury. Simple pleasures mortals accepted as their everyday due were denied her. When she was Merry, she'd thought it was okay. It had been, until she'd met Zeus.

He made her feel warm in places that didn't know touch, let alone warmth. He made her hunger for things she didn't know the taste of, but inexplicably craved. She thirsted for the ambrosia wine like her body was made of desert sand and the wine was sweet water from the heavens. She'd never known this longing.

It was more than sexual. That was something she'd promised her mother she *would* experience before her ascension. It had been nothing but sticky fumbling in the back of an old Mustang, the high school football star rutting between her thighs and rubbing at her labia because he thought it was her clitoris. His ham-fists had been rough on her small breasts, but at least he'd said all the right things.

She'd never touched herself then because she knew she'd later have to deny herself whatever pleasure she'd taken. There was something in Zeus' voice that made her remember that so clearly, like it'd been yesterday. A resonance beneath everything he said that tempted her to every pleasure she could think of, every vice and every excess.

Abstinence had never craved these things before; she hadn't known much of what she was sacrificing. Perhaps that nullified the act itself. She'd sipped the wine and nothing had happened to her. She'd abstained from a full glass—but how long would that last? She knew it was a slippery slope. First it would be abstaining from a full glass, then it would be the full bottle, where did it end? When was she indulging instead of abstaining? She didn't know and she didn't want her sister or her nieces to pay the price.

Why had she ever come to Ambrosia Lane? She shouldn't have moved to Mt. Olympus. She sagged down in the chair. Who was she kidding? If she hadn't come to Olympus, she'd still be sitting outside the window at her sister's house, watching them go about their lives without her. Abstinence didn't bear them any rancor, she loved them all. But she had to do something with her eternity.

The thought made her so very tired. Eternity just like this, never again holding food on her tongue, not drinking or tasting, never being touched. She missed hugging; the feel of being pressed against someone who took away all the bad things in the world. When simply being in their embrace made everything better. She missed her mother. Second best was being hugged by a strong man. Abstinence had liked hugging more than kissing, more than sex.

She supposed it was a cliché, but she wanted to be held. Too bad her traitorous body wanted Zeus to do it. He'd be more than willing, she was sure. It would be too easy for him to go from holding, to touching, to pleasure... He'd do anything to get what he wanted.

The sad part was he didn't even have to be attracted to her to want her. She was something new, something he hadn't had and he'd been told no before he'd even toed up to the starting line.

He was coming over again today. Abstinence didn't remember how he'd gotten an invitation out of her, but apparently, it had fallen out of her mouth like a suicidal lemming and her tongue had been the precipice of the cliff. They were going to watch reruns of Buffy the Vampire Slayer and he was bringing more ambrosia wine. He'd promised to only give her a glass and she was to leave half.

She wanted to tell him not to come. She was only torturing herself by spending any time with him at all. He said he understood her predicament and didn't want anything bad to happen because of him, but she'd have to be sixteen kinds of stupid to believe that. His wrath was vast and terrible when he didn't get his way and he'd been known to hurt those who were supposed to be in his good graces.

Abstinence sensed a presence on her walkway and peered out of the window to see one of the most beautiful women she'd ever set eyes on. She was everything Abstinence was not: thick dark hair hung in perfect ringlets, frosted with purple tips, lush breasts were spilling over her corset with enticing cleavage, her hips were flared and round and her face, her skin... Abstinence was instantly envious. Then she noticed the woman wore a crown. This had to be Hera. Zeus' long-suffering wife.

From the smile on her face, she didn't look to be suffering. Maybe they had one of those open marriages, although mythology said Hera was the super bitch of smiting doom. Abstinence found her gaze drawn to the goddess's cleavage again and then back down at her own sad state. She wasn't sure if she wanted to touch them because she wanted them for her own, or because she was girl-crushing. It couldn't be that, could it? She'd never been attracted to another woman. Ever. She'd never really been attracted to a man before Zeus, either, so she supposed it was all the same. Maybe it was a god/goddess thing. Or maybe it was because she'd denied herself everything for so long, she wanted *everything*. It was like taking a starving homeless guy to a buffet he could sleep in. That explanation made more sense to her and made her much less uncomfortable.

Hera knocked; unceremoniously rattling her from those thoughts and into new ones. Abstinence didn't want to open the door. The Queen of the Gods was paying her a visit the day after her philandering husband had come over and tried to get between her thighs. If she'd been another sort of goddess, he was charismatic enough that she might have let him. Was Hera here to kick her ass into another dimension? Shit, she did not want to deal with this.

"I don't bite, sugar. I promise."

So, Hera knew she was standing there. Might as well open the door, she could probably smite her even if she kept it closed. Abstinence pulled the door open tentatively.

"May I come in?" she asked, a smile on her face.

It looked genuine enough. Abstinence didn't feel like roaches were about to start crawling out of her ears, or her hair turning to snakes so she stepped aside and motioned for the other goddess to enter. She didn't speak though. Her tongue was swollen like a snake that had swallowed a whole raccoon.

"I take it from the look on your face you know who I am?" Hera said as she breezed past her. The scent of roses followed in her wake as her heels clacked on the marble floor.

"You smell lovely," she blurted.

Hera cocked her head to the side for a moment and rewarded her with another smile. "Thank you, you're sweet. I get them from Demeter's garden. Put them in my bath and I smell like roses all day. I'm sure she'd give you some, if you like."

"I haven't met Demeter yet."

"She's a hoot. More into the smiting than me, actually. But you know how rumors are. I throw one little fit and suddenly, I'm a hell bitch."

"I didn't think you were a hell bitch, but I will admit I was afraid to open the door," Abstinence confessed.

"Well, who wouldn't be when the wife of your new shag is at the door, right?"

If Abstinence could have fallen over dead at that precise moment, she would have. Short of that, she was tempted to jam her fingers in her ears and scream: "Na-na-na-na, I can't hear you." She didn't *want* to hear it.

"Gods, don't look so stricken. He's a right bastard, as Nyx is so found of saying. That's not your fault." Hera took her hand in a familiar way and led her into the living room where she sat next to her on the utilitarian futon.

Abstinence let herself be maneuvered, not that she had much say in the matter anyway. There was no use pretending she did. "I don't mean to be rude, but what do you want?"

"I want us to be friends," Hera told her.

"Yes, but what do you want out of that friendship?" Abstinence pushed the issue. She knew Hera wanted something from her and it was better to find out sooner rather than later.

"A few favors here and there. I want you to keep Zeus interested. If you haven't let him in to your bed yet, make him work for it. String him along for as long as you can."

Abstinence choked and gave a spluttering cough. "What?"

"You really are new on the block, aren't you?" Hera patted her hand. "Listen, I'm giving you a free pass to fuck him blue, if you want. No retribution. All I want is for you to make him work for it. He'll appreciate it much more that way. You'll keep him sniffing around longer too. Which, personality wise, not so great. But consider his skills in the sack, oh yeah." Hera nodded knowingly.

Abstinence took a deep breath to steady herself and then took Hera's hand in her own. "I don't think you understand, Hera. I'm more than happy to help you, but do you know who I am?"

Hera blushed. "I am horrible, aren't I? I don't even know

your name. I hatched this plan and charged over without even bringing a hostess gift."

"No, no. You're not horrible at all. Your husband is trying to sleep with another woman, I should count myself lucky you didn't come over here and kick my ass. Everyone knows he's married. It's not like I could claim I didn't know when he came over with that ridiculous gift basket." She shook her head with disgust. "But I can't sleep with him even if I wanted to."

"Why not?" Hera raised a brow that seemed to imply she was dismayed at this turn of events; instead of pleased her husband wouldn't be sticking his thunderbolt in a foreign cloud.

"I'm Abstinence."

"You're shitting me."

"I'd never shit *you*, Hera. If I sleep with your husband, I'll die and my sister or my nieces will have to bear the burden of Abstinence in my place. So, you see, I couldn't do this for you even if I wanted to."

Hera's whole body shook as she tried not to laugh. Especially her bosoms. She looked like she was going to rattle them right out of the corset and Abstinence couldn't stop staring. "I'm sorry, but this is just too funny. Does Zeus know?"

"He does. And he's promised not to seduce me." Abstinence rolled her eyes. "I'll believe that when dog shit tastes like ice cream."

"Oh, good for you." She giggled some more. "I'm sorry, I shouldn't laugh. I know from personal experience that it sucks not getting any."

"You? But he's your—," she began.

"I know. We haven't shared a bed in centuries, but I was

faithful. All but for the sacrificial virgins, but those don't count. Not in my book, anyway."

"But you're so beautiful!" she exclaimed.

Hera blushed again, a genuine expression. "You're kind."

Abstinence hadn't expected this; hadn't expected to like Hera so much. Or still envy her, even though her marriage was a pile of crap. She realized she was still holding her hand and her skin was so soft. She knew her own was calloused and rough. Hera was all that was feminine and for a moment, Abstinence wanted to be her.

"I feel awful. I wanted to hate you. You're so thin and delicate."

"I'm starving. That's not pretty," she replied in a self-deprecating tone.

"It's fashionable," Hera said in a conspiratorial tone.

Why couldn't she hate her? It would make it so much easier not to feel guilty for eye-humping her husband or her for that matter. Her eyes strayed back to the cleavage she envied.

"I'd rather have your figure."

"We're a pair, aren't we?" she sighed. "Are you sure if you sleep with him you'll actually die?"

"Fairly. I don't think any of my ancestors ever pushed the envelope. I never met any of them, but for the office to be open, so to speak, something had to happen that they died, right?"

"What if we could find you a loophole? Would you do it then?" Hera asked tentatively and chewed on her amethyst lower lip.

"Oh, I'll do it anyway. All but the follow-through, of course."

"Wonderful!"

"But if you could find a loophole, there's something I want from you." Was she really going to do this? Common sense had fled, so she didn't stop to reconsider.

"What do you want I can give you?" Hera searched her face.

"A hug."

"Wh—huh?"

"It's what I miss about my mortal life. Hugging. I don't know anyone else and if I ask another god for a hug, he'll think the other is fair game."

"You can have that now. Come here." She held out her arms.

"I can't."

"I don't understand. You asked for it. You can have it. Where does the can't come in?"

It was Abstinence's turn to blush. "I'm just going to be honest. I am totally girl-crushing on you. And..." she trailed off.

"It's okay. What's a little perving between friends?" Hera laughed. "You're amazing for my self-esteem."

Hera dragged her into her embrace and the scent of roses wrapped around her. Abstinence was pleased to notice she didn't perv at all on her new friend and what she'd thought was a crush was nothing more than the instant connection between friends frosted with a bit of boob envy. She'd never had that before and hadn't understood the intensity of the instant camaraderie between them.

Hera seemed to know too. "See, no perving. You're just lonely and don't have a good support system. Although, I did like the idea of being crushed upon."

"I *am* lonely," she said as if she'd only just now realized it. "No one understands I can't do all of the things they do. I can do nothing to excess or extreme pleasure or I get sick. I guess I'm not much fun."

"You're loads of fun. Especially since you're going to keep my husband entertained until I've constructed the perfect...lesson. Not revenge, per se, but a lesson learned." Hera nodded as she spoke, as if agreeing with herself.

Abstinence laughed. "I'm glad you came over, but you have to go."

"Oh, he's coming back today, isn't he? Well, don't let him get his arm around you, because after that, you're screwed. In more ways that one. That god is like a tentacled one from the deep. Once he gets you in his grasp, you're toast. He's so warm and he smells so good." Hera sighed.

"What is that smell anyway? It's like vanilla and rum. Only not drunkardly or girlish. I've always thought of vanilla as a girl's perfume."

"He pulls it off though, doesn't he?" She sighed again. "You should get out more though. *All* of the gods are warm and golden. Except Hades."

"You like him?"

"Zeus?" she deflected.

"You know very well who I mean. You shivered when you said his name, more so than remembering your husband's good qualities."

"Yeah, you caught me. I like sullen and tortured better than GQ asshole."

They both laughed.

"With as crappy as Zeus has been to you if even half of those stories are true, you deserve to find some happiness wherever you can. So, if Hades makes you happy, I'm on the wagon."

Hera regarded her for a moment before she spoke. "It just feels like I can trust you, so I'm going to tell you everything. It's only fair, anyway. I asked you to do something without giving you all the details and possible repercussions. Kind of like the side effects on those prescription drug commercials. You should know what you're getting in to."

"Damn, you make it sound like there's going to be some kind of treasonous coup."

"Aren't all coups treasonous?" Hera asked with a confused look on her face.

"I think so," Abstinence replied.

"Well, there you have it. Zeus has been an Olympic—pun intended—douchebag for long enough. I made him a king and I've decided to unmake him."

"You're going to kill him?" she gasped. Abstinence didn't think she could handle it if that's what she was implying.

"No, of course not. But send him to rot in Tartarus and crown Hades King of Gods? Yep. That's on the to do list."

"What happens if it doesn't go as planned?"

"You mean if his psychotically paranoid ass catches me plotting his downfall?" Hera said lightly.

"Yeah, that." Abstinence nodded.

"I don't know. Hopefully, I can protect myself. If not, maybe Hades will do it for me. We dated before I married Zeus."

"The two most powerful gods of this pantheon and *you* have self-esteem issues?" Abstinence raised a brow. Then her eyes widened right as a knock came on the door that could only be Zeus. "Shit, you know he doesn't wait for a body to answer the door like a regular person. Quick, out the back."

"Wait, are you still in?" Hera asked, wide-eyed.

"Duh. Go on. Back door. Scoot!" She headed for the

door, but then turned back to her. "If you still want me to do this?"

"Yes!" Hera hissed and darted toward the kitchen and the back door.

Zeus appeared inside before Abstinence could get to the door. She spared a glance and noticed the back door had swung wide.

"Why do you never answer the door?"

"Why do you never *wait* for me to answer the door?"

"Was someone here?" he asked carefully.

"Is that your business?"

He looked startled for a moment before he laughed. "I am a jealous god. I want your attentions only for me."

"What if I said the same thing? Hmm? I didn't ask where you were all day."

"You're not my wife."

"And if your wife asked, would you tell her?" she volleyed.

"No."

"Why not?"

"I'm a god. She should mind her place."

Abstinence had a hard time not letting her jaw drop at that one. Her place? Dick. "I wonder how you'd feel about it if you asked her where she'd been and she declined to tell you?"

"I don't care what she does, so I don't ask."

"I bet that would change if she were banging the shit out of, say, Poseidon?"

"Have you heard something?" He narrowed his eyes at her.

"No, just an example." Abstinence shrugged as if she couldn't care less.

He studied her for a moment. "Let's not talk about my wife."

"Why not? I met her today." Abstinence was having more fun with this than she probably should have. It was just that he was so sure of himself, so sure of his place in the universe and really believed he wasn't governed by the rules that applied to everyone else. So the startled look on his face pleased her immensely. It made her wonder what other things she could say that would shock him.

"You what?"

"She's hot." Another blow he wasn't expecting, by the look on his face.

His eyes glazed over. "Yeah? Because you know we could—,"

Why did this reaction not surprise her? She interrupted him. "Maybe. But I don't want to, you know, die to do it. So why don't you work on finding me a loophole?" This flirting thing wasn't as hard as she'd thought it would be. "But you already said you didn't want to talk about your wife. So let's talk about you while we get the DVD fired up." Abstinence gave him a guileless smile. All males like to talk about themselves, or so her sister had been fond of saying. She was about to put all of that sage advice her sister had handed down to her in those midnight whisper sessions to use.

CHAPTER

EIGHT

PERSEPHONE

"You can't be here," Persephone squeaked when she saw Eros coming up the stairs to her room. Holy balls, her mother would skin him like a rabbit and wear him like a winter coat. Demeter would have a two-headed epileptic cow if she knew Eros was not only in the house, but on his way up to see her. In her bedroom. She'd die of the horror and then she'd smite everything for miles. It would be nothing short of Chernobyl.

"No, it's okay. She's the one who let me in." Eros took another step to stand on the foyer.

Persephone narrowed her eyes. "Uh-huh. What kind of arrow did you shoot her with to get her to do that?" It would've had to have been one that knocked her out for oh, say the next year.

"A really sharp one." The corner of his mouth curved up in a smirk.

Seriously, there would have to be something wrong with Demeter on a basic level to let a god in the house. "No, really. Is she okay? She must be sick or something." Persephone stepped around him to go down the stairs, but he grabbed her wrist.

"She'll be okay, but she actually *is* kind of sick. Demeter is resting in her room."

"Oh no! Let go of me. I have to go see if she needs me." She tugged at his grasp and continued down the stairs.

"No, Persephone," he admonished gently. "You don't. You need to let her be on her own and you, you'll come with me."

"Have you lost your mind? I can't leave with you."

"I have her *permission*." He said the last word as if it was a coveted sweet and it stopped her dead in her tracks.

"You're kidding?" Persephone's eyes went wide. She knew she probably looked like a startled anime character, but she couldn't help it. Demeter had told her shit would stick to the moon like peanut butter before she let some sex fiend god take her anywhere. Not that she thought Eros was a sex fiend. In fact, he'd been nothing but a resident of the friend zone (in the good way) the whole time she'd known him. He seemed to be comfortable there. Demeter had always told her gods would do anything to get into her knickers, even lurk in the friend zone until the time to strike was ripe.

"Nope. I can take you out and about today and I told her about the picnic in Elysium."

"She must really be feeling horrible." Persephone wrinkled her nose. "Wait, is she on her death bed or something?"

Eros' face was unreadable, but he shook his head. "She just knows I'm not going to pounce on you like any other number of gods would. She probably thinks I'm gay."

"No, you have to be something special. She *knows*

Hermes is gay and she still wouldn't let me go to a movie with him."

"That was down in the mortal world. Persephone, you're beautiful. Men are as bad as gods. She didn't trust Hermes could protect you. It's the flying shoes."

"Then why wouldn't she let me go have lunch at his house?" She practically stomped her foot. Persephone was still angry about that.

"Because he's shagging Hypnos, who is known to be bisexual."

"I don't understand why keeping me a virgin was so important anyway. I mean, Spring has to fornicate to give birth to the world, right? What's so great about being untouched?"

"I don't know. Maybe she just wanted better for you than what she got from Zeus."

Persephone grew quiet at that. She knew her mother had suffered because of her father. He was such an asshole. She didn't know why all of the goddesses let him get away with it. They had all of this power, why didn't they tighten his leash and jerk it around a few times when he got out of line? So he was King of the Gods. Well, so what?

It was as if Eros could see her thoughts. He held up his hands in a deflective gesture. "Hey, I couldn't do anything with him. Neither could my mother. So I don't know what you expect any of the rest of them to do."

"It's just... it pisses me off."

"You look like your mom when you make that face."

"Shut-up, I do not." Elysium forbid she ever looked like her mother. Although, she had to admit that Demeter's green hair was kind of cool.

"You do. But it's not a bad thing."

"What was that?" She studied him; apprehension and awareness were twin serpents coiled in her belly.

"What was what?" Eros tried to look innocent.

"That. The face you made talking about my— Oh. My. Gods. You've got it for my *mother*. That's kind of icky."

"Why is it icky?" Eros asked as if he couldn't fathom why she'd think it was icky he was crushing on her *mother*.

"Oh, damn. You couldn't even deny it, could you? Why? I really don't want those images in my head."

"Have you ever looked at your mother? She's a woman. She's spent her existence caring for you, but that doesn't mean she doesn't have a woman's desires."

"Yeah, I'm the eternal toddler," she snorted derisively. "I can hear it now. *Sephone's mom has got it goin' on, she's all that I want...*" Persephone sang to the tune of *Stacy's Mom* by Fountains of Wayne.

"It's not that bad, Persephone. Plus, I don't have to tell you 'you're just not the girl for me'." He laughed. "She needs a little help getting past that and everyone is too afraid of her wrath to do it. But I think this will help." Eros pressed a cell phone into her hand.

"Thank you, thank you, thank you!" She threw herself against him in a hug. He kissed her chastely on the forehead.

"Hurry up and get changed. We'll go somewhere private where you can call him, okay?" Persephone got the impression he was herding her like he would a small child, but he'd been too kind and too good a friend for her to let it make her angry. If she didn't want to be treated like a child, she shouldn't still be acting like one.

Persephone darted to her room and began flinging clothes everywhere. She didn't know why she cared about how she looked; it wasn't like Hades would be able to see her over the phone. Unless Eros had popped for one of those smart vid phones, but it was going to be hard enough to make that call as it was without worrying about her hair, her makeup, or if she looked fat on the screen.

All of that aside, Persephone knew in her heart she'd wounded Hades to the very core. She'd taken his heart, something the Lord of the Underworld wouldn't have easily surrendered. She hadn't meant to hurt him, but her leaving had cut her too.

Persephone hadn't understood it at the time when he'd sent her back to Demeter. He hadn't really explained it to her. He'd hauled her topside and without even a goodbye, he'd left her there. He'd said it was because he loved her and she believed him. Not because her mother would kill the world of man, not because Zeus demanded her return. No, Hades couldn't have given two shits less about any of that. Tartarus was a self-sustained community. There were enough souls to keep him in business forever and a day, regardless of what happened on Olympus.

He'd done it because he'd thought she was unhappy, that she didn't want him. But nothing could be further from the truth. Persephone had let her fear of him rule her choices for too long. In all of their time together, he'd frightened her more times than she could count, but he'd never hurt her.

She'd give anything to have his arms around her again, for his harsh whisper in her ear and his hands on her flesh. She dreamt of him touching her, but instead of staying his hand, she surrendered to him. Before she could have any of that, she needed his forgiveness.

While she didn't want to hurt Demeter, it was the way of all living things to leave their nest and fly free to put down their own roots and grow—to form their own seeds and fling them out into the world. Persephone was ready to take that chance. She could only hope it wasn't too late to take it with Hades. She'd been a child long enough. Persephone thought of Eros who'd been born a year after she had and he was a god grown. Even though her mother had been protecting her, she couldn't help but feel Demeter had done her a grave disservice. Not all gods were Zeus.

Persephone hadn't even considered what she'd do if Hades didn't forgive her. Truthfully, it didn't matter. No matter what, she was going to Tartarus. If she had to throw herself on the steps of his castle and wait until he deigned she was worthy of redemption, she would. After all, he'd waited centuries for her. He'd not touched another woman so long as she'd been under his roof. Gods, why hadn't she seen the depth of his devotion? She'd been so utterly stupid to throw it away. Yes, then she'd been the spoiled child everyone thought her to be by playing with her toy until she broken it.

Maybe if she could just tell him she loved him, it would be enough. It was selfish of her to hope for that, she knew. Persephone was aware she deserved every cruelty he could serve her and then some. She'd eat it all with a smile if it would get her back in his arms.

She touched her fingers to her lips, remembering when they'd been swollen with his kisses. They'd been her first and would be her last. Persephone never wanted another kiss on her lips but his.

Eros knocked on her door. "Hurry up."

"I'm coming!"

"You're not even breathing heavy."

"Shut-up, Eros." Persephone laughed.

"Listen," he began as she opened the door. "I have to tell you something before you call him."

Dread slapped her in the face. Had he met someone else? Had he already forgotten her? No, that couldn't be it. A god didn't wait centuries for his would-be lover to say yes and then... Or maybe they did. Persephone strengthened her resolve. She had no right to be angry or hurt about anything he'd done to deal with the pain she'd given him. It was remembering that that would be the most difficult part.

"My mother did something for him. Something I don't know if he can come back from."

"What do you mean?" she cried out more loudly than she meant to.

"Shh."

"Then tell me!"

"She took his heart," he said simply.

"No, she couldn't have. It's mine." Persephone's brows drew together.

Eros smiled sadly. "He begged her, Persephone. The proud, dark Lord of the Underworld on his knees before the Goddess of Love in all her golden light. She took pity on him, his pain was devouring him. She took it beating from his chest and locked it away so nothing could ever hurt him like that again."

Persephone swallowed hard against the despair that threatened to strangle her. Was everything lost to her now? It didn't matter. "I still have to try," she said in a shaky voice.

"I know you do. Your love for him is as bright as anything I've ever seen, Persephone. If anything could spark his heart back to life, I think it would be you. It's not going to be easy though. His heart is gone, all he's got left are shadows. When you light the dark places and the shadows are gone, what will be left?" Eros asked her softly. "Only hollow spaces. You'll have to love him enough for both of you for awhile. Indifference will be kind compared to the hate that will burn inside of him when he begins feeling again. If he ever does."

"I don't understand. I thought he would hate me first, if he had to." Persephone knew she sounded pathetic, but she couldn't help it.

"Oh no, little one. Love and Hate are kissing cousins. Both take much passion, much of the soul. When there's nothing there, you can't have either."

"Can't your mother just put it back? She took it, why can't she put it back?" she cried and buried her face in Eros' shoulder.

"You know it doesn't work that way. If you want him, you're going to have to earn it, Persephone. Through fire, blood and tears. If you truly love him, you won't let that stop you."

"It's just, I had it before. Right in my hands and not only did I let go, I threw it away. I know it's wrong to want to walk back to that point in time and hold on, but I can't help it."

"Come on, we better go. You can only get cell service in Tartarus when the stars are in certain spots, so we have to get moving. You have to decide if you want to do this after all I've told you."

She pulled away from the embrace meant to soothe her. For some reason, it felt important to answer while she was standing on her own two feet, with nothing and no one else supporting her but her own strength.

"Yes." As soon as she said it, Persephone felt something heavy click into place around her. It was weighty like armor, thick like a geis, but was welcome like a vow. She knew for better or worse, she was bound to Hades for eternity.

"Let's go."

"Where are we going? Is there anywhere in Olympus that's private?"

"For matters of the heart, I think the grotto in my mother's temple would appropriate. Plus it gets great reception."

"Thank you for doing this for me, Eros."

"I'm the God of Love. Did I have a choice?" He rolled his eyes.

"You know you did. Thank you for being my friend."

"Of course, Persephone. I love you," he said with ease.

In Persephone's limited experience, she knew he was the only god who could say that out loud and mean it, even to a friend. Demeter had told her gods didn't say things like that and if they did, they meant it only until fluids had been swapped.

"I love you too, Eros. Even if you are trying to get in my mother's toga."

"She doesn't even wear a toga."

"Semantics."

"Which should always be clear when dealing with an immortal," he corrected.

"You sound like my mother."

"She's not wrong about everything, you know." Eros cast her a sly glance.

"I know, but... gods, I need some space."

"I know. I think you're going to get more of it than you bargained for, Persephone."

"Is that a be careful what you ask for sort of thing?"

"Yeah, something like that."

"You're old for your years, Eros. You hand down advice like you're a titan or something." She rolled her eyes.

"What's the one thing people have the most trouble with in life? Men and gods?"

"Love," she replied as if reading from a script.

"So, I do have a tiny bit of experience in the ways of these things."

"I know you do, but what happened to spontaneity? Did you ever think about simply grabbing my mother and planting one on her? I mean, if that's what you want?" She screwed up her face in an expression that proclaimed she couldn't imagine anyone wanting that, but this was her version of being supportive.

"Advice from a self-proclaimed toddler?"

"Yeah. Kids say the darndest things. Or what was that other one? From out of the mouths of babes?" she shot back.

Eros made it a point to look her up and down. "I don't think they meant *that* kind of babe."

"You're not as innocent as you'd have my mother believe."

"Actually..." he shook his head. "Never mind. Are you ready?" Eros didn't wait for her to answer, but willed their transport to his mother's temple.

NYX

"Thanatos!" she cried when she saw her oldest son lounging on her temple steps.

"Hey, Ma." He stood and endured her hug.

"I thought you were working all week. Wasn't there a natural disaster in South America?"

"Wouldn't you know it, it's so cool. Red Cross showed up and the volunteers saved a bunch of people."

Nyx hadn't seen him in what felt like a century. In fact, she almost started counting on her fingers to see if it had been that long. "I suppose you're hungry. Fig cakes with cream cheese frosting?"

Thanatos patted his flat stomach. "You know me so well."

"Why are you outside? You could have gone in, you know." Nyx pushed the door open.

"I didn't want to startle you. Might fall and break a hip and I'd feel bad." He shrugged.

"You little shit," she laughed. He was always teasing her about her age. She was a Titan after all and older than all of the gods. She was one of the last of the old guard; one Zeus was sure wouldn't try to overthrow his power. He was mistaken about that one, only she didn't want the power herself. She wanted him to stop treating Hera like crap. Or divorce her. That at least, would be honest.

He smirked back at her. Of her two sons, Thanatos was most like her. She loved her children the same, but she had a special kinship with Thanatos.

"So uh, what's the deal with Persephone and Hades?" he asked as he followed her inside.

Tartarus on cracker! What was with that girl that these dark types were so stuck on her? Was it because she was blond? Nyx just didn't get it. Not that she had anything against the girl, but it wasn't like she was as pretty as Hera. Or as smart as Athena.

"You have been out of the gossip loop for awhile, yeah? They broke up, so to speak."

"He let her go? Dumbass." Thanatos shook his head.

"What would you have him do? Sacrifice the world for her?"

"Well, yeah," Thanatos answered as if that were the only reasonable response.

Nyx couldn't argue with that, but she tried anyway. "Hades released her from the curse too. He didn't want her to be unhappy."

At that, her son was silent for a moment. "So how hard do you think Demeter would smite me if I asked Persephone out?"

"She better not smite you, or I'll kick her ass up over her shoulders. She has winter, but I'll drench the world in

74

eternal night if she tries." Nyx was thoughtful for a moment. "Unless of course you were unreasonably handsy or demanding. Or acted like Zeus. Or—,"

"I get the picture, Ma. By the way, you look great."

"You're just saying that because my hair looks like yours now." She scowled.

"Moonlight and stardust. No one can resist." He smirked as if it was just his trial to bear, being that attractive.

"Nice deflection. I mean what I said. If you want Persephone, do what you will, but don't be a dick. Got it?"

"Yeah, Ma. Don't be a dick. Got it," he recited dutifully.

"So I have to ask. What's with you dark and tortured types and this girl?"

"I dunno. She's hot. It's not like I want to marry her or anything. It would just be a date. Maybe a kiss." He considered for a moment. "Maybe something else."

"That girl is a virgin, Thanatos." Yes, he was her son and she loved him dearly, but he was one-hundred percent male —thinking with his parts. She had to struggle not to sigh.

"She's probably got a family of bats living in there after all this time. Don't you think it would be okay if she—,"

"You know, we so don't need to have this conversation." She threw her hands up in defeat. Nyx loved that her boys talked to her, confided in her, but there were some things a mother just didn't need to know.

"Why not? Not getting any?"

"What did I say about being a dick? You'll keep a civil tongue in your head if you want fig cakes."

"Sorry," he apologized immediately. "It's just I heard from a friend Apollo was checking you out when you left Jean Pierre's."

"And *he* wanted you to ask me if I was, and I quote, getting any?"

"No." He hung his head. "Yeah."

Nyx took a deep breath and rolled her eyes skyward. "That friend wouldn't happen to *be* Apollo, would it?"

"No, it was Artemis."

"Does everyone know my business?" Nyx complained as she dropped the batter for the cakes in the pan.

"You know how it is on the Lane."

"Is that why you never come see me anymore?" She couldn't resist one little jab.

"Don't start. You know I've got work. If you want me to let you make those fig cakes, you'll knock it off."

The kid had a point. She was more than happy to cook for him and he knew even with his smart mouth he still had her wrapped around his little finger.

"Fine, you win."

"You should really go see what Apollo is up to."

"I know exactly what he's up to. 6'4 and it's no surprise they stack bullshit that high."

"Harsh, Ma. Totally harsh." He shook his head at the indignity.

"When you say 'totally' like that, you sound like some kind of sick hybrid of goth surfer."

"Cool."

"Not so much. Blows your cred."

"My cred can take it." He sat down at the table to wait for his fig cakes. "Are you really not interested in the sun god, or is it because you think he's too young for you?"

"He's one of your friends, Thanatos. That would be weird." She putzed around the kitchen with a few more busy-work chores. Something to keep her hands busy.

76

"If it doesn't bother me, why should it bother you? You were old when the Dead Sea was sick." He snickered.

"One more age joke, just one more," she warned.

"And you'll what? Get younger?" Thanatos didn't simply laugh this time, he cackled like an over-caffeinated hyena.

Nyx threw a pan at him and he easily dodged it.

"You're off your game. You could practice by throwing them at Hypnos."

"He doesn't come over unless he and Hermes are fighting. You know Hermes travels so much and he likes to take Hypnos with him and I understand. Although my aim suffers." She gave a long suffering sigh as if she bore the travails of the world on her shoulders. "They've promised to come for Brumalia."

"Ma, keep up. It's Christmas now."

"I didn't like that Saturnalia fad."

"Again, Ma, when the Dead Sea was sick..."

"Christmas. Fine. Whatever. Call it whatever you want, all I care about is my boy coming to visit. You're coming too, aren't you?" Ha! She'd snuck in the invite while he was there in front of her. Thanatos had no problem telling her no on the phone, but in person? She owned his ass.

"Ma, you know Christmas is always busy for me. I have to work. So many unhappy mortals."

"You're upper management. The peons work the holidays. That's how it's supposed to work."

"They have families too."

"Just for a bit of ambrosia wine and a few canapés? Really, when was the last time you saw your brother?"

"Uh,"

"See? It would make me very happy, Thanatos. And I promise, no nagging if you have to leave."

"Okay, but only if you'll talk to Apollo."

He was picking up some of her better tricks. She'd have to try harder.

"Were you even listening?" No, he probably hadn't been. Thanatos had always had a strong will and he heard exactly what he wanted to. Selected deafness seemed to be something all children suffered from, whether they be mortal or godling. It was enough make her pull out her hair.

"Good, so it's okay I told him to pick you up tonight at eight."

"You've lost your damn mind."

"No, just wait before you whip out the crotch puppet."

"I don't have a *crotch puppet*, son. Do you need an anatomy lesson too, because I thought we had this discussion when you were much younger? Though, given my advanced age, I could be mistaken." Her words dripped with sarcasm like honey from a hive, but definitely not sweet. Maybe honey that had been made from the nectar of the Corpse Flower.

"Look, it's a good idea. He even agreed to take you out at night. When it's your time. You'll be in charge."

"As if I need the cover of darkness to protect me from Apollo. Please." She almost said *bitch,* please. Nyx was always in charge.

"He'll bring his horses and the chariot. He even said you could drive at dawn."

Now this appealed to Nyx. She loved the dawn and watching his fiery horses streak across the sky. She watched every morning before she fell asleep. Not that she'd tell her son or Apollo that little tidbit.

"I guess, but it's just this one time."

"What if you have fun?"

Nyx didn't discount it was a possibility. "Then I'll have fun the one time. I'm not looking for a relationship right now."

"So don't have one."

"I won't."

"Nothing says you can't hit it and quit it." Thanatos gave a pragmatic shrug and tried to goad her further.

"Still not having this discussion."

"Whatever, Ma. What are you going to wear?"

"This?" She motioned down at herself.

"No."

"Are you sure Hypnos is the gay one?" She didn't see what was wrong with what she had on. Jeans and a soft, cotton t-shirt were her favorite things to wear.

"Bisexual, Ma."

"Whatever. He's a brand snob like Jean Pierre. I'm surprised they don't shop together and take you with them."

"You can call me gay until the golden sheep wander home, but that won't change the fact you're not leaving this temple to go out with *my* friend in *that*."

She had to fight a smile. It was odd, but in the old days, none of the gods or goddesses labeled themselves or their orientation. During the time with the Greeks, it was a free for all. The same with the Romans. And then modern civilization happened and suddenly, orientation was a big deal. It pleased her to see that her son wasn't one of those. And it totally blew that stereotype out of the water—Thanatos was as straight as they made them and he had an impeccable sense of style. Although, from his own attire, it wasn't immediately obvious.

"And what would you suggest, Mr. Makeover, The Olympus Edition?"

"The red Dolce."

"No way." She put her foot down. Nyx wasn't wearing that dress on a first date with Apollo or *anyone.*

"Why not?"

"I don't have any shoes." It was true. She didn't.

"You could borrow something from Hera's closet. Her new look is hot."

"Isn't she? I am so proud of her." Nyx clucked like a proud mama.

"Ma, while we're talking about Hera, you should know I've seen that my work will take me very close to her. You too."

"What do you mean?" Nyx knew damn well what he meant, but she had to hear him say it.

"I don't know what you guys are planning, but someone is going to die."

"I'm a titan. I can't die."

"Zeus could kill you. Or make you suffer. Don't do that to me. Don't make me escort you to Elysium."

"Son, I am the night. I am eternal. Not like some of the others."

"Persephone's on the list too," he said quietly, pushing the fig cake around with his fork.

"She can't die either. This is crazy."

"You know if a goddess chooses her own end, or... It doesn't matter. I won't take her. So she won't die. Problem solved."

Nyx kept her mouth shut about his responsibilities and how he couldn't simply pick and choose which souls he did the job for. Thanatos had been Death for a very long time. He knew what his job required and what his responsibilities were. He also knew the consequences if he failed to do his job. He'd decided. Changing his mind was like trying to bail the Aegean with a thimble. She knew better.

"If you're sure that's the wisest course of action," she said in her "mother" tone that told him she knew better than he did and she'd meddle even if the words coming out of her mouth were conciliatory.

"I am." His jaw was a hard line and Nyx knew from the look on his face, he was set on this course of action regardless of what it bought.

"I'll visit you in Tartarus," Nyx sighed.

"Glad you understand."

"I have to say one thing," she began hesitantly.

"I knew you would."

"No, really. It's important. I'm your mother. You'll allow me this and you'll listen."

"Yes, Ma."

He stopped pushing his food around and looked up at her expectantly. His dark eyes were so earnest and in that moment, he looked like his father, Nod. He was long dead to the sands of time and memory, but it comforted her to see that bit of him in her son. At least *that* part of Nod. The bastard part was well-lost and she hoped it was never to be found again.

"You're a good boy," Nyx said as she pulled herself out of her memory.

"Was that what you had to say?"

"No, I was just thinking you looked so much like Nod there for a moment." She worried her lip to keep from saying anything else too emotional. Nyx wasn't a sniffly sort of goddess. She was more balls to the wall, pedal to the metal and only cried if no one would ever see her or those who had seen it weren't only dead, but obliterated from existence.

"Hades had Persephone for centuries. Do you understand what that means?"

"She'll be in her comfort zone if I kidnap her?" He cocked his head to the side.

A dark thundercloud gathered above them.

"Sorry, it was there. I had to take it." He held up his hands. "Okay, not funny. I get it."

"You don't know what happened between them. But Hades let her go because he loved her. She may have feelings for him, Thanatos. Even if you give up everything to save her, she may want to go back to Hades."

"I know that." He looked down at his plate.

"Do you? Do you *really*?"

"I wouldn't want to cause her any pain. Or Hades. He's not a bad guy. Dresses a bit like a douche, what with all the velvet and whatnot. Chicks seem to dig it though." Thanatos scowled.

"Oh, you're bringing it too with your Matrix trench and shades."

"You think so?" he said as if he didn't know it.

"It's already obvious Persephone likes dark and tortured. Just don't let her make you any *more* dark and tortured, okay? I get that you like the dark, you're my son. But don't get lost in it."

"I won't. You taught me well." He crammed the last bit of cake into his mouth. "So it's a no on the red Dolce?"

"Don't talk with your mouth full," she admonished. "Gods, Thanatos. Do you remember to brush your teeth when I'm not there?"

"Sometimes."

"They say for the mortals it's when boys start liking girls they remember to do things like shower. It seems that's not the case with you." Nyx shook her head.

He grinned and showed his teeth. "They're perfect."

"All but that bit of fig you've got stuck in the front." She pointed at the offending fruit.

Thanatos snapped his mouth shut. "We were talking about you."

"I guess."

"Wear something besides black."

"You're one to talk."

"Ma, you're a chick. In case that slipped by you. We like to see women dressed, well, feminine."

"Are you implying I am *not* feminine?"

Thanatos shifted uncomfortably in his chair. "Sometimes. Black has gotten to be your muumuu," he said as if he were almost afraid to say it where she could hear.

"WHAT?" Nyx wasn't a muumuu sort of goddess either. In fact, she'd see herself strung up in Tartarus before she'd ever run around in a muumuu.

"It's your standard house wear, it's no better than PJs."

"Still not wearing the Dolce."

"Fine. What about that silver dress you used to wear to the Fairy Ball?"

Eh, she could do that. It was comfortable, a little jazzy, kind of like a Disney princess dress—which she secretly adored. A little sexy too. It would look great with her hair.

"I'll take that, but I'm wearing flats."

"Good. Apollo is only 6'2. It would be tacky if you were towering over him like some Boudicea."

"Only if he's not secure in his godhood." She flashed a smirk at him. In fact, it was the same one he'd been giving her all day. They were two peas in an immortal pod.

"Why must you be difficult?"

"The same reason you are, I imagine."

Thanatos looked for another cake and promptly shoved

the whole thing in his mouth. "I'm staying the night, so if you want to bang him, do it at his temple, okay?"

"If you're all good with Mom shacking up with your friend, it should be fine if she does it in her own home, shouldn't it?" Nyx said just to be perverse.

"And this is what I'll be telling my shrink next week," he shot back through cake crumbs.

"You have a shrink?"

"No, but I'll probably need one after this." Thanatos sounded certain.

"Good. I haven't done my job as a mother until you need therapy. I'm sorry it's taken this long, darling."

"Wouldn't it be more romantic in the back of his chariot?"

"I should smack you in the mouth. You better not ever have a girl in the back of your chariot."

"I ride a pale horse, Ma."

"Whatever."

"Are you going to get ready or he is going to see you in your muumuu?"

"It's not a muumuu."

"You look like shit."

"Thank you." She employed her long-suffering mommy tone.

"Tell it to your shrink."

"I just might, Thanatos. I just might." She nodded seriously before turning to go to her room to change. "By the way, your room is just like you left it. If you really want to stay."

"I'll be here when you get home in the morning."

"Awfully presumptuous of you to assume I'll be gone all night," Nyx said as she shut the door behind her.

"Common sense. You're going to drive the chariot,

right? Not until dawn. Hello, were you listening?" He taunted her through the door.

Oh. Right. Did she really want to hang out *all night* just to drive some stupid horse across the sky?

Hell yes.

CHAPTER
TEN

DEMETER

Demeter awoke to the sound of a male voice outside her window. Rather than darting to the glass to look outside, she lay quietly in the shadows and listened.

"Heard melodies are sweet, yet those unheard are sweeter. Therefore, ye soft pipes play on..." His voice faded for a moment. "All breathing human passion far above—,"

Keats. He was reciting Keats to Persephone. *Ode on a Grecian Urn.* That had been a favorite of hers. She remembered how the muses had danced when he'd written it; they'd been so bright, so powerful. He'd fed them well and died young. Demeter remembered that too, seeing them ghost around Olympus in their black flowing gowns, their mourning veils and their wails of sorrow.

To be the object of such devotion to inspire such poetry. She wondered if Hades had whispered poetry to Persephone as well, if his words were sweet with soft touches. Demeter was dying anyway and Persephone's misery hadn't saved her. She hated her more for that, but hated herself too.

"Golden absinthe mist will forget, Hemlock whispers passed to these love stained lips." He'd begun another poem, this one she didn't recognize and slipped from the bed and stood in the shadow, peering out into the darkness.

It was Eros as she'd suspected, but he wasn't speaking to Persephone. He was outside of her window reciting from memory, looking up at her window. She closed her eyes against the sensation it wrought in her. A strange, bitter hope, fleeting touches of warmth and a sadness so deep she could drown in it. Until she reminded herself he was nothing but a silly godling.

No, a part of her protested. He was a godling no more, but a god in his own right. Virile and male in every way. He wanted her enough to whisper sweet words outside her temple window where anyone, even her daughter could hear. Demeter knew she should shoo him away, bid him to be quiet and keep such silliness to himself, but she couldn't. One more verse couldn't hurt.

"Folly strings her harp with silver spun tears..."

Oh, but it *did* hurt. His words struck home like an Amazon's spear and pierced all of her soft places. It was folly, all of it and now Demeter would have to pay the piper and the sounds of sorrow would be the only music in her ears.

"An invitation to Lethe's hearth, to drift eternal in the black sea. Eyes luminous like twin stars, overfilling their cups of sorrow and wrath."

Did he know her so well? How could he have looked inside of her; seen her sorrow and wrath and still want her? It wasn't possible. What did a virgin know about the secret depths of a woman's heart, even if he was the God of Love?

The timber of his voice slid over her in a caress. Her fingers were on the window sill, ready to fling it open and invite him in, but something stayed her hand. Her time was over, did it really matter if she took this one bit of pleasure for herself, this one moment out of time to touch and be touched? Yet still, she didn't move, she was frozen.

"Can you hear me, Demeter, or do you sleep still? I don't need to look into your heart to know what's there."

She pressed her palm to the glass and suddenly, his hand was next to hers on the pane. He stood behind her, her body molded to the contours of his. His breath was warm on her neck and the heat of him infused her. His cock was thick against her backside and it was impossible for Demeter not to tilt her hips against him.

His arm slid around her waist to anchor her to him while his other hand explored the length of her thigh and the curve of her hip while hitching her gown out of his way. She didn't speak, she didn't want to shatter the moment, but so many questions burned on the tip of her tongue.

Eros moved the arm around her waist, shifted so it was around her hips and then splayed his hand over her mound. He delved into her wet folds, stroked the engorged flesh with measured motions. As if he'd done this a thousand times before to a thousand different women. She knew he hadn't though. Knew it in the core of her being.

His lips brushed against the delicate skin of her neck and she twisted in his grasp to face him. Demeter looked into his eyes for a long moment before she moved. It wasn't as if she were taking this time to decide what she was going to do; she knew what was going to happen between them. It was somehow inevitable.

She'd savor this moment because nothing would ever be the same after it. A rare thing indeed to stand on the precipice of change and know exactly what it was and to be able to choose accordingly. Irony at its best, because while it *seemed* Demeter was free to choose, she was not. She could no more deny Eros than she could turn the tide. Demeter could give it a damn good try, but she couldn't do it alone.

Eros wanted her and so he would have her there on her bed, but he would leave her empty and needing all the things she told herself she didn't want. As soon as he'd had what he wanted from her, he'd see everything inside of her whether he wanted to or not. All the things that had kept him chaste—kept him from opening himself to another— they were all there waiting to drown him in acid betrayal.

She should stop now, tell him to look, to really see before things went any further, but she couldn't open her mouth, couldn't deny herself this last pleasure. Demeter felt as though she were stealing his innocence even though he'd offered it to her on a platter.

Although his touch belied his innocence. His hands on her skin scalded her, burned right though her flesh and seared secret places that were already scarred.

It was as if he could read her mind when he spoke. "Ah, Demeter. It wasn't innocence I waited on, but you. It's always been you." He took her mouth, but for all his tender words, his kiss was not gentle. It was wild and savage— almost cruel. All of the things Demeter had learned to expect from Love.

She submitted to him, willing to take his savagery, surrendered to his need. Demeter reached between them and took his cock in her hand; ghosted her thumb across the tip. He arched in to her caress.

"Do you know how often I've touched myself this way, imagining your hands doing this now?"

"No, tell me," she invited as she stroked faster.

He covered her hand gently with his own and stilled her motions. "There's something I imagined more than this."

So eager. Who could blame him? He'd waited centuries for her because he thought she was something special. In that moment, she would have given him anything he asked of her. Not only because she burned for him, but because he'd wanted her. He'd never taken anything from her, never demanded. Eros made her feel so many things all at once when all she'd felt for so long had been fear and rage. He made her ache with melancholy, made her want to be better, even though it was too late.

Eros led her to the bed.

Her body tightened in anticipation. He was going to take his pleasure. She wouldn't deny him that, but she could feel something breaking inside of her because she knew this would be the only time he'd want to touch her this way.

Demeter dropped her gown to the floor and displayed herself for him. His eyes were sharp like diamonds and they cut into her, but warmed her too. Eros guided her back on the bed and she opened for him.

But instead of rising above her, he knelt between her thighs like a supplicant. His touch was reverent as he bent his mouth to touch his tongue against her hot flesh. She cried out and he only intensified his caress.

Demeter realized now her visions had been less like dreams and more like memories—the way his mouth and tongue moved over her and drove her need to a frantic pitch. She clenched her teeth against the pleasure she knew was to come because she knew it would be unlike anything she'd ever felt before. She wanted it and feared it at the same time.

Eros made a sound of pure male satisfaction as her slit spasmed against his fingers and the bliss she'd been waiting for took her over the edge. Instead of falling and crashing to the earth, Demeter flew. Wave after wave of ecstasy washed over her, spilling through her veins to tingle all of her nerve endings at once.

Her pleasure manifested, bright blooms of flowers bursting all over the room, vines tangling around the headboard, the windows and dropping down from the ceiling. Grass sprouted from the carpets and berries grew fat and ripe hanging from the sconces.

She became aware of her physical self slowly. Her nails were still gouging his back, her thighs hurt from how she'd kept them flexed and wide, and she'd bitten into her bottom lip when she'd fought the onslaught of sensation.

Eros stayed where he was until she relaxed her hands. He pulled away and placed a gentle kiss on the inside of her thigh.

He was leaving? She bit down on her already bleeding lip again to keep from speaking. This was what she'd expected. It was happening. She'd be lucky if all he did was leave. And then she found herself wrapped in his arms, his hard cock against her thigh, but he made no move to take his own pleasure.

"I don't understand," she said before she could stop herself. If Demeter could have taken the words back, she would have. He didn't need to explain anything to her and it was probably better if he didn't.

Eros ran his fingers through her moss-green hair and dropped a kiss on her forehead. "I want you to know this means something me. I know how your brain works. You think this is some culmination of a godling fantasy. So I'll not take my pleasure with you this time."

His words now overfilled the twin cups of sorrow and wrath he'd been able to describe so clearly.

"Why would you care?"

"I love you," he whispered as he trailed his fingers down her spine.

She stiffened against him. "No, you don't."

"We don't have to have this conversation now, Demeter. Drink the moment, savor it."

"Yes, we do. You think you're feeling something and it's not real. Not if you really *looked*."

"Do you think I haven't? Love isn't about only the shiny things that are new and pink. In fact, it's rarely about those innocent things at all. A temple isn't made solid and enduring by ignoring the cracks in a foundation. Real love, Demeter, isn't only lighting a candle in the dark. It's about turning on the damn sun and accepting what's there, because the rest of it is worth it."

"Eros, you're still young and—,"

"No. That is not an acceptable argument. My age? The hearts of men run deeper than gods, Demeter. There's more darkness, more rage, but more of the beautiful things too. I've seen it all. More so than you, a goddess who's shut herself off from the world because she's afraid."

"Get out." Yes, she was afraid, but what did he know of it? When had he ever been where she was? Never. He didn't have the right to say these things to her.

"If that's what you want. It doesn't change anything. You're still hiding and I still love you. I have for a long time. It was never Persephone and I never pretended it was." He eased himself from the bed and looked at the room. "Has this ever happened with anyone before? This is the life that blooms from love that you feared so much. When you had Persephone, it wasn't because you loved Zeus. Yet you fear her still. Isn't that part of the prophecy? Your mother died long before you had her, long before you ever felt love."

"How do you know?"

"Because for all of your long years, your heart has never bloomed for another."

Demeter wanted to say something, to take away the pain she could see in his eyes, but she didn't know how, she was so full of despair herself. "You can't fix me."

"No, I can't." He nodded. "But you can fix yourself. I love you, Demeter."

"Stop saying that!"

"Not until you believe you deserve it. You don't have to love me back, I know you don't."

He said that with such acceptance, she couldn't fathom it. His tone wasn't hopeless or bereft; it was like he was saying he was simply content to love her. It made no sense.

"Eros?"

He was gone.

She felt his departure like a death. There was a sudden emptiness in the room and all the flowers and berries that had bloomed and ripened now faded before her eyes. They shriveled as they rotted, quickly turning to ash and dust.

Demeter couldn't help but see the similarities between herself and those verdant bits of life that had only had a small taste of existence. While she'd always been comfortable without clothes, she suddenly felt naked. Not just bare, but stripped and flayed open. She manifested a gown, but it did nothing to alleviate anything she was feeling.

There was another bloom, this time in her chest. It was too large to be contained in her body and it spilled forth in a fountain of sadness to streak down her cheeks. They were tears and Demeter realized she was sobbing.

Her door creaked open. "Mama?"

She sobbed harder.

"Oh, Mama. What's wrong?" Persephone rushed to her side and pulled her into her lap as Demeter had done for her. She stroked her hair and hugged her close.

Demeter knew then she deserved to die. For all the suffering she'd wrought in the world. It didn't matter she thought what happened to her had been unfair, it didn't matter what Zeus had done to her. Persephone deserved so much better than what she'd been given. After all, wouldn't her lot be the same as Demeter's when her child came of age?

All of these long, bitter years a waste.

Eros was wrong. She didn't deserve to be loved. She'd never done anything to make herself worthy and her child, her very own flesh and blood who loved her unconditionally had born the brunt of her selfishness. Even after she'd taken away what Persephone had loved most, her daughter was still here holding her in the dark while Demeter grieved for herself.

"Mama, it's cold in here. You have to stop. Come on, tell me what's wrong," Persephone crooned.

Demeter felt the light, yet frigid kiss of snowflakes on her skin. She opened her eyes to see big, fat flakes falling from the ceiling as they blanketed the room. She looked outside and realized it was snowing outside too. All of Olympus would be covered in her frozen misery.

"I'm sorry, Persephone. I'm so sorry." She hugged her daughter close, wondering if she'd ever forgive her for what she'd done.

"What are you sorry for?"

"Taking you away from Hades. Forgive me."

Persephone stopped smoothing her mother's hair for a

moment, then continued. "It's okay, Mama. I know you wanted what was best for me."

Demeter sobbed harder.

"Whatever happened, I love you. It's okay. But you have to stop. By snowing all over Olympus, you're going to incite a war. Come on. Let's make it spring."

"I can't," she hiccupped.

"I'll help you. Think of roses. Bright red roses peeking up out of the snow. It's unnatural. They'll love it."

Demeter felt her daughter's power spike and instead of hating her for it, she surrendered her own and let their powers merge and outside, roses covered Olympus.

"There now, it's beautiful. Come look!" Persephone said excitedly.

"No, I don't think so. I'm tired now."

"Are you still sick, Mama?"

Yes, Demeter was sick, but not only in the way Persephone thought. She was sick, dying. But she was sick at heart too. Demeter sighed heavily. The pain she'd dulled with her rage and her hate came back in a regimented force and she was too tired to put up a defense. She let it take her.

"Yes, little seedling, I am, but I'll be okay. Go on now."

"Eros left his quiver," she said quietly.

"Take it to him, will you? I don't want to see him again."

"He loves you, you know," she ventured.

"I know."

"Mama,"

"Persephone!" she snapped.

"Just one more thing and I'll leave you alone. I think you could be happy with him. You've never been with anyone as long as you've had me and I'll always need you, Mama, but I've learned you and I need something else besides each other."

This was the first time Persephone had ever contradicted her openly and Demeter was proud of her for it. Maybe the damage she'd done to her beautiful child wouldn't be eternal.

"Go back to bed now, seedling." Persephone *wasn't* a seedling any longer, but a long-stemmed rose, lovely and ready to lift her face the sun.

It was the beginning of the long dark for Demeter.

ELEVEN

HERA

"Here to finish what you started?" Hades said darkly, without turning to face her. He'd opened another bottle of Stolichnaya and stood tall and brooding over the wet bar.

"It depends on how many of those you've had." Hera quickly took in his unkempt appearance. Damn if he didn't wear tortured well. Even wallowing in his misery, he exuded sex. She couldn't help but lick her lips in anticipation. There was something to be said for the grudge fuck.

"Drinks or bottles, sweetheart?"

"If you don't have a heart, why are you numbing yourself? Habit?"

"Because I still have a soul. Aphrodite couldn't help me with that one." He took another swallow.

"Aren't you just the tormented creature? Next thing we know, you'll be flinging the gates of Tartarus wide so all those you've punished can find peace in Elysium," Hera sneered.

"What do you *want*?" he growled. "I thought after yesterday's little scene you'd realized your mistake."

"I told you. I want to make you a king and be your woman. But with all that vodka in you, I don't think you're up to either task."

"Keep pushing me, Hera. Without a heart, there's nothing to keep my temper reined." The expression he wore was hard and unforgiving.

"Do you want me to be afraid of you? I don't fear you, Hades. I never have."

He spun on his booted heel and crossed the room, backed her against the cold stone of the wall. Hera was breathless and maybe a little nervous of his intent, but whatever he wanted to do to her, she wanted it.

"Not even when you were young?" His whisper was close enough to brush her lips. "You were very much afraid of me then. I watched you in the shadows and when you fell down the rabbit hole to Tartarus, I thought you were a gift from powers greater than Olympus."

She shivered, remembering his eyes on her all the time, how vulnerable she'd felt, exposed. What Hera would give to feel that again with him, vulnerable but soft, protected. Safe. Hera had feared him as a male, but she'd trusted him to keep her safe down here in the recesses of the world.

"You were beautiful, Hades. I was afraid, but I wanted you too," she confessed.

His gaze dropped to her mouth and for one glorious moment, Hera thought he was going to kiss her. She wet her lips with the tip of her tongue.

"So why didn't you say yes when I asked your father for

you?" he asked, his tone still seductive, but with an edge like a knife beneath every word.

"My mother said you were dangerous and wild, that you'd take me down to Tartarus and I'd never see Olympus again."

"Do you remember when I kissed you the first time?"

"In Aphrodite's grotto." She leaned closer, but Hades captured her wrists and held them above her head. She yearned for more of his touch, but he kept a careful distance between them.

"You were asleep beneath the stars, with daydreams on your lips and moonbeams on your brow." He took one lock of her hair between his fingers. "Your hair was a pool of crimson spread out behind you and your skin so luminous in that pale light." He brushed the pad of his thumb over her lower lip. "Your lips were rose petals—parted in sweet invitation."

She gasped and arched against him in an involuntary movement, her body reliving those memories on a cellular level.

"I awoke in your arms. Your hands were all over me and I wanted you to stop, but I wanted more too. I felt like I was on fire and frozen at once. Yes, Hades, I confess, I was afraid of everything you made me feel."

"And now, what are you afraid of?"

"You'll stop and I'll never feel those things again," Hera confessed and tilted her face up, hoping for his kiss.

"What if I told you that you won't? That I'll never touch you again?"

"I'd tell you to get your damn hands off me then because you're touching me now and whether you want to admit it or not, your body still wants mine even if the rest of you doesn't."

"This is quite the change from little Miss Vulnerable yesterday. Zeus take another runner at it? Give you a little confidence boost?" he sneered.

"Don't be a bastard to me because someone else hurt you."

"There's where you're mistaken, sweetheart. I'm being a bastard to you because you hurt me," Hades explained nonchalantly.

"A millennia ago," she shot back.

"Now you want something from me. Something my brother doesn't give you, maybe never did. And I'm supposed to be thankful, eager even, that you deign to come down from on high and offer me my brother's leavings. I should take his castoffs and be grateful for it?" Disgust was written on his countenance.

He knew that wasn't how she'd intended it. "So, I'm forever to be something big brother didn't want—a hand me down whore? Should I have been a virgin forever?"

"Yes."

"What about Persephone?"

"What about her?"

"You would have fucked her seventy-five deviations from Sunday."

"A hundred. A thousand," he swore.

"What's good for the gander, Hades," Hera said defiantly.

"Obviously, it wasn't good, was it? Because I was left with this." He flung the box on the floor that held his heart.

Hades released her and stalked from the room. She sank to her knees to catch her breath and she saw that the box had sprung open and the husk of his heart had fallen to the floor. Hera reached out to touch it. It was so small—the sight of it dark and still twisted her insides.

She picked it up carefully like she would have had it been a baby bluebird. Hera feared it was going to crumble to nothing in her fingers, but it sat still and hard. She stroked her finger down the side of it in a tender motion and found it to be so cold it burned her. Hera brought the dark thing to her lips and blew soft, warm breath over it. Surely, if it was so hard, that wouldn't hurt it. It was dirty, after all, and she didn't want to put it back in the box that way.

A little bit of the charred edge flaked off and Hera gasped. For one horrible moment, she thought it was going to dissolve. Until she saw a bit of something beneath. It was ashen and gray, but it wasn't black. Hera brought it to her lips again and this time, she touched that new place with her mouth as she blew.

Another layer peeled away, like the shell of a hard-boiled egg. What she held in her hand now looked to be a stone. It was heavy and bleak, but was solid. It wasn't a fey thing of ashes and soot.

Hera placed it tenderly in the box and closed it. She put it back up on the mantle and traced her fingers over it lightly before turning to figure out where tall, dark and sullen had gotten to.

She crept through the long corridors carefully until she remembered which passage led to his chambers and was astonished when she heard a feminine voice. Well, the tart would just have to go, whoever she was. Hera had a plan and Hades was the lynchpin. Hell or high water, she would have her way in this. Hera hadn't come this far to be thwarted by what was between *anyone's* thighs.

"Hades, I can't find the towels and I... Sorry. Didn't see you were on the phone." She heard through the door.

Oh, hell no. It was not happening like this. He'd left her

to fend for herself to come up here and shag this hooker, whoever she was, while he knew she wanted him? That was too big of a slap to Hera's ego to let it pass.

Maybe that's why he hadn't already succumbed to her charms? Part of why she'd wanted Hades was because he was monogamous. If he had a woman, whether he loved her or not, he wasn't running around trying to stick his dick or thunderbolt into anything that would stand still long enough.

Damn it.

One little look wouldn't hurt, would it? She peered through the door and saw the same snarling gargoyle from the day previous and a woman's voice issuing from its mouth. It looked just as pissed off at this day's indignity. At first she thought the charade was for her, but she could see he actually was on the phone.

Thank the powers for cell phones. All that prophecy stuff was a colossal pain in the taco. Gods talking to each other through oracles, shit never came through clearly.

It was obvious he was talking to Persephone from his tone of voice, the look on his face. But rather than be frustrated about the possible wrinkle in her plans, she felt sorrow. If he'd had that heart in his chest, Hera was sure it would be breaking now.

From the sound of things, it seemed she wanted him back. Why was he telling her no? Hera was both elated and miserable at the same time. Why were things with him so complicated? He was a god. Gods were simple. Ambrosia. Sports. Sex. That was supposed to be the extent of it. But no. Hades was *complex*.

Having a wild affair with Abstinence sounded better all the time.

He hung up the phone. It was a testament to the kind of

god he was when he didn't throw the phone across the room as she would have after such an exchange, but closed it carefully and set it down on the table beside the bed. He raked his fingers through his hair and sighed.

Hera opened the door the rest of the way and moved to sit beside him.

"You're still here? You must be desperate."

"I am," she admitted freely. A long moment of silence made the air thick. "Why didn't you let her come back?"

He turned to study her, his blue-flamed irises flaring. "It's the best I could do for her."

"Isn't this what you wanted? She loves you."

"No, she doesn't. Suddenly, she's alone and doesn't have me to take care of her. It's a sad state of affairs when *I* am the constant. She loves how she felt when she was with me, she doesn't actually love me."

"She asked to come back. Take her now and she'll give you everything you could have asked for." Hera knew this to be true, because it's what she would have done when she was a young godling easily led by her mother.

"It won't be real," he answered as if he'd only now awakened from a dream.

"Is anything?"

"It doesn't matter now."

Oh, but it did. Hera thought back to where his heart lay in the box. It mattered more than he could know. How did he not see it? He was *still* sacrificing for this woman. No matter if his heart beat within his chest or shriveled to nothing outside of it, he loved Persephone.

Hera wondered what it would feel like to be loved with that kind of devotion. Zeus had never loved her so thoroughly. Not even in the beginning. She swallowed against the emotion rising in her and reached out to touch his face, grazed her thumb over his cheek.

"No, I don't suppose it does."

"Why do you want this, Hera? Are you another Persephone, here because you remembered me as a young god and what you felt then is better than what you have now?"

"That's part of it, but not the big picture. You already told me you can't love me. I accept that. I mean, Zeus doesn't so it's not like I don't know what I'm offering. You've never lied to me, Hades. We could build a good life on that, a strong monarchy. Zeus cares only for himself and where his next bit of pussy is coming from. You may never love me, but with trust and fidelity, we could find a bit of happiness," she promised.

"And punish my brother."

"That's definitely one of the benefits. Is that what you don't like? Do you think I'm using you to punish Zeus?"

"Aren't you?" he said as he cupped her cheek and mirrored her caress.

"Yes, but I was honest about it. I've spent enough years being unhappy and this thing? I'm talking about forever. Commitment. Not just revenge. Why would I damn myself to more misery?"

"Because knowing Zeus is miserable too would be worth the price." Hades sounded as if he were an expert in such matters.

"Not to me, it's not. Our existences are too long to spend them in misery." She leaned into him and he allowed her to brush her lips against his cheek. "I've often wondered what would have happened had I not listened to my mother and accepted when you asked for me. I regret that I didn't."

"I have my faults, Hera. It sounds as if you've made me into some redeemable hero who just got lost in the dark."

That was exactly what she'd made him out to be and she made no bones about it. He was so damn noble it made her ache, but he was flawed enough to be real. She kissed his cheek again, this time closer to the bitter slash of his mouth. And closer again until her lips brushed his. It was bitter, but not like what she'd expected. It was sweet too, like dark chocolate. "Yes."

"This thing, it will crash and burn for all the reasons your mother gave you and more. I'm not the guy who wins, Hera. I'll only hurt you."

"Then hurt me." She crashed her mouth into his; she was the aggressor, taking what she wanted from him, demanding everything he had. "I've told you if pain is all you have, mark me with it. Dance with me in the dark, Hades."

He conquered with his surrender and pushed her back on the bed. Hades slid up the length of her body and he studied her, their gazes locked for a long moment before he took any other action. She didn't know what he was looking for, but she didn't turn her eyes away. Let him look, let him see anything he wanted to see. There would be no secrets between them, no lies.

He pushed her hair out of her face carefully and his attention was drawn to her mouth, her lips parted in expectation and her breath hitched. She wanted to taste him again. He stroked his fingers down her side to her hip and Hera was surprised at how gentle he was.

How could he be so blind? He had so much more to give than the dark. If only she could make him see. In that moment, she was determined he'd know the kind of god he was and she'd keep his heart safe. She'd never let anything hurt him like that again; Hades would never need to question his worth with her.

"I'm not going to break," she promised.

He looked away from her now, dragged his cheek against hers and buried his face in her hair.

This must have been all Persephone had allowed him. From his reaction, this was where she would become afraid and Hera couldn't blame her. Hades' cock was pressed against her belly and while Hera was an experienced goddess and she was wet for him, she was a little afraid. Zeus had never been packing anything like this.

"Would you still want this if I refuse my brother's throne?" he whispered against her ear.

Hera hooked her legs around his and eased him more firmly against her. "Yes."

"Then gods help you." He said this as if he actually pitied her, but it didn't stop him from moving his hands up over her body to cup her breasts.

She made short work of his velvet coat and bemoaned his penchant for dress-up. It looked so fucking good on him, but it would have been easier to peel him out of a t-shirt and jeans. He'd look good in that too, with his muscular thighs and perfect ass. He'd look even better naked.

Hera wondered if he was thinking the same thing about her costume, but he didn't seem to mind unlacing her corset. He took his time, each eyelet that was released bared a bit more of her skin and Hades devoured each new vision of flesh.

Her nipples tightened in expectation of his touch and he skimmed his fingers over the exposed globes of her breasts. When he'd finally unlaced her completely, Hades pulled back from her and his intent stare on her naked skin made her as hot as anything he could have done with his hands.

The way his eyes raked over her made her feel like she was the most beautiful thing he'd ever seen. Again, Hera wondered if he'd looked at Persephone like that, with dark promise burning his countenance. How had she turned him away, tossed this worship aside like it was nothing? Stupid girl.

He dipped his head and touched his lips to her stomach, before unbuttoning her leather pants with his teeth and tugging them down her legs. Her panties were next and he paused, as if expecting her to refuse him, but she lifted her hips and in a moment, she was completely bare to him, but he was still wearing his breeches and boots.

And he was beautiful in the candlelight. Mortals used "built like a Greek god" as a model for perfection, but Hades surpassed them all. His body was like living marble, so hard and smooth—sculpted by a master. But it wasn't cold, it was infused with warmth. His shoulders were wide, as wide as Atlas', his corded arms were strong, but the safety in his embrace didn't come from only that strength. It came from somewhere deep beneath that dark, jagged scar where his heart had been.

What was he waiting for? Didn't he want her?

"Please," she begged.

"Why are you here, Hera? You're too beautiful to want this with me," Hades said in a defeated tone.

His words twisted her gut as she remembered the young, arrogant god who'd tried to seduce her in Aphrodite's grotto. He hadn't thought anything above him —all the world was his for the choosing.

Hera leaned up to him and kissed him softly. "Touch me, Hades. I need you."

She did need him, whereas before she'd decided she wanted him, she'd slipped somewhere and fallen into something she wasn't ready to face. All she knew was that if he didn't touch her now, she'd die. Her body would incinerate with her need.

He groaned at her entreaty and bent over her, his mouth ready to pleasure her.

"No," Hera growled and tugged on his hair to pull him back up to her face.

"No pleasure? Do you want pain, then?" he asked, ready to indulge her desires.

"Feel how wet I am for you already." She guided his hand between her thighs. "I don't need an orgasm to want you inside me."

It was true, she'd had mouths on her slit, tongues working her clit and while they'd made her come, it was nothing compared to bliss Hera felt from the brush of his fingers, his breath on her neck, or what she knew she'd feel when he was thrusting into her.

The dark slashes of his brows came together over his blue-flamed eyes. "But I want to, Hera. I want to taste you on my lips and feel you clench around my fingers and tongue. I want to hear you scream my name and when I do fuck you, I want your nails so deep in my back I bleed."

His words sent shivers of expectation shooting through her. His dark promises resonated in her core. She kept her fingers clenched in his hair and he kept his eyes fixed on hers as he descended between her thighs.

The first touch was all that he vowed and the intensity made her want to close her eyes, but she couldn't look away from him. She imagined this was much like how a rabbit felt before a hungry wolf tore it to pieces. Hera was poised on a precipice and she couldn't see the bottom, but she knew in a moment the ground would crumble away and she'd fall into the pitch.

She trembled with her need and when fear would have made her retreat, Hera rallied. She guided him closer to his task. He pushed two fingers inside of her with no preamble. His caress was rough, but practiced and he knew how he filled her, stretched her. Made her feel marked. Just as she'd demanded.

Hera gasped when he started to thrust with his fingers and he leaned back, his lips wet with her essence and his forefinger replaced his tongue on her clit. He licked his lips slowly, savoring what he found there and she clenched hard, her hands fisted in the sheets.

"Already?" Hades raised a brow and smirked; an expression of supreme male confidence.

Her body was an instrument and he was a master musician. He knew which notes to play and how to strum the threads that held her together. Hades could take her apart at will, touch her note by note, or give her sensation in a symphony.

He stopped the caress, knowing she was on edge and leaned back over her and pressed his mouth to her hip in a chaste kissed that had no business on the seductive curve of his lips. Yet, he wasn't as unaffected as he would have had her believe. There was the occasional tremor in his hands, as if he waited for her to tell him no, to deny him whatever he would have of her next.

"It's been so long," she confessed without shame. "And you're too good, Hades. You know just how to touch me.

Hades was above her again and brushed her mouth with a kiss. "I've dreamt about having you at my mercy like this for so long, now that I have you naked and wanting, all I can think about is spending inside you."

The images his words painted were only the same things she wanted; only the same fantasies she'd touched herself to in her cold bed all alone. "Shall I tell you about my lonely nights spent bringing myself off fantasizing about this moment?"

He groaned and shed his boots and breaches in a way only a god could, by the force of his will. Hades entered her sure and fast, just as he had with his fingers, but it was exactly what she craved. Hera dug her nails into his back and bucked to meet his thrust and he buried himself to the hilt in her slick heat.

She cried out and he drove into her again and again. His fingers marked half moons into the tender flesh of her hips and she answered by digging her nails deeper into his back. At the twinge of pain, Hades growled against her throat.

"You're mine now, Hera. Say it," he demanded.

"I'm yours, Hades," she said through clenched teeth.

"Until the stars burn to nothing and the earth is dust and ash. Mine."

He continued to thrust in to her with a barely restrained violence that tempted her to see how far she could push him—because it was a tender brutality. Hades had put his mark on her now, branded her.

She clenched again, her inner channel spasming around his cock and Hera tried to fight it. She wasn't ready to come, for this first time to be over. She arched involuntarily as bliss took her over the edge as quickly as it had approached.

"More," he rasped.

Hera knew what he wanted and dug her nails deeper until she was sure she'd broken skin—marked him in her way—and he spilled his seed inside of her. They rode the waves of pleasure together until he was spent and Hades reclined beside her.

Her body was still spasming, aftershocks radiated from her clit all the way to her toes, like little electric jolts. When they were over, things would change. Because they had for her. Hera thought she could do this—that she could accept what she'd had with Zeus with Hades because he'd be faithful. That it was okay if he couldn't love her.

But it wasn't.

She wanted everything from this god. Hera wanted forever and when she'd told him she belonged to him, it was because she did. She closed her eyes and begged for sleep. If she could have called Nyx without him seeing, she would have. The Goddess of the Night could have laid a blanket of silent stars over them and allowed Hera to hide and regroup—find her strength. If only for a little while.

He gathered her to him carefully, as if that would break her when fucking her hadn't. Something tremulous welled inside of her and Hera realized he'd be right. This soft touching, this mockery of affection, this was what she couldn't handle.

"You don't have to."

"Don't I?" he asked cautiously.

She hated it when he answered her with a question. No, he didn't need to hold her. In fact, she'd prefer it if he didn't. Or she'd shatter right there in the sanctuary of his arms.

"I don't want to be held."

"I see." He stiffened against her.

But he didn't see. "No, I don't..." *I don't want anything that isn't real.* Hera remembered her earlier conversation with him—why he'd turned Persephone away. She understood and with that understanding came a little death. In a dimly lit corner of her heart, hope died alone and unshriven. She understood why he'd let Persephone go more than she wanted to. "Not if you don't feel it, Hades. And it's okay if you don't. I had my big goddess panties on when I propositioned you. I knew what I was signing up for."

She just didn't know it would hurt so much.

CHAPTER

TWELVE

ABSTINENCE

Z eus had come over again. He'd brought another
season of Buffy the Vampire Slayer and had opted
for the musical episode: *Once More, With Feeling*.
This was the one where in the end Spike plants a knicker-
twisting kiss on Buffy and she lets him. It was one of her
favorite episodes and Abstinence wondered if Zeus had
used some kind of god-mojo on her to pick her brain. As if
vampire/slayer make-out sessions would be enough to
break down the walls she'd erected against him and god-
whore/goddess make-out sessions would ensue.

"This is my favorite episode," he said.

Liar. It was not. Was it? Only because he thought it
would get him laid.

On the outside, this looked like every girl's dream date.
(If one had to stay home for said date.) There was a guilty
pleasure on the television, milk chocolate fig truffles, pizza,
and ambrosia wine all served up by the hottest male in
existence that enjoyed each guilty pleasure in turn himself.

It wasn't fair. She'd repeated that to herself so many times Abstinence was sure the next step would be to hold her breath and kick her feet. That had the same effect on the situation as complaining it wasn't fair. Abstinence turned to study him again while he was watching the screen.

He'd sat on the opposite end of the futon, but his massive body took up more than half. He was huge by any standard. Abstinence could feel the heat from his body without even touching him.

She hadn't expected him to look so good. All of the legends had painted him past middle-aged with long, white hair. Nothing could be further from the truth. He looked like a man in his prime. Although, she'd noticed he'd aged oddly in these few days. When she'd first met him, he'd been so young, like a college frat boy. Now he looked like he had a few lines around his eyes and damn him, it just made him sexier.

"Are you going to take a bite of this truffle, or do I have to eat it all by myself?"

"Definitely all by yourself." She nodded emphatically.

"Just a bite. It's so good. If you don't eat the whole thing—,"

"It's abstaining," she finished for him with a shake of her head. "But when is it indulging?"

He looked serious for a moment. "I don't know."

"Exactly."

"It won't hurt..."

"But it will, Zeus. It will kill me. Is that what you want?"

"No." He hung his head like a child who'd been denied a lolly. Then he perked. "Do you trust me?"

"Hell no."

"That wasn't the right answer." He looked as if he'd actually expected a different answer.

"Then ask another question."

"What if I could promise you nothing would happen to you if you indulge only with me?"

"Wish in one hand and shi—," she started.

She was cut off by his kiss.

He hadn't even gotten his arm around her, like Hera had warned, and she was already *fucked*. Fucked face down like an ugly whore because he tasted of milk chocolate and figs. Abstinence wanted to fight him—she did, but there was something about him, like a spider that injected his prey with venom, but instead of fangs it was his kiss. It paralyzed her and she had no doubt he was going to consume her exactly as such a predator would.

But it was okay, because his venom was sweet like chocolate and figs. Her logical mind knew she was dying, knew she had to fight to keep her sister and her nieces safe, they were at the forefront of her awareness, but her pleasure centers were on overload and she melted into liquid ecstasy. It was like drowning.

The world faded and all she knew was his mouth and his hands. Her breath faded too and soon she was breathing only him, his scent and the life he gave her from his own body. Awareness slipped from her like a silken gown and pooled somewhere in the darkness that waited to welcome her with open arms.

His strong hand kneaded her breast and she was vaguely aware when he pulled her into his lap to straddle him. Sweet bliss slammed into her again and it knocked the tenuous hold of existence out of her grasp.

Zeus was a tide that pulled her out to the deep waters of a shoreless sea where she'd drift until it swallowed her whole—there were stars exploding in her veins and the veil of the eternal dark had fallen over her eyes.

"Abstinence!" His voice shattered the silence that had been screaming in her ears as her heart thudded to a halt.

That shoreless sea wasn't water at all, but the pools of his eyes. They were trained on her with concern as her vision returned to her in pixels of gray and blue. His hand slid down her spine to steady her and she swayed.

"I'm sorry, I didn't..." he said helplessly.

Abstinence couldn't say he didn't know, because he did. She'd told him. One more than one occasion. He was going to kill her to get what she wanted and it wasn't the death that Abstinence feared, but it was what it would do to her family. She couldn't fight him, not when he had power like that.

Tears gathered and slipped down her face. Abstinence didn't know if it was from the pleasure he'd given her or the fact even though her life and those of those she loved depended on her denial, she wouldn't be able to refuse him.

"You didn't what? Know? I told you."

"I didn't believe you, Abstinence. I'm sorry." He was stricken.

"Please let go of me." She couldn't tolerate his hands on her another moment, but she wasn't sure if she could stand on her own.

"You'll fall on your face, Abi." He clucked like a mother hen, a mannerism not at home on the King of the Gods. "I did this. Let me try to make it right."

"You can make it right by leaving. You want me to trust you and then you do this? You could have killed me."

"I don't want to leave," Zeus said, as if he were surprised by it himself.

"Then you've decided?" Abstinence tried to keep the

tremor out of her voice. She'd seen what his wrath had wrought on the world. Her death wouldn't matter to him, or anyone else, only to the next woman who had to bear Abstinence.

A cold gust of wind blew the door to her temple open with such force the handle was imbedded into the wall. The sharp sound startled them both and they turned to see an unwelcome visitor. Death, in his pale glory, had come to call.

Abstinence instinctively knew he was the twilight of all things, this man who stood with a kind smile on his face. She could see the depths of eternity in his eyes, they were bright with the swirling mist of souls, alternately like darkest midnight and then threaded with the purples and oranges of the dawn.

Hera had said all the gods were golden but Hades. This one wasn't either, he was pale, his skin blue-veined ice and his lashes were like snowflakes. He was unmistakably male, but beautiful and terrible like she'd always imagined the elemental gods to be.

He held out his hand to her, the dark blue of his nail beds strangely comforting to her. Abstinence reached out to take his hand as if in a trance and Zeus snatched her hand away. "Stop that."

"I have to go," she whispered.

"What did you do, Zeus, that I've been called to do my job here on Olympus?" Death demanded in a voice that brooked no argument or deflection.

"I..." he trailed off.

"Zeus!" he demanded again, but this time when he spoke, the wine on the table turned a brackish color, the fig truffles wasted away and the very walls of the temple shook, for Death would eventually own all things.

"I kissed her," he replied softly.

"And she must pay the price for your lust with the light in her eyes?"

"I'm the King of Gods, damn it."

Death continued to hold out his hand for Abstinence. "Regardless of who you are, you've brought her time about."

"No."

Death sighed. "Don't make this more difficult than it must be. Can't you see she's afraid? You've done this to her, don't make it worse."

"I'm..." Zeus looked to be searching for the word. "Sorry."

"I know," Death returned quietly. "So does she."

"No, you don't understand. I. Am. Sorry. I feel it here," he said and splayed his hand on his stomach.

"Sorry doesn't erase the fact you took what she had."

"Can I give it back?"

Death sighed and frost covered the windows. "Yes, but it will hurt."

"Nothing could hurt more than this... regret. How do mortals stand it? It's like food poisoning." Zeus still looked startled.

"Yes, my King. Regret is a poison." Death nodded.

Abstinence had stood on her own and moved like a wraith toward Death. She felt so light, as if she floated. When she'd been lost to the pleasure and the sensation, it felt like two forces bearing down on her and lifting her simultaneously. This was simply as if she'd become a part of the air.

"Don't be frightened, Merry. It doesn't hurt. There is no sorrow or pain. Only this."

"As your King, I command you to go and leave this

goddess," Zeus stood, his voice also shaking the temple walls.

"You are the King of Gods, Zeus. But no being has power over Death, but Fate."

"Then choose. Choose to leave her with me."

"Why should I, Zeus? What have you done for me or any other being that I should risk the consequences of denying my purpose?"

"Because it's not her fault. It's mine. She doesn't deserve to pay for my actions."

"My actions were my own," Abstinence said as she found her voice. "Those who don't deserve to pay are those who will bear the mantle of Abstinence after I've gone."

"A deal with Death does not come easy," he warned. "Every day I see love for fellow beings burn in the hearts of those who would trade themselves to spare others and I do not make these bargains. Why should I make yours?"

Zeus looked defeated. "I don't know."

Death smiled. "That's the right answer. I'll do this for you. This one time, but there are conditions."

Zeus scowled. "I figured. What are they?"

"You give back what you took."

"As soon as I figure out how."

"The same way you took it," Death explained as if Zeus were a schoolboy asking how to return a piece of candy he'd stolen.

"What are you talking about?" She still wasn't sure what he'd taken. At first, she thought he'd been talking about the fey idea of her life, but it seemed to be they were talking about something more tangible he'd taken from her; something physical he could put in his hand and walk away with.

"Later, Abi." He brushed her off as if this conversation had nothing to do with her. "What's the second?"

"You owe me."

"I know that too, Thanatos."

"No, Zeus. You *owe* me. A boon. And when I ask for it, no matter what it is, you must grant it. Swear it on your godhood." Death looked pleased with himself.

"I don't swear anything on my godhood. What if it's something I can't grant?"

"No, what you mean is, what if it's something you won't grant, something you're not willing to sacrifice. And my answer to that is tough shit."

Death's aura of power was thinning—Abstinence could tell he hadn't lost anything, but he'd pulled his strength back inside of him and while he was still all of the things he'd appeared when she'd first seen him, he wasn't as horrible. He was a person—more real—than the dark ideal of his office.

She found it funny. Abstinence had thought something was more real than death. It didn't get much more real or in your face than the end of all things. She giggled.

"I don't see why you're laughing." Zeus' face was dark as a thundercloud.

Abstinence found this even funnier. He'd been so nonchalant about the whole thing, it was only her existence. He'd wanted to play and laugh and now, he was serious as... well... death. She laughed some more.

"Laugh or cry," Thanatos shrugged.

"Stop it, Abi. You could have died."

What did he care? Had someone just miracled him a soul? He'd come to her house with every intention of seducing her, knowing what it would do to her. Then when it happened, he was upset about it. Maybe it was because he'd only gotten a kiss and not the whole enchilada.

"You knew I could have died when you came over and decided to tempt me with wine and chocolate."

"I said I was sorry."

"Yeah, sure. You're sorry. My nieces or my sister would have been doomed to this loveless, pleasureless, misery and you're sorry."

"I'd love to leave you two to battle this out, but I need my answer, Zeus. Yes or no. It's up to you."

"You don't need his answer, Death. I'll go with you. I don't want anything from him."

"What about your family?" Thanatos asked.

"Ah, you need something from this too." Abstinence was disappointed. For a second, she'd thought Death was different.

"I do, but I'm asking because I agreed to make this deal because of your selflessness."

She sagged, although she was relieved to see her instincts had been correct. "If Abstinence passes to them, I know my sister wouldn't last a day. Is there a goddess of excess? She'd be prime to fill that role. Living as Abstinence would do her in and she wouldn't suffer long. Neither would my nieces."

"So, Zeus. Do I take her?"

"It's actually not up to him, Death. If Fate says I'm to go, I'll go," Abstinence answered for him.

"There are things at work here bigger than any of us. So yes, this does hinge on what the god-king has to say." His eyes flashed and she fell into a dark future where not just her family suffered, but the whole of the world was draped in misery.

"I don't understand," Zeus said.

"You aren't meant to. Not yet."

"Then yes."

"Yes, what, my King?" Thanatos prodded.

"Yes, I will give her back what I took. And yes, damn you, you can have your bloody boon—whatever it is. I promise on my godhood. Are you happy now?"

"No, but I can leave."

And Death was gone with his cold that chilled her marrow and froze her heart. Abstinence was left alone with duality of her would-be murderer and savior.

"Come here," he said grimly.

Like hell. "No."

"Listen, I can't make good on my promise unless you do."

"I don't care. I'm not getting within ten feet of you."

"Abi,"

"Stop calling me that."

"Why?" His serious demeanor was gone.

Abstinence could feel her resistance melting away. "What are you doing?"

"Besides fucking myself in the ass?" He took a step toward her.

"What?"

"Look, you're making me use my power to gain your compliance. Now, I made a promise on my godhood. So I have to do this or lose everything."

"Hmm, this conversation sounds familiar," she quipped with a smirk that was supposed to be a scowl.

He was already past her walls and she didn't stand a chance against him, although she was going to try.

"Abi, I'm not going to hurt you. But the more you make me use my energy compelling you, the more I'll have to take from someone else."

"You will have to explain that statement before I agree to anything, your godhood or no."

He sighed into his hand before he spoke. "I need sex, okay? That's where my youth comes from. Sexual energy keeps me healthy. Without it, I'd be only immortal, but what's immortality without youth? I feed off of the energy."

"Like an incubus?"

"A what?"

"It's a demon."

"Whatever. It doesn't really hurt anyone, but me if I don't get it."

"Tell that to my corpse, jackass." Abstinence backed away another step.

"I didn't think a kiss would hurt you. It wasn't sex."

"It was. For me."

Zeus looked like she'd just hit him in the mouth with a dog rocket and told him to open wider. "A kiss?"

"Yeah, a kiss. It was the kind of bliss I've never known and something I don't want to live without now that I've had it."

"I'm sorry." He looked as if he wanted it to all go away, so harried and tortured. Even though she was the one he'd almost killed.

Why did he care anyway? She'd told him what his seduction would do to her and he'd done it anyway—yes, for all of his contrition and "sorry" it came back down to that every time. Zeus was like a child who'd been caught tracking mud on his mother's white carpet and he'd apologize, he felt badly for it while he was being scolded, but he'd do it again.

"You keep saying that, but what does it mean, really? You're sorry. So what? It doesn't change what you did to me."

"I have to give you back what I took, Abi. One more moment of pleasure? Will it still be so euphoric if it's not forbidden?"

"I—," she broke off, at a loss.

"I can promise it will be quick. In a few moments, my youth will fade and wither. My shoulders will shrivel and narrow and my back will bend. Your bliss will wilt under the ugliness of age. If you force me to compel those feelings in you to get close enough, I'll be nothing but a talking husk."

It all made sense to her now. Why he threw Hera's love away, why he was always fucking some other goddess or mortal. He had to. She knew how the world worked and how much easier it was for him to keep his reserves full when he was already young and strong.

"You don't have to give it back, Zeus. Keep it. A gift. Only never come back to my temple."

"I can't, Abi. I have to give it back. It's part of my oath. Now, please come to me," he entreated. "I've never had to work this hard for a simple kiss. You don't understand what it's like."

Abstinence was moved by the plea on his face and the sincerity in his voice. "Then tell me, Zeus. Help me understand why I should care about your godhood after what you did."

"Asking for this kiss is like a crack addict asking you to take his hit for him."

"Sex is your drug?"

"Yes and it's an addiction I can't ever be free of. To survive, I have to feed it. I can't go cold turkey, or take twelve steps, it's always there. I won't lie to you, Abi. It feels so good. It's a rush unlike any other and feeling that youth wash over me, it's a high I'd kill to have."

"I know. You almost killed me."

"But I didn't want to. I've never felt any remorse for anything I've done to feed myself. And now... gods, just let me do this and get it over with. Then I can leave and you'll never have to see me again."

Abstinence didn't trust him, but she did trust Death. She had a feeling if Zeus tried to screw this up, there would be a horrible reckoning. Death was a surety, a constant. More so than even taxes. Everything had an end and that was a universal truth, so it stood reason Death himself would be much the same.

Abstinence let him hold her and tilted her face up to meet his kiss. When his lips brushed hers, it wasn't what she'd expected. She'd thought it would be the passion and fire that burned her before, but it was bitter and cold. She wondered how sick that made her because she wanted more. She desired the chill of his suffering more than the heat.

Suddenly, where his shoulder had been golden and hard was ashen and flaked away like bits of burned paper. It quickly spread to his whole body and as his legs crumbled beneath him, he rasped, "Get my wife."

CHAPTER
THIRTEEN

PERSEPHONE

Persephone had given up all pretense of hiding the fact she was trying to call Hades. She frankly didn't care who knew about it: from Zeus, to her mother, to those powers higher than those on Olympus. She didn't give a feathered damn. Proven by the fact she was sitting outside Pomegranate Pizza where anyone who cared to see what she was doing could.

And he had yet to answer.

She dialed again and expected his voicemail. So when she heard the echo of his voice on the other end of the line, Persephone found her mouth open and no sound coming out. She knew if she didn't say something he was going to hang up.

"Hades?" Well, no shit, Sherlock. Who the hell else would be answering his phone?

Dead silence answered her. She couldn't even hear him breathing.

"Hades? It's Persephone."

"I know who it is." His response was cold and empty.

Her first instinct was to throw the phone and bawl until her face hurt and she passed out from lack of ambrosia, but she'd known this wasn't going to be easy. She still didn't know what to say. So she was going to be honest. Her pride wouldn't keep her warm at night.

"I miss you," she said in a rush.

"Does your mother know you're talking to me?" This was said evenly, no trace of emotion either way. No anger, no joy, no anything.

"No, but I don't care. I'll tell her," she promised passionately.

"Why would you do that?" Hades asked as if he really had no idea why.

"I want to come home." Yeah, home. That forbidding castle nestled in the dark places of the universe, it was *home*. Anywhere Hades happened to be was home to her now.

"You are home." His words had a finality to them that dropped a lead weight on her chest, she couldn't breathe.

"No, I'm not." She shook her head as if he could see her. "I need you."

"I'm not in the hero business, Persephone. Save yourself from whatever mess you've landed in."

"I'm trying to, Hades. I fucked up, okay? And I'm sorry. I'm more sorry than I can say for how I've hurt you."

"It doesn't matter. It's done."

"No, it's not done. Say you forgive me."

"I forgive you," he parroted. Persephone knew he didn't mean it, didn't feel it. What had she expected? Eros had told her he would be indifferent. He was right though, it cut her more deeply than his rage ever could.

"If you forgive me, then come get me. Right now, I'm

ready to be yours in all ways." She swallowed hard. "I love you."

He actually laughed and it was hollow and dark, all the things she'd been told to expect from him before he'd held her tenderly. "Then I *am* sorry. Truly."

"What do you have to be sorry for? I'm the one who didn't understand this thing between us; I'm the one who was afraid. Why are *you* sorry?" She didn't comprehend what he was saying.

"Because you're going to hurt, Persephone. It's going to feel like someone is taking a razorblade to your beating heart every minute of every day until you find something that numbs the pain, the memory. Something that makes you forget the scent—" he broke off.

"Bay and Sandalwood. That's your scent and I haven't forgotten. Nothing could make me forget the way you smell, the feel of your hands on my body, your arms around me. Nothing, Hades! Do you hear me?" Persephone realized she was bordering on hysterical, but she didn't care.

"I hear you, little one. But you're not hearing me. What you think you're feeling isn't real and if it is, gods help you. I feel nothing for you."

"You kept me for centuries, Hades. How can you say that?"

"Because a lovely goddess took pity on this wretched bastard and took my heart from my chest. There is nothing there to feel."

"Then it won't matter one way or another if I'm there with you, will it?" Persephone forged ahead. "I'm coming and I'm going to live with you and you don't have to call me wife, I don't care. Only keep me."

"Only keep you?" He laughed again.

It was bitter, but the knowledge warmed her. Bitter was something he *could* feel. Her cause wasn't lost.

"And what do I get out of this keeping? A pretty little godling under foot? You're a child, Persephone. I have no use for you."

Her heart cracked in her chest as earthquakes of sorrow changed the terrain. "No use at all?" she whispered. "Not even my body?"

"I was celibate for centuries for you. When I offered you your freedom and you took it, did you really think I'd stay that way?"

"Offered me my... You didn't *offer* anything, you ass. You dumped me on the surface and told my mother to take me back. You didn't ask me what I wanted. You didn't offer..." she stopped mid-thought. He'd just implied he'd been with another woman.

Persephone felt sick. She crumpled to her knees and that weight that had seemed to press on her chest crashed into her again and again. Nameless, faceless women all danced through her imagination and she could see him touching them, those strong hands on breasts fuller than her own, smaller than her own, on curves of hip and pouting lips. She could see the look of pleasure on his face, like the one when he'd spilled in her hand after offering to ease him if he'd teach her how. He was watching these other women with the same intensity he'd once watched her.

Maybe he'd only said it to hurt her. He'd promised her eternal fidelity and Hades, for all of his faults, had never broken a promise to her.

"I don't care. You can have me now, you don't need them."

"Little one, you're still under the impression I want you."

Another knife to her heart. "You're wrong, Hades."

He laughed again. "About what I want?"

"No. They're not razorblades," she said slowly. "They're knives."

"See, you don't need this pain and that's all I have left to give. Don't call me again, Persephone."

No, no, no! This couldn't be the end. She wouldn't let it be. "What if I'll take it?"

"Take what?"

"The pain. What if I'll take whatever you want to do to me to punish me?"

"I don't want to punish you, little one. I don't want anything from you at all. Save yourself this misery. It's not worth it."

Persephone felt like she was dying. "How about we make a trade?"

"What kind of trade?" he asked as if they were discussing nothing more than the fire lake outside his window.

Persephone was flooded with memories of being wrapped in his arms out on the terrace, the chilled wind blowing cold over them and watching the lava burst into the air over the lake. She wanted that again, needed it.

"I'll take your heart."

"You already did."

"No, I'll trade you. My heart for yours."

"You don't know what you're offering," he said lightly.

Maybe she didn't. Persephone knew she wasn't wise in the ways of the world and it didn't matter. "I don't care."

"It's nothing but soot and ash in a box on the mantle.

You wouldn't want that dead black thing inside of you," he said quietly.

Her own heart finished breaking, but it wasn't for her own loss. It was for his. "I do. You shouldn't live without the capacity to love. Even I know that's no kind of existence. You loved me longer than I deserved. So yes, I do want it. Let me bear it."

Tears slipped down her face. If he agreed, she'd do it. In a second. She wanted him to find some happiness and while she wanted them to have their happily ever after, Persephone knew in reality there wasn't always a horse to ride into the sunset, no matter how badly she wanted it. If anyone deserved to suffer, it was her. She'd been a selfish, spoiled, scared child. He deserved better.

"What would a jaded old bastard like me do with a heart as innocent as yours? No, Persephone. Find another godling to love you. Love him back. Forget the time you spent with me and let it fade like a nightmare with the dawn."

Even in his desolation, he could still turn a phrase with such beauty it made her soul ache.

"I love *you*, Hades. There will be no godlings for me. No men. None but you."

Persephone heard a woman's voice. "Hades, I can't find the towels and I... Sorry. Didn't see you were on the phone."

"I'm almost done. You don't need a towel. I'm just going to get you dirty again," he said with wicked seduction in voice.

"I'm not going to stop, Hades. You can hurt me as much as you like. Whatever you need to do, only at the end, let me be with you," she said.

He sighed. "Persephone, you're suffering needlessly.

The woman you heard in the background? Do you know what's going to happen when I hang up?"

Again, Persephone knew this wasn't the time to hold on to her pride. "You're going to fuck her." She almost choked on the word. "And I don't care." He didn't say anything so she kept pushing. "Do you know why I don't care? Because it's just a fuck. It won't mean anything to you. And while I was too afraid to let you take my virginity, all those nights I spent in your arms? They meant something to you. To me too. All of those soft words, and touches? The way you kissed me? You were making love to me, Hades. You can deny it all you want, but whoever is there with you now, she's not me and you don't love her."

"No, I don't love her. But I don't love you either."

"You don't just stop loving someone. It's not a switch that can be flipped because Aphrodite Criss Angeled your ass. Did she take your soul too?"

"When did you start saying ass?"

"Don't change the subject." That was just like him. Touch on something that hurt and he'd change the subject faster than she could blink.

"You're the one who said ass."

"Are you going to be on the phone all day talking about ass, because if you are, I've got other things to do with *my* ass." The other voice interrupted them.

Oh, that... Persephone made claws with her hands and then curled them into fists before releasing them. It didn't help to be made at the woman, whoever she happened to be. There was nothing more to say, but that didn't mean it was over. She wouldn't let it be over.

"No, you don't. Come here."

He didn't even bother to hang up, she realized as the sounds of their encounter echoed in her ears. He was kissing her now, his mouth hot and sweet on hers. The memory of his lips wrapped around her like a shroud.

And when she would have sobbed, Persephone remembered he'd felt this way for her for what must have been an eternity. Her pain now was only a drop in an endless ocean of suffering he'd endured. For her.

She flipped the phone closed slowly and wondered how he did it—how he walked around broken?

Persephone dashed at the tears on her cheeks with the back of her hand and tried to find her resolve, but it was like digging for gold in a mine field. Eros had warned her, but somehow, part of her had still hoped when Hades heard her voice he would have simply appeared and taken her into his arms—all forgiven.

She was a silly girl with silly dreams to imagine after she'd cut him so deeply, she deserved to have his love handed back to her on a platter; that he'd carry her off into the night without any consequences or any penance.

"Persephone?"

She swallowed another wave of grief and looked up into the dark, soulful eyes of Death. "Thanatos," she acknowledged.

"Are you okay?" he asked and pushed his long, silver hair out of his face.

"I don't think so. No." She shook her head.

"Do you want to talk about it?"

"No."

"My mother always feeds her misery. Want some ice cream?"

Suddenly, ice cream sounded better than ambrosia. She sniffed. "Chocolate. With chocolate syrup. And chocolate sprinkles. And hot fudge."

"Isn't that chocolate syrup?"

"No. They're different and I want them both. On a brownie sundae."

"Whatever you want, little one."

Her throat constricted at his casual use of Hades' endearment. "Thanatos?" Persephone felt her bottom lip quiver.

"Hey, whoa. All I did was offer to buy you ice cream. Don't fucking cry. Please don't fucking cry. I take it back, whatever I did." He took a step back and mumbled, "My mother is going to smite my balls off."

"What? No. I'm sorry. I just... don't call me that, okay?"

"No problem."

"Why would your mother smite you for making me cry?"

"I mentioned we were friends. She said to be nice to you. Actually, verbatim was: Don't be a dick."

"I love your mom. She's cool. I wish my mom was as laid back as yours is."

"I think it happens with age. Nyx is older than dirt." He flashed her a smile.

"Niiice. I dare you to say that to her face."

"I did, just a few hours ago. And she made me fig cakes with cream cheese frosting."

"You are so spoiled."

"Yeah, and I like it that way."

"Wait, you just had fig cakes and now you want ice cream?" She eyed him. "You better be careful or you'll be fat as Dionysus."

"And look at the tail he still pulls down. Last week he was—," he broke off. "Sorry. I'm doing it again."

"Doing what?"

"Being a dick. You don't want to hear this stuff."

"No, it's fine. You and Eros are the only ones who don't

treat me like I'm going to break. So please, don't stop being you. Talk about whatever you want. Even tail, I don't care. It's time I learned something of the world, I think." She smiled at him.

"In that case, I'm your god." Thanatos grinned. "Give me that smile again and I'll let you drive my pale horse." He winked.

"Was that a euphemism?" She wrinkled her nose.

"What? No." They were suddenly sitting inside of a white '69 Ford Mustang convertible. "He's been with me for awhile now. His name is Jimmy."

"And you're still telling me that's not a euphemism?"

"Time for your first lesson, Persephone. Keep referring to that and a god will think it's a euphemism for a euphemism. Get my drift?"

"No."

"Flirting, pretty girl. You're being flirty."

"You think I'm pretty?" Suddenly, inspiration flashed. She could feel Thalia's presence all around her and knew it to be divine.

"Come on. You know you're pretty."

"No, I mean, am I pretty to you? There are some girls who are pretty by any standard, some who are pretty to a few and some who are beautiful. Some who are more like works of art than something feminine to be touched. What am I to you? Would it be a hardship to kiss me?" she asked thoughtfully.

Thanatos looked like a deer caught in the blaring lights of an oncoming Mack truck.

"Look, you know I love Hades, right?" Persephone ventured.

"I assumed that's what you didn't want to talk about."

"Cute and smart." She grinned. "You said this is my first lesson? Well, I've got a lesson to teach too. To Hades."

"I see. You want me to make him jealous." Thanatos rolled his eyes. "This has *ends badly* written all over it with a red Sharpie."

"You're the only other god he'd buy me falling for. You both have that bad boy dark thing going on. You're also one of the only other gods whose ass he can't hand back to them like a Happy Meal."

He leaned back in the seat. "Persephone, what if you only had a week to live? Would you want to spend it trying to inflict more misery on the god you profess to love?"

"Yes. In the hopes he'd realize he still loves me before I'm gone."

"Have you ever considered that maybe he does?"

"I know he does."

"No, he loved you enough to let you go. It's not that he doesn't realize it. Maybe he wants better for you. I know if you'd been my goddess and I had to see you with someone else, it would tear me apart. If you still love him, don't shred what he's got left for a game."

"What he's got left? You know what he's got? He's got some woman in the castle where I used to live asking him where the damn the towels are. He's telling her she doesn't need them because he'll just get her dirty again."

"How do you know that?"

"Because I was on the phone with him when it happened."

"Maybe it wasn't—okay, it probably was. I have to be honest though, what did you expect?"

"I didn't know what to expect!" she cried. "Please, Thanatos. Please help me. He told me to move on, I want to show him what it would be like if I did. Being away from him, it taught me how much I want to be with him. Why couldn't it do the same for him?"

He still looked unsure.

"Just one kiss here on the Lane where everyone can see. Is it too much to ask for a kiss from Death?"

"Persephone, it's not that you're not kissable..."

Was he really telling her no? After the day she'd had? Screw the ice cream. He was going to kiss her and like it.

"Did you know Hades calls himself the Master of the Dead?"

"He is." Thanatos shrugged.

"No, I think he thinks of himself as the Master of *Death*."

"Oh, what, like saying he thinks he's the 'boss of me' is going incite rebellion?"

"Doesn't it?"

"You're damn right it does." Thanatos threaded his fingers through Persephone's golden hair and dragged her to him for a hard kiss, there with the top down on his pale horse convertible.

CHAPTER
FOURTEEN

NYX

This is a bad idea, Nyx thought as she walked up to the front door of Pomegranate Pizza.

Probably the worst in the history of bad ideas and that was saying a lot, but Nyx hadn't actually been out on a real date in centuries. Sure, she got hers, but it was always a "hit it and quit it" sort of arrangement as her son was so fond of saying.

It wasn't that Apollo wasn't handsome, or witty, or any of the things she would look for, it was simply that he seemed so very young to her. He was friends with her son— a Lifetime movie waiting to happen: My Son's Best Friend, My Lover. (She was ashamed to admit, she loved LMN.)If that wasn't bad enough, like most of the gods he was Zeus' get and Nyx had been old when Zeus had taken his first breath. Youth wasn't the issue when it was only sex, but this was a date. A date implied interest in a relationship. Unless he'd been afraid to ask his best friend to set him up with his mom for a shag... Perfectly reasonable excuse. Nyx vowed to put that out there as soon as she saw him. Get it out of the way. So, depending on his answer, she could be nervous later.

Meeting a boy at the pizza parlor? Nyx felt stupid. She also felt every single eye on Ambrosia Lane watching her. Even the Cyclops who ran the parlor was looking at her and he had fourteen ovens to watch. No mean feat with one freaking eye.

Nyx darted into the bathroom to check her reflection one last time. She'd opted out of the fairy dress. As much as she liked it, she had no idea what to expect. It wasn't like she couldn't change if they did something that required more formal attire. She'd gone with jeans and while they were black, they definitely *weren't* a muumuu. They were what the mortals were calling "apple-bottom". She'd gone with a shimmery peasant style blouse that could be low-cut or demure, as she chose. Depending on how the evening was going.

"Heya!" Artemis appeared beside her and Nyx shrieked like an arachnophobe with a tarantula in her knickers. "Gods, Nyx. It's only me."

"Hello, Artemis. You know, a bathroom isn't really a place where one pops uninvited."

"I'm not invited?" she pouted. "That's just as well. I have to say something and I don't know if you're going like it."

"Don't be shitty to Apollo and if I'm only after sex to say so, so he doesn't get the wrong idea?" Nyx supplied.

"Yep. That about covers it." Artemis ticked off her talking points on her fingers and deemed them to have all been addressed.

"And if I did break his heart?" she asked gently. Artemis was ditzy like a game show blond. Wait, she *was* a game show blond—on the Game Show Channel. It was a hobby of hers.

"Not sure. I'd have to do something though, you know? It's like the brother-sister-best pal sort of code." Artemis nodded.

"Sure, I get it."

"You're ace, Nyx. I knew you'd understand. I mean, he's never been real commitment minded, but you're special. You're different from the other goddesses. And the way he looked at you, wow. The god was head over arse. So, be kind."

"I recently had this conversation with my son." Nyx commiserated.

"Right? Why is he tangled up over *Persephone*." Artemis made a sound like she was vomiting. "If he had to go for the blond virginal type, why did it have to be her? I don't see the attraction."

"Me either." Nyx curled her lip in disgust. "She's not ugly or anything, but she's spoiled and cruel. At least from what I've seen. Granted, I don't know her, so I shouldn't be making that judgment, but I don't think she'd be best for Thanatos."

"Then there's her horrible mother. Who'd want Demeter for an in-law?"

"That's mean, Artemis. Demeter's... not so bad," she managed half-heartedly.

Artemis snorted and choked. "Puh-lease. She's awful— the horrible monster-in-law archetype."

Nyx hadn't known Artemis used words like archetype. She was impressed. "I will admit if I were a god, I wouldn't go sniffing up that tree if you paid me."

"So, do you think you could put in a good word to Thanatos for me? I'm a blond virginal type." Artemis looked hopeful. "At least if you don't think I'm too horrible a tree to be sniffing." She colored. "I mean, well, you know what I mean."

"I do and as much as I hate to say it, because really, the friends longing to be more category sucks..."

"I know," she sighed. "Be his friend. When this thing for Persephone bursts into flame, be there for him. I *do* know. I just..." she growled and clenched her fingers.

"Gods are frustrating." Nyx patted her hand in a motherly way.

"Are you going to give me the don't break his heart talk too?"

Nyx looked at her for a long time. "No, dear. I think you already know."

Artemis rewarded her with a smile and then perked. "Apollo is here. Have fun!" And she popped out of the bathroom.

Poor goddess. She was stuck like glue on Thanatos and he only had eyes for Persephone who was stuck on Hades who was going to be fucking Hera who was still married to Zeus who was hell-bent on shagging Abstinence who wanted none of it from anyone. She could design a new game with all of this mess: Six Degrees of a Migraine. Patching all of that together made her head hurt. The worst part was that none of it was necessary. It made Nyx thankful she wasn't a godling and had been through all the Oh-My-Gods-Angst of relationshipping. Then she wondered if she was going to have something to throw in the mix tomorrow that would have her calling Hera in one of those same godling dramas. She shook her head at herself and went out to meet Apollo.

The first thing she noticed was that he was wearing black.

Muumuu, indeed. The slacks and designer turtleneck made him look very US East Coast Prep. It was sexy on him.

He gave her a genuine smile that reached his eyes. "Wanna get out of here?"

Damn if that wasn't fast. So much for being nervous about it being a real date. This was her comfort zone. She could do this. Nyx nodded and he held the door for her. There were still a hundred eyes on her, but at least out in the evening air she could breathe.

"Where would you like to go?" he asked.

"It's up to you, really." Nyx was good, wherever he thought was best. Although, if he said her place, she'd have to demure. No matter what she'd told Thanatos, she wasn't brining Apollo back to the temple for a quick in/out.

"Do you like dancing?"

What did that have to do with anything? Was this going to be some joke about the horizontal mambo? If so, she'd have reconsider the whole experience. She nodded experimentally—she waited to see what else he was going to say.

"There's a great discothèque in Greece. There'll be live music tonight."

Oh shit. He really did want to take her somewhere.

Out in public.

Together.

Nyx's stomach flipped and she was sure she was going to hurl. She hadn't been out with a god in... she couldn't remember how long.

She must have gone pale—from ghostly white to incandescent because he said something. "Not a fan of the discothèque, then?"

"I'm going to be brutally honest."

"I thought Night was supposed to hide our sins, not

shine a light." He gave her a half smile that could have been a grin or a smirk, she wasn't sure which.

"Nothing that happens at night is ever really a secret. So, might as well save us both the trouble, right?"

"You don't really want to go out with me?" His smile never wavered. "Is Thanatos holding his visits hostage or something?"

"It's not that. Well, it is that. But not like you think," she babbled.

He waited patiently for her to continue. It felt odd, but it was like he was the grown up and she was child who had something on her shoe she'd tracked through the house and he was waiting for a reasonable explanation.

"You just surprised me is all." Yeah, that wasn't going to fly. She knew he was going to want details, but suddenly, with him so close and the very real possibility of having him in her bed, she didn't want to mess it up. Who knew?

"Nyx, I know you don't really date. So this is new. How about we just have fun, okay? No pressure. We'll go hang out, you can drive the chariot at dawn and I'll drop you safe and sound at your temple."

"What if I don't mind the pressure?" Damn it, how had that escaped her mouth? She needed to have a new filter installed; one that actually did what it was supposed to do and kept her from running off at the suck.

"Now I'm confused. I'm just a god, so you're going to have to spell it out."

"That's how you surprised me. You wanted to take me somewhere."

"That's generally what one does on a date, Nyx," he mock whispered.

"I know, but I thought this was…something else."

Apollo laughed and it was a deep, rich sound that

reminded Nyx of summer. "You thought I was trying to get laid?"

"Well, yeah." She grinned awkwardly.

"Nyx," he tsked. "Getting laid is easy. Finding a goddess or a woman I can talk to, or want to spend time with other than fucking, that's tough."

"Correction. I *do* mind the pressure." She laughed.

He laughed again. "So, a quick roll in the proverbial hay and you were good to go, but talking about really getting to know each other scares you?"

"Most definitely," she admitted cheerfully, pleased he understood.

"And here I thought you were going out with me to drive the chariot."

"That too." She nodded enthusiastically.

"When I was a young god, I made it a condition to be in the chariot, you had to put out."

"I know. You were a bad influence on Thanatos," she admonished.

"And yet, here we are." The look on his face promised the same when he got her into the chariot.

"What do you think it is we have to talk about?" she challenged.

"I don't know. Maybe we should just go back to your temple and call it a night." He winked at her playfully.

"I like that id—I don't. Can't, I mean. I promised Thanatos I wouldn't bring you back for a quickie because he's staying over."

"I've got one of my kids at my place too." He shrugged helplessly. "Looks like we have to find something to go do instead. Like a real date."

"Dancing it is. Unless you want to sneak into the bathroom here? It would save on the cover charge."

"Nyx, you're not getting out of this. If you don't want to go out with me again after, I can take it. But we're going to do something that isn't horizontal."

"Don't you like horizontal? I mean, you do have a lot of children."

"To be fair, I haven't fathered any children in a century."

"So, you *don't* like it?" she needled.

"I guess not." Apollo was completely unruffled by her jibe.

Nyx liked that, probably more than she should have. In fact, after her initial discomfort, she liked the whole exchange. He wasn't intimidated by her age, or her mouth and he obviously wasn't thinking of her as Thanatos' mother. She'd been worried this had been some godling spank bank fantasy and he'd be...well, not like this.

"Okay, fine. Have it your way." She softened her words with a genuine smile.

"I plan to."

His lighthearted flirting sent warmth fluttering through her. She was giddy and scared all at once. Nyx was surprised to find she liked this too. It had been a long time since her interest had been piqued. What would Hera say?

She wondered how her friend was doing with her plans for total Olympic domination. But all other thoughts fell out of her head like candy in a piñata when Apollo put his hand on her waist.

"Are you ready?"

Nyx's cheeks warmed in a blush and she nodded her head. She was going to have whiplash before the night was over, yo-yoing between feeling like the old lady on the block to the giddy girl whose heart was a butterfly in her chest.

They were immediately inside the club, the music

thumping in a seductive beat. She was sure she recognized the strains of Lady Gaga. She looked up at Apollo and noticed he was wearing rimless glasses.

She gave him a questioning glance. Somehow, those chic glasses made his hair look even better. The dark of the arms lost in the feathered sides of his hair struck her as incredibly sexy—made her want to push her hands through it.

Rather than moving away from her or offering to get her a drink, he pulled her closer and fell in step with the music. A god who could dance, another slash in the plus column. Or maybe it was the minus column. They way their bodies undulated together to the thrumming of the music made her want to see what his other moves were like. Until she remembered seeing him and Thanatos making cosmic mud pies in the yard outside the temple—Demeter making it rain so the mud would be pliable and Zeus with the breath of life animating their creations. The boys had laughed and giggled, burying their chubby fingers in the dirt.

Nyx was the most horrible lech.

She consoled herself with the knowledge he was a baby no longer and by the way he was touching her, he hadn't been in a long time. Was she so old mortal morality was coming in to play? She wasn't just a goddess, she was a titan. To be truthful, there wasn't anyone she could have a toss with who wasn't Thanatos' age. It didn't matter.

"Nice, Apollo." A young woman snorted as she danced beside them. She looked Nyx up and down and seemed to find her lacking.

Okay, so it did matter. If this was what she had to deal with, Nyx was out. She didn't have the patience to deal with some baby mama drama or whatever was about to ensue. She'd either walk away or smite and neither option appealed to her. She'd rather not deal with it at all.

He rolled his eyes. "Aren't you supposed to be at home, Hyacinth?"

"Aren't you supposed to be hanging out with Thanatos?"

Nyx snapped her head sideways to look at him. Oh, hell no. He'd lied about who he was going to be with? She called bullshit to all of the crap he'd said earlier. Apollo had game, she'd give him that.

"Oh, didn't know he lied to me about where he was, did you?" The golden girl put her fists on her hips.

Nyx was about to turn and walk away when Apollo caught her wrist. When she tugged and he didn't let go, she narrowed her eyes and all the light disappeared from the dance floor. Shadows had swallowed the strobes and spotlights; even the glo-stick jewelry went dark. Everyone in the club gasped, but rather than panic, they continued to dance.

"Nyx, this is my daughter. Hyacinth. Rebellious ruin my date child type, this is Nyx—Goddess of Night."

"Cool! I thought the Goddess of Night was old," Hyacinth grinned.

"She is," Nyx replied dryly and the light came back.

"That was awesome. Can you do it again?" She looked to Nyx eagerly. "Oh, and sorry about the whole looking like a jealous girlfriend thing. I knew he was going on a date, but Apollo has notoriously bad taste in women."

"You call your dad Apollo? Thanatos still calls me mom."

"Wow, he's so hot. Is he single?" Hyacinth asked eagerly.

Was every immortal chick this side of Olympus hot for

her youngest son? She wasn't sure whether to be proud or completely squicked.

"Aren't you supposed to be at home?" Apollo cut in.

"I figured you'd be out all night and wouldn't notice."

"Your mom won't let you come to Olympus anymore if you jet to Greece when you're supposed to be at my temple."

"What my mother doesn't know..."

"Will kill me. Come on. Go home."

Hyacinth's face fell and Nyx noticed someone waiting for her. It was Boreas—God of the North Wind. She realized Apollo hadn't let go of her wrist and she slipped her hand into his. "She'll be fine. Boreas will take good care of her."

He looked like he'd been junk punched with a rhinoceros.

"I know him. He's a good god," Nyx said soothingly.

"Fine, but can we get out of here?"

Nyx laughed. "What happened to the no-pressure party guy?"

"Knowing his daughter is going to be violated tonight kind of puts a damper on it."

She laughed harder. "I definitely had it easier with all boys."

"She runs wild. Her mother isn't any help. All she does is yell at me about it, drink and pop pills. I may be a god, but there's nothing I can do about the behavior of a teenage girl. I want her to come live with me full time, but she's mortal."

"At least with mortals the rebellious stage only lasts a couple years. With godlings, it can be centuries."

"Gods, woman. Don't remind me. I've petitioned Zeus to give her ambrosia."

"It's hard to imagine you as a father." She cocked her head to the side, trying to picture it.

"And yet, I've done it so many times."

"At least you support all of your children." She frowned thinking of Zeus.

"I was determined not to be my dad." He seemed to know the train of her thoughts.

Apollo held the door for her as they stepped out into the Greek night. "I guess I don't have a kid at my temple anymore. Want to go be old and have a quiet night with a flick and some ambrosia wine while we sit up and wait for my daughter who I know won't be home until tomorrow?"

Nyx smiled. That actually sounded like a much better time to her than clubbing anyway. "Yeah. It sounds fun, actually. I still get to drive the chariot, though, right?"

"Why is it all women want to drive my chariot?"

"We're all car hos at heart."

"You've got a saucy mouth."

"All the better to—," she broke off. Nyx had no idea where she was going with that, but was sure she didn't want to find out.

"All the better to what, my dear? I'd like to know." He grinned suggestively.

"I'm sure you would." She smirked.

"You're not going to tell me?"

"Nope." Nyx shook her head.

"We'll just have to see about that," he promised and stroked his hand down her spine as he pulled her close to teleport.

FIFTEEN

DEMETER

Demeter thought it funny how the granules through the hourglass of eternity slowed to a sickly crawl when one marked them off with misery. She'd always thought there'd never be enough time. She didn't know how the mortals stood it—learning from birth they would have an end and careening closer to it every day.

She'd hidden from Death for so long, now it seemed she'd have to invite him in. Demeter wished she'd met him before Love, that these memories weren't so stark and ambulatory. A movie that played over and over again in black and white. Regret was a word she'd vowed never to learn, yet here it was ashen and bitter on the tip of her tongue.

Demeter regretted not only singular moments, but every choice she'd made. They were all wrong and she didn't know how to fix them before her time was up and she didn't want to correct them only for herself. She'd done Persephone a great wrong.

She hadn't seen her in days and Demeter hoped she'd gone back to Hades. Hoped that she'd found something beautiful that would sustain her in the long dark. More than that, she didn't want to leave Persephone alone and unprotected in the world. By keeping her cloistered and innocent of everything, she'd never really lived yet either.

What would happen to Persephone without the fear of Demeter's wintry wrath to ward off those who would hurt her? She'd be alone.

The word echoed hollow in her ears and settled in a dead weight on her stomach. Alone. The last place Demeter wanted to be. Once upon a time, Demeter had dreamed quiet dreams of green and growing things; she'd heard the voices of these tiny lives all around her. They'd sung to her songs of joy and rebirth. Until she'd brought the winter in her heart with her fear.

"Spring is never an easy time, rebirth never gentle," Eros spoke softly as he materialized in the garden chair next to her.

Love was to be found in the strangest of places, or so she'd always heard. She'd never been so happy to see him or so distraught at the same time.

"I don't remember inviting you back, Eros."

"That is the nature of Love, is it not? To come unbidden?"

"I suppose it is. Does that mean when I need you most, you'll be nowhere to be found?" Demeter wouldn't turn her head to look at him.

"I'm always here, Demeter. Whenever you need anything, whether you know your need or not."

"I gave Persephone your quiver."

"She called," he acknowledged.

"I told her to give it to you," she replied, sullen.

"She told me to come and get it."

"I'm sure she did. She thinks she's helping."

"Isn't she?"

"How? By throwing us together? There's only one way this can end, Eros."

"And how do you know this? Are you Fate now, to tell us all what paths we'll take?"

"I know how it will end because it's time for *my* end. Don't you understand?"

"Then why don't you want to spend the time in joy and happiness? Because you don't deserve it? Again, are you Fate to make that choice?" Eros asked her quietly.

"Why should I be happy when my daughter will be frightened and alone? When I took the one god from her who loved her?"

"You overestimate your power, Demeter. Hades isn't the only god who will love her. I love her."

"Do you love her as a god, or as a friend?" Demeter asked.

"You know very well the answer to that, Demeter. But if she needs me, she knows how to ask me for help. She's done it before."

"Tell me then, will Hades love her? Surely that is within your sight."

"Hades has loved her and loved her well. He let her go. As to what he feels now, no, I cannot see. His heart has been torn from his chest. But her path is not with him."

"Then where is it?" She finally turned to look at him and he wore a mask of quiet sorrow.

"She will walk with Death, Demeter. Into the long dark,

but she will not be cold. She will not be alone. He will hold her tenderly."

"She'll die, then." Demeter couldn't keep the bitterness out of her tone.

"No," he shook his head. "She won't. Death's love becomes her in the fading dawn, the birds will sing and flowers will bloom in her step and he will love her well. But only if you allow her to become what she was meant to be."

Tears streaked down her face, for Demeter knew this to be her redemption. Persephone would only become the Goddess of the Spring when Demeter let go of her power—when she laid down her breath and surrendered. It was the only way to make sure her daughter would be safe and finally, after all of these long years, Demeter had been granted a second chance to be a good mother. To love her child more than she loved herself.

And such was the way of the mother and the earth, the old god dies and the new one is reborn. The lifecycle of the seasons and all things green and growing.

Snowdrops bloomed at her feet where her tears fell and Eros took her hand in his own, a tender gesture.

"Do you see, Demeter? Will you let me hold you now?"

"I'm afraid, Eros."

"I know." He lifted her easily and gathered her to him.

He didn't tell her not to be afraid, but it was okay somehow. The way he held her in his arms was comfort enough and more than she deserved. She loved the way he smelled, of summer and bright things. His scent brought to mind sweet simplicity, uncomplicated purity. She remembered being a child and picking flowers in Elysium, she remembered when she first discovered she could make them grow.

There'd been fields upon fields of flowers growing as they would, all hungry for the power she held—the elixir of life she could share with only her will. She'd been so eager to share it then, to blanket the world in abundance. The trees and vines grew heavy with fruits and the roots grew large and strong deep in the ground.

She should have done that for Persephone.

"Demeter, go back to that place you were. The place with the sun and the ripe berries," Eros commanded her.

She couldn't find it again though; it had slipped through her fingers like the crumbled petals of a dried rose.

"Open your eyes. Look at what you've wrought in your joy, yet again."

Demeter looked and saw the fields behind her temple bursting with life. Things she'd had to wring like water from a desert out of her power these last years now flowed freely.

"It's you. It was your scent, Eros. You wrought this, not me."

"This came from you. From your love. Remember what I said to you and the prophecy? Love will save you, Demeter."

"Will you?"

"Not me, though I would if I could. The love inside of yourself."

"I have none."

Eros stroked her hair. "Then just let me hold you."

"You can do whatever you like, only..." she bit her lip.

"I'll grant you whatever is in my power, but I can't do it unless you ask."

"Stay with me?" Demeter asked in a small voice.

"Always."

"When it's time," she clarified. It was selfish, but she wanted him to hold her hand. Demeter knew she'd have to go into that final dark by herself, but it would be nice to have his warmth to see her off.

"Yes."

"You promise so easily." Did he know what he was promising? If he did, could he really love her as he professed? How did one let go of someone they loved? She didn't understand.

"I love you. I'd never let you face this alone. Pain is transient, but the impressions of love stay with us into the Elysian Fields and even Tartarus."

"How easily you speak of love and death." She sighed and rested her cheek on his shoulder. "If I could love, Eros, I would want to love you."

He didn't speak and he didn't need to. Demeter knew he could see into her heart and for once, she was thankful. She could never express the fountains of sorrow or the raindrops of joy—the darkness and the light that warred within her. Eros could see it all. She almost believed he loved her despite it all. It was a beautiful fantasy and she'd waltz with it into the twilight of her existence.

Demeter wanted to give him something, but she had nothing to offer but herself. "Eros?"

He didn't speak but dragged his cheek along her hair.

"Do you still want to..." she trailed off. Demeter had been going to ask him if he wanted to fuck her, but she knew he didn't. He wanted to *love* her. "Make love to me?" She felt stupid saying it that way; she didn't think anyone said things like that anymore.

Eros cupped her cheek as he carried her inside the temple and stroked his thumb over her bottom lip.

"More than my next breath." He kissed her then, with those honeyed words on his lips and they were sweet.

He tasted not of saccharine lies, but of truth and the poetry that had been tattooed on his soul. For a moment, Demeter felt as if letting him kiss her would tarnish all of that beauty he had inside of him, but wave after wave of something warm washed over her. It was endless and eternal, a never-ending sea; it sparkled with everything that made Eros who and what he was. It was his power, his mantle.

It was Love.

In its purest form and inexhaustible, it filled her. He trailed it over her skin with his lips, sparked it inside of her with his hands and while it was like lava; molten and gold, it didn't burn. It made her feel strong and it bathed her in an innocence she thought she'd never touch again.

"Eros?"

"Don't be afraid," he murmured against her lips.

And she wasn't.

Demeter opened herself to him and allowed all that he wanted to give her to come rushing in. It was tsunami, an earthquake and an apocalypse. It was vast and sharp, but it cut her strategically. It lanced the darkness and the misery; bared her wounds and tore them open.

But it eased her pain too in a sweet balm.

Her knees were weak and Demeter couldn't stand on her own when Eros shifted her so that her feet were on the cherry wood planks of her temple.

"I don't want to be here anymore."

"Where do you want to be?" Eros asked as his mouth fastened to the curve of her neck.

"Somewhere else. Not Olympus. Not this temple where so many dark thoughts have moldered and infected the walls. Somewhere in the world. Make love to me on a beach at sunset, in a gondola in Venice, the top of the Eiffel Tower, or maybe even the moon. I'd like to see earthrise."

They were suddenly in a gondola that steered itself down the canals of Venice and the full moon hung round and gravid in the dark sky, the stars splashed across the velvet pitch like glitter.

Her back was against his chest and her cheek was close to his. Her arm was draped around the back of his neck and his fingers stroked down the sensitive skin of her inner arm. Every touch was a benediction and this time, she didn't want to fight it.

SIXTEEN

HERA

Hera wrinkled her nose. "Really? What a centaurhole. Yeah and then to ask you to call his wife? Dick move." She snorted with another laugh. "No, I have no idea what's wrong with him. He what? WHAT? I'm coming." She snapped her phone off, but stayed put. Partly because she wasn't hurrying anywhere under Zeus' command and partly because she wasn't sure if she could move. Hera hadn't been able to sit correctly since she'd started this mad affair with Hades. On the one hand, she loved it, or the other, it was hard to keep her feelings compartmentalized.

On second thought, that was a lie. They *weren't* compartmentalized. She had feelings for Hades, regardless of what was happening between them or what he felt. She simply had to accept that and get on with the business of living. Hera couldn't change anything either of them felt; she could only control how she reacted to it.

"What's happened?" he asked, pushing a damp lock of hair behind her ear.

She leaned into the touch, wanting more of it and less of the rest of the world that would take a sledgehammer to the foundations of their idyll. "Zeus. He's had some sort of episode at Abstinence's temple."

"What kind of episode?" Hades wore a look of concern.

"He passed out and turned all flaky. I guess he didn't drink his ambrosia. Now, he expects me to come haul his ass home and tend him like a loving wife. It's not that big a deal."

"No, Hera. It is a big deal. I'm afraid you do have to help him."

"Why? I mean, I will help him, but it'll be on my schedule, damn it." She wanted to roll over and pull the blankets up over her head.

"Do you want him to die?" he asked quietly.

"He can't die." Was that even an option?

"He can. And if you don't help him, he will."

How come this was the first she'd heard of this? Hera wanted to say that she didn't care—that he had it coming for treating her so badly and making her feel like shit. For all of the mortals and gods he'd punished because he didn't get his way.

"Ye—no." She slumped down further in the bed. "How do you know what's wrong with him anyway?"

"I can't believe he didn't tell you this. You've been married for an eon."

"Tell me *what*?" she almost screeched.

"It's his secret to tell you, Hera. Although, the irony today will amuse you to no end, I'm sure." Hades smirked at her and moved to dress.

"What are you doing?"

"Coming with you of course."

"Why?"

"Been doing it all day, why stop now?" He eyed her lasciviously and she felt his appraisal in the throbbing between her thighs.

"Stop that." Hera shivered.

"Or what? You'll fuck me again?"

"Yes! It's gotten to be where I need it like I do ambrosia and taunting me with it doesn't help."

"Pleasure on par with ambrosia." He made a big show of stopping to consider the possibilities. "That's certainly something to be avoided." Hades' voice was silk over her skin and his long strides took him around the bed and he'd hauled her up against him. "Be a good goddess and get your delectable ass in gear and I promise when we get home, I'll lick *your* ambrosia until you scream."

His words made her need intensify, but it wasn't only the promise of his tongue working her flesh until she came. He'd said home. *When we get home.* Hera knew she shouldn't read so much into what he'd said, it was a word said casually. It meant little or nothing to him, so it shouldn't mean anything to her either.

But it did.

The implications were they would go to see Zeus, to help him, but that Hera wasn't going to stay where her ailing husband was. She was going to stay with Hades. Her god. Her future. This was *their* home and she wouldn't lose it to Persephone, or anyone else.

She smiled brightly. "I'll let you drive then." Hera struggled into her clothes. "Wait, should we cleanse first?"

"No, definitely not."

"You're bad."

"Actually, you'll need it."

"I don't like the sound of that." She narrowed her eyes, but before she could question him, he'd anchored her against him and they were standing in front of Abstinence's door. "Damn it. You didn't even let me do my hair."

Abstinence opened the door, a panicked look on her face. "He's in the front room."

Hades stood straighter. "Death was here."

"He was," Abstinence acknowledged. "He came for me."

"Okay, you need to tell me everything. These half-assed explanations are going to make me rip my hair out," Hera grumbled.

She followed Abstinence into the front room and saw a pitiful figure—a skeleton prone in a pile of dust on the floor. He was emaciated and week, unable to move—his chest sunken and shriveled. There was nothing about him Hera found to be familiar except for the glacial blue of his eyes. Those were eyes she'd stared into for centuries, eyes that had seen all of the horror and pleasure the world had to offer. They were ancient and youthful both.

Zeus.

"What did you do to yourself, you ass?" Hera whispered almost tenderly. She sighed. "And then you told your would-be mistress to call your wife. Do you know how tacky that is?"

"Hera, you can ream his ass later if you so choose. Right now, you need to hold his hand," Hades told her.

Hera wrinkled her nose. "Nuh-uh."

"I will hold his hand." Abstinence took the barely animated bones in her own tiny hand.

Hades put a reassuring touch on the thin goddess's shoulder. "I'm sorry, Abstinence. It must be Hera. She has the energy to share."

"Oh." It all seemed to click for Abstinence, but Hera felt

like she still had goat cheese for brains. She didn't understand at all.

Hades sank to his haunches behind her and traced his fingers down her bare arm and Hera breathed deeply as those light touches sparked sensation through her body. She didn't feel the least bit guilty about it either. Zeus was lucky she'd even bothered to show up after all he'd done to her.

He whispered in her ear. "Think about this afternoon. Remember what I said to you before we left?"

About licking her? She shuddered and wondered how perverse Hades really was. Until she saw that it wasn't punishing Zeus or tormenting him, at least not obviously. In fact, his form had become more solid, fleshy. The more aroused she became, the more it healed her god-husband.

Hades kissed her neck and took the tender skin near her carotid between his teeth and this sent jolts of healing energy to Zeus. As Hades ran his hands down Hera's sides to her hips, Zeus sprang to his feet and ripped Hera away from him.

"Thanks for your help, brother. But your work here is done." Zeus snarled.

"No, Zeus. It's not. I'm not your wife anymore." Hera jerked away from him. It felt so good to say the words, to release the bonds that chained them together. Hera felt free.

"Are you *his* wife, then? You know you'll never be as young or beautiful as Persephone. He will never love you the way he loved her."

Hera had her arm drawn ready to slap him, but it fell useless to her side. She didn't need him to tell her that she wasn't Persephone. Hera knew that. She wasn't an idiot.

And now it was so obvious how his barb had stuck home because she had nothing to say.

Abstinence slapped him for her.

The undernourished goddess packed quite a punch. She knocked Zeus back a good two feet and he wobbled for a moment like he was going to fall. He braced himself on the fireplace and rubbed his jaw.

"What was that for?"

"Saying something that horrible to your *wife* who came here to help you when by all rights she should have let you rot," Abstinence snapped. "Gods know I would have."

"Saved me?" Zeus smirked.

"Left you here to think about what you'd done all of these years, you bastard. You know, I thought I saw a glimmer of redemption in you today, but I was mistaken," Abstinence snarled.

From the look on his face, Zeus had been hit harder by her words than her fist.

Hades had been right; the irony of the situation was killing her. Only not how he'd thought. Their sexual energy had healed him. By cuckolding her husband, she'd done him a favor. But that wasn't what caused her to mourn the irony of the situation. It was that Hera and Zeus' hearts both were breaking now, but it was their lovers who'd done the breaking and not each other.

She was amazed at this change in Zeus at how one word from the goddess had caused him pain. He'd never been like that with her, even in the beginning.

"I think you owe your wife an explanation," Hades said quietly.

"Fuck yourself," Zeus snapped. "She's not my wife anymore, remember?"

"Fine. I will tell her then. She deserves to know."

"You only think that because she's not yours."

"Not mine? She was mine twelve different ways this afternoon, brother. She bears my mark; she's vowed herself to me. No, I have her. She's mine no matter what happens here."

Zeus used his renewed strength to catch Hades in a choke hold and Hades didn't fight him. He allowed the violence, but smiled coldly, as if it didn't matter. "Choking me doesn't change what happened. Nor does it change the fact she *wasn't going to come*."

The fire of his rage was extinguished and he released Hades. "What do you mean?"

Hera answered for herself. "After all that I've given up for you and how you've treated me, did you really expect me to drop what I was doing and run to see how I could serve my god-king?" she snarled.

"Yes, you're my wife." His face was twisted with anger.

"A fact you conveniently forget when you're trying to fuck our new neighbor. Or all the countless others you've ridden. Even though you haven't touched your willing wife in more centuries than I care to count. Your mighty thunderbolt is a bad porn joke, Zeus."

"You never wanted sex, Hera."

"Oh, I did. I wanted it, but with my husband and only my husband. Not the entire extended family of the Emperor of Rome at one sitting."

"You said no, so I left you alone. What did you want from me?"

"Fidelity. Trust. Honor."

"You sound like you've been reading Grail Romances. Wrong pantheon."

"I know. I do know. Your brother is more worthy of your crown that you are."

"Be careful what you say, Hera. If you try to take my crown, wife or no..." He let the threat hang.

Hera screamed. She screamed so loudly all the glass shattered and splashed out onto Ambrosia Lane like a waterfall. "It isn't your crown! It never has been. It's mine. Mine. *Mine!* Do you hear me?"

"Hera, everyone can hear you." Hades put a steadying hand on her shoulder.

Zeus made a face like she'd kicked him in the sac, bit it wasn't enough.

"It's mine. I made you King of Gods and if I so choose I will unmake you and there is nothing, absolutely *nothing* you can do about it. You've frightened everyone else with that little stunt you pulled with Prometheus, but just try that with me and you will find out how great and terrible my wrath really is," she seethed through her clenched teeth.

"Oh and what would you do with *my* crown?"

"Give it to Hades." she shot back. "You're lucky he didn't want it."

"You treacherous bitch." He took a step toward her.

Hades was between them before Zeus could blink and a long, dark shadow filled the room. It billowed out from behind Hades in wings of darkness and sucked all of the light from the space. The Lord of the Underworld grew taller, broader and the blue flame that burned in his eyes spread; now crackling over his palms and up his forearms.

That living shadow wrapped itself around Hera and moved her further behind him. The voices of the damned lived in that breathing darkness and they whispered to her —a cacophony of suffering—but they touched her hair and her face softly and she recognized her lover in those caresses. His power was greater than anyone on Olympus.

The crown of the gods was his by right. With a certainty, Hera realized it always had been.

She felt a rush of desire, not just because of the power he held, but for how he wielded it. That quiet confidence in himself, he didn't need a crown to know who he was. He didn't need to take something from another only to prove he could, not when he knew how much Zeus needed that crown to define himself.

Hera had another epiphany.

It was something she'd known was there, so she supposed maybe it wasn't the lightning strike of an epiphany after all, but an acceptance of an irrefutable truth.

Hera loved Hades.

It wasn't a silly godling infatuation, it wasn't something that had sprouted in her fantasies because he'd made her come, she loved him for all of the things he was as a god; a male. For all of his darkness, his soul was a bright beacon and it was beautiful. It had made her want to be a better goddess. He'd changed her without trying, without wanting anything from her other than what she could give.

With that realization, she knew what she had to do. Hera had given him her heart—metaphorically speaking. Now, she was going to do it for real.

CHAPTER
SEVENTEEN

ABSTINENCE

When Hades released his power, Abstinence was reminded of every foul thing she'd feared lurked under the bed and watched her in the darkness. While he terrified her, she thought Hera was lucky to have a god such as Hades who treated her gently and protected her as if she were the most valuable of jewels.

"I said get out of my way, brother. This is between me and my wife," Zeus growled and thunderbolts gathered in a quiver strapped to his broad back.

Abstinence hated to admit it, but she was pretty sure Zeus would be the one who had his ass handed to him with a bow on it. Then there was the fact he was *wrong*. It occurred to her Zeus had always taken or been given everything he'd ever wanted with no one to gainsay him. Now, he was learning a hard lesson and he was acting like a spoiled child who'd been forced to give up a toy.

"Be that as it may, Zeus, I won't allow you to hurt her," Hades said evenly.

"She's my *wife*."

"No, not anymore." Hades said gently.

"You'll never love her. Does she know that?" Zeus spat.

"You don't either."

Zeus turned his rage on Hades. "She didn't want you all those years ago. Neither did Persephone. Even after all of your gallantry. What makes you think Hera has any use for you besides your cock?"

For a moment, Hades and Hera both looked like they were about to shatter. Abstinence wished they could see each other's faces. Nothing else would ever need to be said, but they couldn't. Such a pity. Abstinence shook her head.

"What makes you think I want to be used for anything besides my cock?" Hades said in another measured tone. He seemed indifferent to everything but Hera.

Abstinence couldn't let this go on. It was a feast of betrayal and rage, pain and suffering. They weren't going to resolve anything. They were only going to twist the knives a little deeper, a little harder.

She grabbed his arm. "Stop it."

He swatted her away lightly, but he didn't know his own strength and it sent her reeling. "This doesn't concern you."

Abstinence quickly righted herself and for the first time, her power showed itself. A great warmth filled her and spread through her veins—a balm for her soul. She'd never felt strong before, but at this moment, Abstinence felt like she could tear down the walls of Olympus with her bare hands.

"You have had enough, King of the Gods. You've glutted yourself on your own fanfare and power until you can't taste or feel anything else. Everyone has catered to your needs your entire existence and now it's going to stop."

"My crown—,"

"Is a one-hit wonder on a broken record. By all rights, it belongs to Hades. You're lucky he doesn't want it. It isn't what defines you as a god. But you will learn. Abstinence is my gift to you, Zeus." She reached out to brush her fingers across his brow with her meager blessing.

"You've murdered me," he said in a monotone voice when her skin touched his.

Though, she had to wonder why he didn't move away from her, try to avoid the benediction he thought would be his end. Some part of him wanted this lesson and that gave her hope.

"No, Zeus. You will live. You will only be able to feed on energy that's freely given. No more taking, no more gluttony. No more ripped abs unless you work for them. You've never worked for anything you've had in all of your existence. How can you lead people if you don't understand them?"

"They aren't people, they're gods."

"They're much more human than you'd like to think, Zeus. Even you. Right now, you embody selfishness and excess, but not pleasure. Why is that, do you think? Why is it you aren't happy with what you've become?"

"Existence isn't about being happy," he countered grimly.

"It should be, Zeus." Hera crept out from behind Hades. "Our existences are too long to spend them in misery."

"Oh, now you're the Oracle at Delphi? You're selfish too."

Hera nodded. "I never said I wasn't, Zeus. I am selfish. Finally. After a forever of living to someone else's standards,

I am taking control and doing what I choose to do because it's what I want. Not what I'm supposed to do."

"You've all turned against me." He sagged against the wall and sank to the floor. "Betrayed me."

"Zeus, you betrayed them. Again and again." Abstinence went to touch his arm in a gesture of comfort.

"Don't touch me! After what you've done?" He jerked away from her.

Instead of letting herself be hurt, she eased down beside him. "Zeus, this is a prime example. A few hours ago, I almost died. You expected me to forgive you because you said you were sorry. Even when it seemed I would still have to go with Death. Why do you deserve forgiveness and trust, but I don't?"

"I didn't know. You did this to me wantonly."

"Stop being a victim," Hera snarled.

Abstinence held up her hand to stop her. "No, it's alright. He believes himself to be a victim and that won't change until he decides it will. I think I can handle it from here." She was surprised to realize that she could and it showed in the tone of her voice.

"I think you can, little goddess." Hades nodded his approval. "Come, Hera. Let's celebrate your divorce." He guided her out of the door, the shadow wings still splayed out behind him.

Abstinence turned her attention back to Zeus. "You can't say you didn't know because I told you. We've already been over this. You thought your needs were more important than anyone else's and you didn't care about the consequences. Now, you'll have to learn your lessons like anyone else."

"I don't want to."

"I know. Do you think I wanted to be Abstinence? Do

you think I wanted to be alone with you when I knew you wanted to touch me and I wanted you to? Even knowing what it would mean for me?"

"You wanted me before I used my power on you?" He looked up at her, his sky blue eyes uncertain.

"Yes. I did. You were so witty and confident, sexy. I'd never been attracted to anyone before you."

"Only because I was young. How I looked."

She realized Zeus, for all of his gifts and glory, was insecure. "No, didn't you feel me hold your hand while we waited for Hera to get here?"

"She'd never fed me so well from a touch. I didn't even have to..." He buried his face in his hands. "It was Hades spurring that energy, the lust that fed me. I still hated seeing his hands and mouth on her. She's mine."

He seemed prime to learning things and she felt she owed it to Hera to try and make him see this now, while he was open. "Hades has never asked you for anything, has he? He's never tried to take anything from you. And now your ex-wife—who still came to save your existence even after all the times you've betrayed her—she wants him. They give each other peace. Why can't you let go of her, something you didn't want, haven't wanted in a long time, and let her be happy?" When he didn't say anything she continued. "Hera has a great capacity to love. She's very passionate. I think the betrayal that cut her the most wasn't all of those you cheated on her with, but the fact you didn't tell her why you did it. In the beginning, I know she loved you. If you would have told her, she would have tried to help you in any way she could. Even if it meant seeing you with another. You need to think about that."

"Why do I always need to think about others? Who will think about me, if I don't?" Zeus demanded.

"That's the nature of leadership. You've fathered all of these gods and goddesses, but have you ever really been a *father*?"

"What do you know of it? You've abstained from everything your whole life so you wouldn't have to sacrifice it later," he growled.

Abstinence couldn't deny he was right. "Nothing," she admitted.

"Why did I let you do this? What is it about you I can't resist?"

"I don't know. You'd be the first who couldn't." Abstinence pulled him to his feet and led him to the bedroom. "You sleep here for a little while. You shouldn't be alone."

She knew this had been traumatic for him. Part of her screamed this had been traumatic for her too. What about her? But Abstinence knew she had coping tools whereas Zeus had never had to develop any. This was where the detachment of her mortal job came in handy. Who knew Olympus needed a resident psychiatrist?

Abstinence felt his pain as keenly as she felt her own. There was something broken about his perfection that had called to her and now she'd peeled away that pretty outer shell and found a rotted husk on the inside, but she could still see the beginnings of the god he could be.

This was a dangerous path. She knew that well. Abstinence had long warned clients against getting attached to a "fixer upper" type. People weren't like old houses one could flip and get back all they'd invested or even make a profit.

Healthy relationships came from acceptance and honest feelings for whatever qualities the other person already had on the table—not expected winnings at Karmic poker. Even for all of his selfishness and faults, Abstinence couldn't help but focus on the god he could be and feel a tender pity for the god he was.

He'd lost a lot today and she'd tried to change the way he viewed the world. That was never easy, even when one *wanted* to see things differently.

"You shouldn't let me stay here, Abstinence."

"Why not?" she asked as she tucked his golden head against her breast.

"I'll hurt you when I'm stronger. I hate you."

He wanted to hate her, she'd give him that one, but he didn't. Some part of him knew he needed what she'd done. He'd lived his eternity as a child and it was time for him to be a man. Otherwise, he wouldn't have tried to warn her away.

The analytical part of her brain wondered if maybe he would do to her as he had to Prometheus—chain her to a rock to have her heart ripped out every day, only to grow back every night and see it done again.

Her only hope against that sort of punishment was that Fate would see it as excess and Abstinence wasn't permitted any excess of any kind. She looked down at him as he slept and smoothed his hair from his brow.

This had been a lesson for her too.

She'd never before seen the purpose of what she'd become; of Abstinence. This was what she could do that no one else could. Abstinence realized it wasn't a punishment, neither was what her power could do.

Abstinence taught that once on the roller coaster was a joy, but twenty would feel awful. That taste of chocolate on the tongue was divine, but too much led to sickness. Excess wasn't to be coveted, but avoided. As was complete abstinence.

She'd been living on the wrong side of the spectrum

too. She'd been avoiding everything so she wouldn't have to give anything up. Who lived like that? No one. People made choices to stop doing things that felt good, or tasted good, or they enjoyed every day to be enjoyed again later. To keep them special. Pleasure was like a word that lost its meaning when repeated too often, made your tongue and lips numb if one did it all at once.

None of the other gods and goddesses were named after their power—although some of their names had become synonymous with their power. She wasn't Abstinence—she was Merry who only bore the mantle of Abstinence.

For the first time in a long time, Merry felt a glimmer of hope spark inside of her.

CHAPTER

EIGHTEEN

PERSEPHONE

Persephone heard her cell phone ring for the millionth time that day and she reluctantly turned it off. She'd hoped with every ring it would be Hades calling to tell her he'd changed his mind—that he wanted her back and couldn't live without her.

Word of her impromptu kiss with Thanatos had spread over Olympus like wildfire. Everyone wanted to know if it was true. A few gods had called to ask *twice* so word should have reached Hades by now. It had been a week. He should be seething in Tartarus over the fact some other god had dared put a hand on his goddess.

Still no phone call.

It was just as well. Persephone knew she wouldn't be able to ignore his call when it came, so turning the phone off was for the best. Let him think she'd moved on. He was a bold god to take what he wanted. He'd done it before; nothing would stand in his way if he wanted her back.

She flopped back on the bed. Rolled over. And over.

Only to sit up and flop again. This wasn't doing her any good at all. She turned her phone back on and dialed Thanatos.

"No," he said before she could get anything out.

"I haven't even asked you yet. Do you know who this is?" Persephone asked in an accusatory tone.

"This is Persephone and you want me to come pick you up to torment Hades. Same answer. No."

"Please?" she wheedled.

"You horrible tart. You don't even deny it." He gave an exaggerated and oh-so put upon sigh.

"Why should I? You want me to lie to you?" She didn't think he did, but why would he want her to deny it?

"No. But it would be nice if you'd called to, you know, talk to me," Thanatos admonished.

"I did call to talk to you. But about Hades. Pretty please with a kiss on top?"

"A kiss where everyone can see? What do I get out of kissing you? I've kissed lots of women, Seph."

"What about a kiss that's only for you?"

"What did I tell you about being a flirty little goddess?" he teased.

"It won't get me in trouble with you. You're one of the good guys."

"Don't be too sure about that." His voice sent shivers down her spine.

Why did she like the bad boys so much? The more noble a god was, the less interested she was. She might as well put a sign on her head that read "Treat me like shit, I'll follow you anywhere." Persephone was starting to realize she'd needed Hades to take what he wanted from her. She'd been willing—it wouldn't have been anything ugly—he knew her body craved his, but he'd still asked her. Offered her a choice and she'd been afraid—that choice, room to breathe, it gave her time to give in to her fear and to back away from what she wanted. Not a very feminist attitude, but he was a caveman sort. It was to be expected, wasn't it?

"Well, I am. I'm very sure about that." She drummed her fingers on her copy of *Wuthering Heights*. Heathcliff was a lot like Hades. They were both "H" names. She wondered if that had to do with the high levels of angst in their lives. "Are you going to tell me you don't want to kiss me again? I know you liked it."

"And how would you know that?"

Aside from the fact she'd liked it too? Gods, how she'd liked it. His mouth on hers had made her hot and cold at the same time, made places ache she thought only Hades could find and when she'd come home, she'd laid on her bed with her legs spread wide and touched herself, thinking of his kiss.

She didn't feel the least bit guilty about it either. She'd imagined him doing the same thing to himself and thinking of her. Several of the poems she'd worked on with Eros came back to her and she wondered what it would do to Thanatos if she were to speak to him that way—if it would make him do what she wanted?

Persephone knew kissing her had turned him on, he'd pulled her into his lap and she'd felt his erection. He wanted her. Persephone wanted him too, lusted for him. Eros had told her that was natural, it was okay. She could lust after one and still love another. Maybe Thanatos would take that in trade, her virginity. She'd wanted to give it to Hades, but he was banging some chick right now. She didn't even know who she was because she couldn't get to Tartarus to see for herself. So why wouldn't it be okay for Persephone to do the same? Maybe

Hades would even be pleased if she came to him with more experience.

She took a breath before she replied. "Because your cock was hard." Persephone blushed and her whole body heated, but she got a little thrill from saying such a naughty word.

"Seph, do you kiss your mother with that mouth?"

"No, but I want to kiss you with it and you want me to, so I don't see what the problem is."

"How do you know that my *cock*," he emphasized the word, "was hard for *you*?"

"Don't play with me, Thanatos."

"But you asked me to so prettily," he taunted. "Hot and then cold, typical goddess. First you want me to play with you and now you don't. Make up your mind."

"Wasn't it though?" She barged ahead, wondering if her mouth was going to cooperate with her brain. Persephone would do anything to get what she wanted. "Weren't you hard for me, Thanatos? Didn't kissing me make you want to touch me?"

It made her want him to touch her.

"And what if I said yes?" he rasped in to the phone.

"I'd ask where you wanted to touch me." Persephone leaned back on the bed again and splayed her hands on her stomach. She could imagine it was his hand so easily.

"Persephone, what are you doing?"

"I'm getting what I want. All the way around," she confessed and trailed her fingers lower.

"At any price?"

"Any at all," she promised breathlessly. "How does that sound? Do those words move you? Tell me. Are you imagining the price you want me to pay for your help? Are scenarios running through your mind to see what would test the boundaries of 'anything'?"

"Stop it."

"Why? I thought this was what all gods were after."

"I'll help you, just stop it."

"What if I don't want to stop?" She choked back a cry as she slid her fingers into her slit. Persephone had never felt this sensual. It was a heady rush to know she could wield such power.

"Persephone?" he asked in a strangled voice.

"Don't you want to ask me what I'm doing again?" she asked as she struggled to even her breathing.

"No, I'm going to hang up and forget this call. You'll thank me for it."

"But I won't. I'm so wet and all I can think about are your fingers doing this instead of my own. Wouldn't that be better than a kiss?"

Silence reigned for a second that felt like eternity before he spoke. "Suppose I was there now, what would have me do, Persephone? Tell me," he whispered.

"What I imagined after our kiss—your hands on me, inside me. Your hair brushing over the tips of my breasts as you work your way down my body. Your mouth suckling at all the places where I touched myself. Even your cock, so hard inside of me. I know it will hurt, but I want it." She gasped as the sensation roiled through her. Persephone loved telling him this—not only for what it did to her, but she knew intrinsically he was as affected as she.

"You don't want to give your virginity to someone you don't love."

"Why not? It would feel so good. Tell me, Thanatos, aren't you touching yourself now?"

"If I was, what would you say?" His voice was low.

"I'd ask if I could watch—if I could look into your eyes while you come and know you were thinking about me. I watched Hades all the time. I asked him to show me how to help him. I've even tasted him in my mouth."

"Seph, if I was a god of another sort, I'd be there now, fucking you hard and fast with no care to how you'll feel about it later. You can't play these games with just anyone."

"I know. That's why I'm playing them with you." She cried out again as her release built, but flagged. "Please, Thanatos."

"Please, what?"

"I—I—," she struggled to speak, but flicked her fingers faster over her clit.

"Please come kiss you? Or please kiss you until you come?"

She mumbled something unintelligible and she knew she'd lost control of the game, but she didn't care. Persephone just wanted his hands on her, his mouth. Anything to break the sensation building inside of her.

Demeter had a ward against teleporting into her daughter's room, but Thanatos was suddenly outside her window, his palm spread across the glass.

Persephone was very aware of herself in that moment, the way her breasts were exposed in the unbuttoned nightshirt she wore. He could see her through the window, her hand between her own thighs. Once upon a time, she would have been embarrassed to be caught in such a state, but seeing his eyes flash from the black endlessness of death to the purple of the dawn told her he liked what he saw.

She stopped her caress and opened the window for him; the cool air caused her nipples to tighten further. Persephone didn't stop him when he reached out to cup the heavy globe. The hands of Death weren't cold and unfeeling at all and the heat of his skin on hers intensified the ache in her core.

He took her phone from her hand and dropped it on the floor with no care to where it fell. Persephone braced her hands on his shoulders and his hands moved to her bare hips.

"Now what? Tell me, Persephone. Can you use your tongue boldly now that I'm here in front of you?"

"Oh yes, Thanatos."

"And that's who I am to you?" He raised her leg around his waist and stroked the velvet entrance to her channel. "You know who touches you? I'm not Hades. I won't ask if you're sure. I'll just take what you've offered me."

"You're asking me now."

"No, I'm not. I want to be sure you know it's my cock that breaks your maidenhead, my tongue and my fingers that make you come as you've demanded. That it's the kiss of Death you've begged for."

"Yes, Thanatos." She dropped down to the bed and reached for the grinning maw of the Venetian carnival skull belt buckle he wore.

He didn't stop her as Hades had, didn't cater to her maidenly fears. Thanatos was all hard demanding god. She pulled his mesh shirt from the waist of his black fatigues and was amazed to find his skin was silver everywhere.

"You're beautiful," she said, unable to look away from the starshine.

"As beautiful as your precious Hades?" he asked coldly, his voice at odds with the fire in his touch.

"Yes," she admitted. It was the truth. He was every bit as dark, dangerous and brutally sexy as the Lord of the Underworld. His flesh was as pleasing to her—although maybe that was a lie. His flesh pleased her *more*. Whereas she'd feared

Hades, she didn't fear Thanatos. She couldn't think about that right now. "Help me?" Persephone tugged at his belt.

He looked for a moment as if he might say no, but she watched with fascination as he stripped for her. When he freed his cock, she licked her lips and surrendered to her desire to taste him.

She met his eyes over her task and took him fully into her mouth as Hades had shown her. Persephone bobbed her head down his long length and back again. She flicked her tongue over the head and then dipped again, taking as much of him as she could manage.

His hands were fisted at his sides and he stood stoic under her ministrations. The only evidence he was affected was the pre-come she could taste on her tongue. She wanted to break his control and have him spill his pleasure on her lips.

She applied more pressure with her tongue and closed her fingers around his shaft and stroked as she laved him. His cock surged and she was pleased with how fast she'd taken him to the edge.

Just as he was about to come, he tangled his hands in her hair and pulled her back roughly. "Not yet." She licked her lips and his eyes darkened again. "I want to see you, Seph."

"You are seeing me."

"No, like you promised on the phone. Like you were when I got here."

Persephone was ashamed of herself, not because of what she'd done, but because it made her blush. Heat infused her cheeks.

"So dirty on the tease, but nothing for follow through?"

"I want to…"

"Then do it."

He pushed her back on the bed, but his hands weren't rough. Thanatos unbuttoned the few buttons on her night-shirt and let it fall open to his gaze. His hands followed where his gaze traveled and the intensity in his appraisal made her feel beautiful; powerful.

Thanatos took her hand in his own and pressed it to her sex. He worked her own fingers over her engorged clit and eased one finger inside of her until he hit her maidenhead. She bucked her hips against him, begging him to go deeper to give her more, but he refused.

She manipulated herself to the point of orgasm, but still couldn't push herself over the edge. It *hurt* and she realized then what Hades had done for her by denying himself all of those times. She'd have to think about that later too, right now, all she knew was that she needed what Thanatos held just out of reach.

"Please."

Thanatos eased onto the bed next to her and when she would have kissed him, he guided her down toward his cock. She didn't demure. He held her release in his purview; she'd do whatever he wanted to get it.

Persephone bent to take his cock in her mouth and when she did, he grabbed her hips and maneuvered her so that her slit was positioned over his face. She tightened with anticipation, knowing he was going to put his mouth on her as she was doing the same to him. Persephone relaxed against him and the heat of his tongue pushing inside of her brought her quickly to the edge.

It was a challenge to concentrate on what she was doing to him, to still stroke him and lick him in the ways she'd been taught. It was like an assault in a way, a strategic battle plan to bring him pleasure, but his forces had beaten her to the pass.

She was coming against his mouth and the ecstasy that quaked through her was stronger than her will to continue sucking him. Persephone went limp and sagged against him. Thanatos eased her from him gently and stood; buckled his belt as he went.

"Where are you going?"

"Home to jerk off with the taste of you on my tongue. I'm going to do it again and again—until it hurts to think of you, Persephone. Maybe until it bleeds. Then perhaps you'll be out of my head."

She propped herself up on her elbows. "Is this some noble sacrifice? Because you said you'd take what I offered. No asking if I was sure, no self-sacrifice. Was that a lie?"

"No, Seph." He shook his head and pulled his shades back into place over his eyes, a symbolic end to their connection. "Not self-sacrifice. More like preservation. I don't want to end up like Hades, on my knees begging Aphrodite to pull my heart out of my chest." He was gone the same way he'd appeared, her window open to the night.

Persephone curled up and pulled her blanket over her, loving how it smelled of him, and cried herself to sleep wondering what she'd done wrong.

CHAPTER

NINETEEN

NYX

Nyx awoke naked and sore in the Stable of the Sun. Apollo's chariot was gone and so were the winged horses. Her head pounded in a tartaran rhythm and her eyes felt like they'd been crusted shut with barnacles.

She felt around blindly for her knickers, hoping she wouldn't find them in a pile of horse shit. When she managed to pry her eyes open, she realized there was to be no such luck. Well, they could stay there. The Stables were notorious for godling hookups and finding a pair of stray lacies wouldn't be at all remarked upon.

Nyx couldn't fathom it. What was it about girls and horseflesh? Why stables? It wasn't that cool.

Okay, so that was a big, fat lie. It had been nothing short of spectacular driving the dawn across the sky. All that power in her hands and Apollo's strong, steady presence behind her. When he'd kissed her after their flight, her blood had already been racing and her heartbeat thundered a hundred miles a minute. The polarity between them had been undeniable—a heat stronger than the sun itself and just as irrefutable.

Double damn that ambrosia wine.

She never would have—another lie. Nyx totally would have banged him blue. He'd kept his glasses on, she remembered that much. She shuddered as another wave of desire shot through her, but then moaned as the pounding in her head doubled.

To her horror, she realized it wasn't in her head.

Ohfuckohfuckohfuckohfuck…

Nyx, most-aged of the goddess titans, was knocked up higher than a kite and the pounding she heard was that of another heartbeat inside of her body.

To reiterate: *Ohfuckohfuckohfuckohfuck.*

Nyx should have known something like this could happen, what with how many other children Apollo had. He was fertile like a damn virus. She'd thought her child-bearing days were long over. She'd *counted* on them being long over. What would she do with another baby? Worse, what would his/her powers be? She'd already birthed Death and Sleep. She was frightened for what they'd created, because no matter what it would be her child.

She felt like crying and Nyx didn't cry. She consoled herself with the fact that she wasn't mortal. Mortals never found out until they were farther along. Goddesses knew as soon as it happened.

She still felt like crying. Unlike Zeus who could drop children by brushing his hair, or other goddesses who were lucky enough to have a mortal gestation, Nyx was more like an immortal elephant, she'd be pregnant for nine mortal years. That made her cry too.

Sonofabitch.

She had to call Hera.

Nyx should have listened to that voice nagging inside of her head last night. The one that warned she was going to have some sort of drama to call her best friend about in the morning. Where the hell were her shoes? Fuck it. She could make Thanatos come get them. She wouldn't want him to run out of stuff to talk to his shrink about.

Oh, this was so, so, so very bad.

How was she going to get home? Why had he just left her there by herself? What an—oh, right. She could teleport. Nyx was feeling a little fragile and she wanted something to be pissed at Apollo about, but she couldn't find anything. She'd been a willing participant every step of the way. Even when her knickers ended up in flying horse shit. The horses flew, not the shit. Gods, why wouldn't her brain be still?

"Hey, gorgeous. Did you sleep well?" Apollo came around the corner with two steaming mugs in his hand. One had whipped cream on top. He handed that one to her.

"I'm not really a morning person," she grumbled.

"Really? Because you look beautiful. I didn't think the Goddess of Night was allowed to glow during the day."

She narrowed her eyes sharply. Was he talking shit? "It's too early for bad pick up lines."

"It's not a pick up line if I already—," he broke off and stared at her. "What's wrong?"

"Nothing. Just not a morning person. Can you take me home?"

"Only after you drink you cocoa and promise to tell me the truth later."

Yeah, she could promise that. Nyx didn't have a choice. She looked down at the cocoa in her hands and liked the warmth from the cup. It soothed her. He'd been paying attention. It was Godiva cocoa. She could tell by the aroma. Nyx took a diminutive sip and waited for the waves of nausea to hit. With Thanatos and Hypnos both within seconds of conceiving the smell of anything she enjoyed made her yark like a siren with a bone twisted in her gut.

"It's a deal." She tried to hand the cocoa back to him but he raised a brow and she brought it to her lips again dutifully.

"It's got my signature ambrosia hangover cure, so drink it all up or your head will pound unmercifully for days."

Well, no shit. Her head was going to be pounding for the next nine damn years. She froze—she didn't know what he'd put in the cure. Some gods put some nasty stuff in those supposed cures.

"What's in it?"

"Mostly extra vitamin C and electrolytes. It's the dehydration that makes you sick."

Okay, so he was kind of doctor-y. That was sexy too. She chided herself for thinking along those lines. It was those kinds of ideas that got her in this mess to begin with.

Then he laughed. "Oh, I actually used science to create my cure. It's not something my mother told me. One of my sons is the God of Medicine, after all. I should have some vague idea what I'm about, don't you think?"

She nodded and took another sip. Nyx found it made her stomach rather *happy*. She felt good. With a sigh, she wondered how many times he'd buy she'd overindulged before he got suspicious of how often she wanted his cure.

It didn't matter, she had to tell him. That way, he could just make her the cure. He could at least do that. It's not like they were in a relationship or anything, but if he wanted her to keep this baby and not starve it to death because she couldn't keep anything down, he'd do it. She knew he would anyway and felt bad for even thinking it.

Nod had been such a bastard the first time she'd told him she was pregnant. That was why they'd had to get married. Nyx's mother had been none too pleased and she was the scary bitch kitty deluxe in her family. Her father had just gone along for the ride.

Oh, she didn't want to do this. Nyx had two beautiful boys who were wonderful and more importantly, they were *grown*. She was too old to be waddling around in a maternity toga and wiping snotty noses.

Her stomach roiled and she put a soothing hand to her belly. Whoever had taken up residence in there didn't like the train of her thoughts. Yep, it was another boy, she was sure. Girls were never this demanding until they made it to the outside.

"Nyx, you spaced off again. Are you sure you're okay?"

"Yeah, I guess. I'll be fine." In NINE fucking years. She took another gulp of cocoa before her little darling could protest. "This is really good. You'll have to give me the recipe."

"Oh, no. It's a secret. You'll have to come see me if you want some."

"Double entendre much?"

"Occasionally." He smiled and took her cup and set it down where the stable hands would see to it. "Will you let me see you to your door?"

"That would be nice."

He put his arms around her and teleported to her temple steps. "I'd like to see you again."

There were all sorts of quick and sharp relies on her tongue about "I'll call you" and other phrases people didn't mean, but she managed to keep them to herself. He'd definitely be seeing her again, but as to the prospects of another date, she wasn't sure.

He noticed her silence and spoke again. "Really. It's not one of those brush off things. In fact, I'd spend today with you if you'd let me, but it looks like you need some rest."

Waste not, want not, right? If he wanted to come over later, fine. She could tell him then. "Do you want to come over for dinner later?"

"Shall I bring the wine?"

"Gods no," she laughed. "How about some more of that cocoa?"

"I can do that." He looked down at her tenderly. "Rest well, Nyx." He smoothed her hair from her brow and kissed her forehead before he teleported home.

Yeah, she'd see how tenderly he felt toward her when she told him he was going to have another godling to take care of.

She flopped on her couch and noticed from the feel of the temple that Thanatos wasn't there either. He must have had a very good night, doing whatever it was. Hopefully it wasn't Persephone. Nyx had a feeling that would end poorly for both of them.

Knowing she wouldn't be able to sleep until she talked to Hera, she grabbed her cell and dialed the goddess.

"Oh my gods, Nyx, have I got things to tell you," Hera said by way of a greeting. "Can you make it to Jean Pierre's?"

The thought of going to JP's so early made her feel like she'd been sucking on a dirt pop. "How about a quick recap and Jean Pierre's tomorrow? I have news too and it's sort of made me take to my bed."

"Spill then. If it keeps you from Jean Pierre's it must be apocalyptic."

"It is." She sighed heavily. "I'm pregnant."

"Excuse me, I think I had a something in my ear the size of a planet because you know what I *thought* you said?"

"Yeah, I'm knocked up. Preggo—it's in there. Ripe. Breeding. Bun in the oven. Bringing forth life, etc. and so forth."

"Shit."

"No kidding."

"So, I guess that negates the need for the question about how your date went. Did you tell Apollo?"

"No, not yet. He's coming back over later. I figured I might as well get it over with and tell him. I have a few years before I start to show, but I don't want to lie to him. I'm nervous though, Nod was a cock when I told him about Hypnos."

"Do you want me to come over?" Hera said supportively.

"No, I really want to sleep, but I had to tell you or I knew I'd toss and turn until I did."

"Wow. Makes my news kind of trivial in comparison."

"Your turn."

"I don't want to dump on an already gianormous pile. We'll talk tomorrow."

"Hera. It's already built up. Come on. I want to know," Nyx pleaded.

"If you insist."

"I do."

"I told Zeus I was leaving him."

"What did he say? When did this happen? How did it happen? Details," Nyx demanded.

"Actually, it happened at the new goddess's temple."

"Abstinence?"

"Yeah. She's really a doll. I like her. Weird, that. I don't think I'm supposed to like my husband's would-be mistress. Poor thing can't have sex or she'll die."

"I'd have to die."

"I know; me too." Hera sighed. "Anyway, Zeus kissed her and almost killed her. Your son came to the door like a gentleman and Zeus managed to talk him into some kind of bargain."

"Oh, that's a good idea. Wait until I see him."

"It gets better. All of those eons I've been married to Zeus he never told me he needs ambrosia *and* sexual energy to survive."

"See, that would piss me off more than the cheating."

"Right? Asshole. Anyway, he gives back the energy he took from her and *he* almost dies. So, he has her call me to come save him."

"Classy."

"Dick move, was what I told Abstinence. We had a good laugh. Anyway, you know I've been with Hades and the irony was just gold. It was our energy that fed him, Nyx." She laughed. "But then he got all caveman trying to mark his territory and I told him we were done. Finished."

"What did he do? I mean, you're still here because we're on the phone, but..." she let it hang.

"He acted like he was going to do something and I was ready for him. I could smite him."

"I know you could."

"Hades wouldn't let him. I've never seen power like that, Nyx. It filled the room and wrapped around me. It was the most terrifying and sensual experience I've ever had. He didn't need me to give him Zeus' crown. If he wanted it, he could reach out and take it. He doesn't want it. Oh, he breaks my heart."

"Because he doesn't want to rule?"

"No. Because even though he's so broken, he's still so noble. His suffering is like my suffering."

"Hera. You love him."

"I do. With everything that's in me."

"Have you told him?"

"You know I can't. He keeps his heart in a box over the fireplace."

"I know you, though. You're going to do something."

"I'm going to give him my heart. I'll take his. It may be broken, but it's healing. It can live in me until it's whole."

"What if he still loves Persephone?"

"I know he does. And that's okay. A true, honest love never dies. If he could turn from her so easily, it wasn't real. She's called and asked to come back."

"Thanatos wants her too. I don't see the appeal."

"Me either." She laughed gently. "She's a nice girl, but she's a child and Hades is a god long grown."

"What did he say when she asked to come back?"

"He told her he didn't want her. I caught him forcing his gargoyles to role play so she'd think there was a woman in the room with him. He told her to be happy. Hades told me he knew she missed what was familiar and that was him, that she didn't really love him. I was so stupid, Nyx. I asked him why that mattered. Fate has a wicked sense of humor because after we had sex, he wanted to hold me and I found the same words coming out of my mouth about wanting something real. That's what I get for asking, right?" Hera has a tremulous sound to her voice.

"Aww, do you need me? I'll come right over. I can sleep when I'm dead."

"It's okay. I'm about to leave with Hades again. You know, even if he never loves me, I love him. I hope it's enough."

"It's not, but how could he not love you, Hera?"

"Zeus didn't."

"And we all know we should measure everyone by that goat scroat. Come on. You know better."

"I've gotta go. I love you."

"I love you too, sweetpea. I'll see you at JP's tomorrow."

"If Apollo lets you out of bed. You can't get knocked up any higher, after all." Hera hung up and Nyx was aware of just how much she loved to have the last word.

She sighed and it struck her even though they were eternal, how much their existences could change in one blink of an eye.

The door blew open and Thanatos staggered in, a half bottle of pomegranate Stolichnaya in one hand and an empty bottle of George Dickel bourbon in the other. Nyx raised an eyebrow.

"Don't fucking ask, Ma." He stumbled up the stairs to his room.

Nyx hadn't even opened her mouth and had no plans to do so. She didn't want to know. Unless he wanted her to smite someone, but he had his big boy trench coat on. He was Death, after all. She drew the chenille blanket up over herself and sighed.

She'd thought she'd been done with this teenaged angst with him too. Maybe it would never end. That thought was enough to take the rest of the starch out of her knickers— had she been wearing any and hers not still baking in a warm pile of flying horse shit.

Nyx slept. Yes, when all else failed, the Goddess of Night was adept at dodging the slings and arrows of Fate by sleeping through them.

CHAPTER

TWENTY

DEMETER

Demeter awoke in Eros' arms to a beautiful Venetian dawn. Fingers of gold shot through the sky and tugged at blues and purples, the brightening sky pink with the soft, new breath of the day. She was amazed at the simple beauty. Because while Demeter had seen a million dawns, she'd never seen one where the bright colors reminded her of an artist's palette. They were the first sure brushes of a master expertly mixing color and texture. The landscape had branded itself into her memory. She breathed deeply, hoping to capture the scents of the morning air and the fresh coffee from the cafes.

Their gondola had been anchored by the sudden burst of lily pads that had bloomed to maturity with the magic of their lovemaking. She used her power to release the life in them so as not to impede the waterways and directed it to plants blooming in window box gardens.

Ivy ripe with fruit and vegetables spread over walls and balconies and the scent of fresh herbs filled the air. Demeter sighed. She hadn't felt this complete, this right with the world in what seemed like an eternity.

She realized she would have happily traded all of her long years for a few days such as this one. Maybe that's what it was like for the mortals too. They knew they had an end and made better choices with the time they'd been given, because unlike Demeter, they had no way to prolong their existence.

Her power came to her with ease now. She was the alpha and omega, the energy flowing from her and to her at once. Demeter wasn't at all tired and she knew with a certainty she could cover the world in Spring and her strength wouldn't flag. These last years it had gotten so it tired her to make a single bud bloom. She'd thought it was from invoking an endless winter, but she knew now it was because she'd cut herself off from her source of power by denying the life cycle.

Demeter sighed and reveled in the heat of the god who held her. In his arms, she felt certain nothing but joy could ever touch her. She didn't know why he loved her, but she was willing to accept that he did.

Last night had been his first time with a woman and he'd wanted it to be special for *her*. Demeter was thankful for him. He'd opened her eyes with his deeds, not words. Eros had given her so much and she couldn't think of anything she'd ever done for him. Even making love with him had been about her, despite her better intentions.

It saddened her she wouldn't have the time to make room in her heart for love. She wanted desperately to love him, but she knew her heart had been too full of hatred and fear to love anyone. He was already inside of her soul though and she wanted to tell him, but didn't have the words.

The deep, even movement of his chest signified he still slept and Demeter was content to lie in his arms and drift endlessly through the canals. She wanted to thank Venice for this morning and she called the Honeysuckle to burst into bloom over bridges and tangle itself over fountains and statuary.

It felt so good; Demeter wanted to cover the whole world in flowers. She resisted the urge, though. It wasn't fair to them to call them forth in the deep set of winter in the frozen north, or in the desert where they would thirst and suffer.

A frantic plea interrupted her utopia and Demeter bolted from her repose to see who had called her name. Eros stirred and with a sleepy endearment, pulled her back against him. She didn't see the owner of the voice so she settled back against her lover.

His warmth was like a blanket and she sighed again. Demeter was happy. Until she heard the damn voice again. She bolted up with such force the gondola teetered precariously. She still didn't see anyone who could be talking to her.

She seriously considered this experience with Eros, all of it, was simply a figment of her tormented imagination. She'd wanted to be done with misery for so long now, perhaps her mind had made it happen and she was a couple pomegranates short of a bushel.

It would be unfortunate if that were the case, but if it was, Demeter didn't want to know. She liked this new existence she'd made for herself—granted it had to end, but not yet.

"Demeter, what's wrong?" Eros asked, alerted by her distress.

"I keep hearing someone calling my name, but I don't see anyone." She studied their surroundings again.

"It's prayers."

"No one prays to the old gods anymore, Eros. I'm not like Love, people don't invoke me or even wish for me like they do love. I haven't heard a prayer since 1852 when Lord Helmsely Hunsaker had a likeness of me erected in his garden and his Greek maid left honey and milk to ensure a bountiful harvest of mandrake so she could rid herself of his bastard."

"And did you grant her prayer?"

"Certainly. I gave her some Belladonna as well to keep him out of her thighs permanently."

"He loved her, you know," Eros informed her with a brush of his lips on her cheek.

"I doubt that. If he loved her, he would have married her instead of whelping a bastard on her."

"We all love in different ways."

"Did she love him? She never prayed to me again and I quite forgot to look in on her." Demeter found herself wondering what happened to the girl who had pleaded so earnestly for deliverance.

"No, she didn't. There was a boy in Greece she'd loved as a girl."

Demeter was quiet for a moment. "Did she have an unhappy life?"

"Yes."

"What was the point of it then?"

"Only Fate can answer that, Demeter."

"What about the voices in my head? Can she answer those?"

"Those are strictly within your purview, but it wouldn't

surprise me if Fate already knew what you were going to do."

"I don't even want to think about the implications of that. I am a goddess. I'm supposed to have free will." Demeter knew she sounded a bit petulant, but couldn't help herself. It was the vocal equivalent of stomping her foot.

"Just because she knows the choice you're going to make and has planned accordingly doesn't mean it's any less your choice."

"It's too early to be philosophical, Eros," she grumped.

"You were happy when you woke up. What happened?"

"Besides the voice in my head? Nothing. It disturbed me. I wondered if I was losing it and if I was losing it, if all of this with you was nothing more than a mad dream."

"No. I'm yours always, Demeter."

"A figment of my imagination would say that," she teased.

"How may I prove to you this is real?" Eros asked with sincerity.

"You can't. But you can tell me how to answer this prayer. It's been so long, I don't remember."

"Concentrate on the voice and will yourself to see its owner and his need. You know mortals often pray for what they think they want, not what it is they need. Sometimes, it's crueler to answer a prayer than ignore it."

Demeter did as he instructed and concentrated all of her energy on finding the owner of that voice. It was a farmer in the United States, Missouri. She didn't want to give up her gondola, but her selfishness was keeping her from seeing what she wanted to see. So she let go.

She was soaring through the space and time, through the

real and the layers beneath. It was not a farmer at all, but a small child sitting in the middle of a desolate corn field. There were a few shoots pushing up through the dry, cracked soil and she could feel the pain of the plants as they starved. It was probably not unlike what the young boy was feeling.

He was too thin, ragged. His overalls hung loose on his tiny frame and she could feel his hunger as well. He had a social studies textbook open to a section on Greek Mythology.

"Can you hear me, Demeter? I don't know if you're real, but I hope you are. We need a little help this season. I'm not asking so we have more than our neighbors or so I can have a Wii after harvest. I'd like to eat and be able to feed our animals."

When he looked up with solemn brown eyes, it was like he saw her and knew what he was looking at.

Eros was suddenly beside her in the ether. "He has the heart of a man grown, Demeter. Full of love for the land and sacrifice for his family. Will you answer his prayer?"

The unfairness of it hit her like tidal wave. Earlier this morning, she'd been bringing life and bounty to those already blessed and this boy who loved the land like a child of spring could do nothing to help himself but pray to a goddess he wasn't sure he believed in.

She materialized before she had a chance to think better of it. Upon further reflection, it would have been as easy to bless his crops go on about her day, but it had been so long since anyone had prayed to her, she couldn't help herself.

When she became solid, the look on his face told her she'd probably scared the sense right out of him. His eyes grew wide and for a moment, she thought he'd scream. Or cry. But he did none of those things.

"Are you Demeter?" he asked carefully, as if she was a snake and he was unsure if she was poisonous or not.

"I am. You prayed to me, so I came."

"Where were you last year?"

That wasn't even in the same ballpark with what she'd expected from him and back in the old days, had a mortal spoken to her or any of the gods in such a way, they would have been smited. Or would that be smitten? No, smitten was something all together different. But all hell would have broken loose, to put it in more modern terms.

"I don't have a good answer for you." And she didn't. There was nothing she could say that could make up for the fact she'd let her power go fallow like an abandoned field.

"No one ever does." He sighed as the weight of the world pressed down on him.

"What are we going to do about this field?" Demeter asked gently.

"I don't know. I was hoping you had an answer."

"I think I might."

"So, what do you want in return? A cow? We've only got one, but you can have it."

"No, I've got something different in mind. How about if I give *you* my blessing? Not your field, or the land, but you."

"Why would you do that?" he eyed her.

"Didn't you ask for my help?" she reminded him.

"I did, but in all of the stories with those great gifts come pain and sacrifice."

"Such big words for such a little boy." Demeter was amazed to feel her heart warm toward this mortal child.

"I'm in the gifted program."

She nodded. "Well, do you want my help?"

"Nothing too extravagant. Like I said, I don't want to be greedy."

"No, your request isn't greedy. That's why I want to give you my blessing. I don't think you'll abuse it."

"Terms?"

"If you insist." She smiled. "For every bountiful harvest after this one, you must donate a percentage to a food bank. And no nasty herbicides or pesticides, no genetically modified seeds. All organic crops."

"What percentage?" he asked, not balking at any of her requests.

"I'll leave that up to you." She tried not to smile again, he was so serious.

"You're awfully trusting."

"I can freeze the world with eternal winter. I can afford to be."

He nodded as if he understood exactly where she was coming from. "Okay, I think I'm ready."

"Come, embrace me." She knelt down to where he was.

He approached her tentatively, as if he still thought she would bite. When he reached her, she kissed the top of his head in a benediction and the rows of corn shot up around them.

"My blessing to you, little seedling. May you grow as your crops, strong and tall. Always keep me in your heart and I'll keep you in mine. Love the green and growing things well and they will love you in return."

She made herself invisible before he could thank her and Demeter felt a strange sense of peace. Almost as if she'd moved by a power greater than herself, yet... She went to visit their one cow before she could think about the further implications of greater powers. That always made her uncomfortable.

Demeter fed the cow from her own hand and watched its lines fill in with muscle and health. She rubbed its belly twice and called forth twin beams of light that became the spark of life inside and she disappeared back into the ether.

"Have you never done these things, Demeter?" Eros asked her.

"I don't think so. If I ever did, I don't remember."

"Didn't your mother teach you these things?" He sounded incredulous.

"No. Never."

"You have to teach Persephone before it's her time."

"I don't know what to teach her," Demeter said helplessly.

"You'll figure it out, you're a smart goddess. Now, do you have any more prayers on the docket, or are you mine again?"

"I'm always yours," she replied before she could think about what it meant.

"Do you mean that?"

"Eros, look and see." Demeter bared herself to him, determined there would be no more shadows inside of her for him to fight. He could look with his power and see.

"I don't want to."

She felt that like a knife that pierced her heart and her soul. It was a physical pain.

"No, not because I don't want to see what's inside you, Demeter. Because I don't want to have to look. Does that make sense?"

"Not really."

He made them corporeal and they were on the Riviera. It wasn't the moon, but it would do. Eros was ever thoughtful and had manifested a double lounger.

"Let me explain. To simplify, I don't want to bring my work home. If you feel something for me, I shouldn't have to dig for it. You should tell me because you feel it and you want me to know you feel it. I may be the God of Love, but I'm still male. And you are my goddess. Poking around in your soul is like digging through your purse for a tampon."

"Did you just compare my feelings for you to a tampon?"

"They're both used to cork—," he began, but broke off when she hit him.

"Proof all men are the same. It was poetry and sweet words that melted my soul and now that you've had me, you're wisecracking about tampons. What's next? Burping with your hand down your toga while you wait for me to make you dinner?"

"Sweet Demeter, if it's poetry you wish, it's poetry you shall have." But instead of reciting words of verses composed by other hearts and other hands, it was his lips on hers.

And it was poetry like no other, the sensation he wrought in her, the bliss that felt like home.

HERA

"Hera and Hades, sittin' in a tree, K-I-S-S-I-N-G," the gargoyle sang loudly.

"Shut the fuck up, you little troll." Hera wasn't about to take any lip off of this creature.

"Not a troll. Gargoyle. Stupid goddess."

Hera gave it a sly look and then kicked it on her way by. Hard. Too hard for her poor

little toes. She howled and it laughed with malicious glee. "Oh yeah?" She hauled it up over her the shoulder and the stone creature yelped.

"What are you doing?"

"Yeah, Hera. What *are* you doing?" Hades asked as he entered the room.

"Throwing this smart-mouthed piece of furniture out the window."

"And what has Peri done to merit such action, may I ask?"

"It has a name? Well, Peri the Penis is mocking me."

"I see. Would you like me to toss it out the window for you? He looks heavy."

"Nooo," it yowled.

"No, indeed. He needs to learn to respect me and he won't do it if I don't handle this myself."

Hades nodded along as if weighing the merits of her argument. "Open the window before you throw him out of it. Getting stained glass down here is a bitch."

Hera held him high above her head and she wanted to let go. She tried to force her arms to fling him forward and send him hurtling out into the fiery lake beneath the balcony, but she couldn't do it. She wanted to, oh how she wanted to, but he was a living creature.

She placed him down on the floor next to the balcony door. "I'm not going to do it this time because I think melting would hurt. A lot. So, you get a reprieve. Sing that damn song just once more though and I'll chuck you out into that lava so fast the knobs on your head will spin. Got me?"

"Yes, Hera." He made a sullen face. "I was just playing. And you called me a penis."

"I did and I'll call you worse if you don't behave."

He grumbled and pouted, then went quiet. It didn't even giver her a nasty look before he closed his eyes and hardened into unreadable stone.

"Look at that. Before you know it, you'll be propping

your feet on him while you read those Lusha Lovelace books."

"How do you know what I'm reading?"

"I know more than you'd think, Hera," he promised.

"Is that another innuendo, because I can't take it, Hades. Not again. I can't even walk."

"At the risk of sounding like my brother, you're a goddess. Why do you need to walk?"

"Oh, because I should be on my back all the time?"

He gave her a wicked grin. "No, because you should have a strong god to carry you wherever you'd like to go."

"That would only lead to more fucking. I'm out."

Hades laughed. "You're delicious, Hera."

"Stop it," she pleaded.

"But I like it." The corner of his mouth curved in the beginning of a mischievous grin.

He sounded so earnest; she wasn't sure if he was still playing with her or if he'd confessed something important. Gods were like that—unable to speak of softer things unless in jest.

"I guess if you like it, I don't have a choice."

"How about we get out of the castle tonight? Dinner?" he offered.

This was the first time he'd suggested they do anything but roll around naked. Not that she was complaining, well, her nether bits were protesting loudly, but Hera had a lot of time to make up for. Somebody could have told her she shouldn't try to make up for it all at once.

"Can we go to—,"

"Red Lobster?" he supplied. "I don't know why you're not sleeping with Poseidon. He could set you up with all the scallops you could ever want."

"They wouldn't be bacon-wrapped. You know how I

love my bacon." She shrugged as if that were the only reason she wasn't interested in the God of the Sea. That and he and Nyx had dated. Even among goddesses there were rules about dating your BFF's ex.

"Everything is better with bacon." Hades swatted her on the ass.

Hera gasped and slapped his arm playfully.

She wondered if he'd done these things with Persephone. Hera wished she could stop coming back to that, but every experience she shared with him, she wondered if Persephone had done it first. Or worse, she'd done it better.

Of course she did, you silly bitch. He hadn't begged Aphrodite on his knees to rip his heart out to stop the pain after she'd turned down his suit. What was it that made that goddess so special that she was worth all the pain and sacrifice done in her name? Was it something secret in the way she smiled? The way she laughed? The way she held her thighs closed tight and pretended to be so virtuous her feet never touched dirt when she walked?

Would anything ever belong solely to Hera? A moment that was just theirs, a look he reserved only for her, a certain touch... She wondered if she was naïve to want those things. Zeus had never given her any cause to think she could have them from him or anyone else. Were they only in fairy tales and stories once told to frightened brides on their wedding nights?

She hadn't noticed his approach, so he startled her when he pulled her to him. He searched her face with an intensity that made her squirm—she wanted to turn away so he didn't see the need in her soul or the love that burned for him not a flickering beacon in the dark, but a bonfire.

"You're so beautiful, Hera. It's like you were made to belong to me."

Hera wanted to cry out that was the truth of it on his lips. She *had* been made for him, only for him. The hollow of her throat curved for his lips, the shape of her hip for his hands, her legs to lock around his waist and her heart a great chasm to be filled by all that he was and all he wanted to be.

"I keep wondering why you're here."

She forced a smile. Hera wasn't ready to talk about this —they'd found a comfortable routine, they were together. For a moment, Hera had forgotten she'd assured him what he could give would be enough. She didn't want to shatter their idyll, not until she had a foundation built to replace it with something better. "I told you why I'm here. To be with you."

"Why?"

What sort of answer did he expect to that? He was either being purposefully obtuse or he was mocking her. Either way she didn't like it.

"Why not?" she tossed back, just to be difficult.

"Hera, I saw that look. I've known you long enough to know when something makes you unhappy. You just made a face like you were chewing on barbed wire."

"You can't expect me to be happy 24-7."

"Give me some credit. I know the difference between your expressions of casual displeasure, irritation, and all out misery. That face you made, something is hurting you. Tell me."

You are. You're hurting me, Hades, tearing up my insides with that same barbed wire and twisting it around my heart. But it's not your fault because when you would have let go, I demanded you twist it again for good measure.

As if she'd ever tell him anything of the sort. "Nothing. I'm hungry."

"You're not breeding are you?" He sounded scandalized —something out of a Georgette Heyer novel.

"I'm not a horse, Hades. I don't *breed*."

"That's not an answer." He looked stricken.

"No, of course not," she reassured him. "But Nyx is. Maybe I'm having sympathy cravings." She wanted to ask him if it would be so bad if she was. Hera realized the futility of her thoughts. Hades wouldn't be a good father without his heart.

"You guys are that close? Is she going to slap me for making you both walk funny?"

"Sorry, sugar. Apollo is the one who made her walk funny. Waddle, to be specific, the poor dear."

"Isn't she a little old to be having godlings?"

"Aren't you a little shitty to be asking?" Hera rushed to Nyx's defense.

"Probably." His gaze drifted down to her lips.

"Oh, no! Don't even start that. At least not until later," she said as she pulled away from him. "You offered me dinner and you're not getting out of it."

"Fine." Hades sighed as if she'd taken away a favorite sweet.

She rather liked that comparison. Hera could be happy being his favorite indulgence. Contrary to the earlier path of her thoughts that made her scowl as if she'd been forced to lick between a centaur's hooves.

"You can't go out like that."

"Like what?" he looked down at himself. "Oh. Right. 1800's gentleman wouldn't go over well at old Red, would it?"

He blinked out of the room and Hera released a breath she didn't know she'd been holding. She shook her head sharply—like that would rattle out whatever was loose and her brain could go back to working in a way that wouldn't break her heart.

Hera thought of hearts then, but not of her own—of Hades' heart sitting alone on the mantle. Her gaze was drawn to the box unwillingly. She didn't want to look—she wanted to leave things alone and let them be.

Although, this goddess couldn't leave well enough alone, not when she knew she could ease the pain of the one she loved. Even if it meant she'd lose him.

She took a few halting steps, afraid he was going to catch her peeking. Hera didn't know how she'd explain it, but then decided she wouldn't. If he cared so little about the thing he'd shoved it in a box to rot, then why would he care if she wanted to poke at it? He couldn't feel it.

Hera drew the box down to her and cradled it against her chest before she peaked inside. She blew warm breath on it again as she had before and more of the soot and ash blew away from the gray mass. In one place, she saw something pink and it had spread.

"Give yourself to my keeping," she whispered.

It shuddered against the confines of its tomb.

"I swear I'll treat you tenderly. I know there's darkness in him and I know Persephone was afraid, but I'm not. The only thing I fear is eternity without him."

With the next shudder, all of the ash and the gray fell away to reveal something smooth and pink. When it shuddered again, Hera realized it wasn't a shudder at all, but a beat so loud and strong it echoed through the room.

"Oh, you can't do that just yet. Hades is going to kill me." Hera looked around for a panicked moment and wondered where she'd hide her lover's newly animated heart. She'd have to worry about that when they got back. There was no time.

At her distress, the movement stopped and Hera almost let out a wail of abject despair. It was almost as if it could sense all of her feelings. When it felt warmth from her, it knew it was safe to breathe, to be. When it felt her fear it played dead.

Who knew a man's heart could be so complicated?

"I love him, you're safe," she cooed before she snapped the lid shut.

"What are you doing?" Hades demanded as he appeared.

Fuck.

Well, she wasn't going to lie, but that didn't mean she had to give up the ghost either.

"Talking to your heart."

He cocked his head and looked at her as if she were some strange new kind of beetle he'd found mashed under his boot, with that same clinical detachment. For one horrible moment, she thought he would ask her why.

"Take the damn thing if it amuses you. I've got no use for it."

Hera was torn between soaring on wings of elation that he would give his heart into her keeping and feeling the darkest depth of despair that he had such little care for a part of himself.

"Thank you," she said simply.

It would be easier to hide the fact it now beat; it didn't have a regular rhythm, but contrary to his desires, it lived.

Hera would make good on her promise, she'd never let anything cruel touch that tender flesh, she'd hold it dear for all of her days. She vowed it on her goddesshood.

"Can you quit playing with it so we can go?" he grumbled.

She smiled and stepped into his arms to teleport.

"Are you sure you don't want to stay in?" Hades asked in a suggestive tone and traced his fingertips up the base of her spine.

"Hades, what part of you broke it wasn't clear?"

He laughed and rather than being a calculated sound to seduce or mock, there was genuine mirth in his tone. "Did I really? You know I'll have to brag about this one."

"There's no one to brag to, oh Prince of Darkness. Every being in Tartarus heard me screaming that last time. I'm actually rather embarrassed."

"Your pleasure should never embarrass you, sweet-heart. Especially when it's me doing the pleasuring."

She slapped his arm. "No, Hades. Stop saying pleasure. Or anything coitus related. It hurts."

His eyes darkened. "Isn't that what I promised when you *came*, sweet Hera? That it would hurt? You said you'd take everything I had to give you."

They'd gone from splashing in the wading pool to the drowning water in an instant. Rather than struggle to stay above the murky depths, Hera let go. Any momentary discomfort she felt would be worth proving to him she was wholly his and more than that, he could trust her promises.

"Yes, I did promise. And I always keep my promises, Hades." She drew herself up on her tiptoes to close the distance between their lips. "Always," she repeated before kissing him hard.

"Good," he said as he relented. "I didn't want you to get any little girl ideas simply because I gave you a box with a piece of rotten meat inside."

"Hades, you have such a way with words. I don't know how any goddess could resist you." She rolled her eyes.

A loud thump echoed through the room and Hera's eyes went wide. His heart must not have cared for her sarcasm, or the comment cut him deeper than she'd intended. They were going to have to come to an understanding when she got back. No way was she going to spend eternity mincing words while he got to call the pot *and* the kettle whatever he wished.

"What was that?"

"Who cares? I'm hungry. Let's go." His eyes scanned the room again. "Listen here; if we don't teleport right now, I'm going to have a full-blown goddess style temper tantrum. Smiting will ensue."

Hades laughed again. "You're so cute. Would you hit me with one of your little mini lightning bolts?"

"My lightning bolts are bigger than Zeus', just so you know."

"I'm sure they are, my Queen."

"I like the sound of that. So, later, when I tell you to get on your knees and lick my boot..."

"You don't have to be Queen of the Gods for that. You want me to lick anything all you have to do is ask."

Why did she get into these word games with him? He always won. Everything he said or did oozed sex and power. He could wield both sharp as any blade.

"Right now, I want to go somewhere to lick bacon grease off my fingers." Hera hoped the visual was too icky to encourage any sort of innuendo, but she should have known better.

"Kinky."

"You're such a dick."

"You like my dick."

"Not right now I don't." Hera winced in pain as her battered body protested her arousal.

He laughed again. "I'll make you a deal. I'll behave—,"

She snorted.

"I promise, I will. But you have to eat your dinner from my hand. I want you taking those scallops from my fingers. Bacon grease and all," he said with a smug grin.

The thought of taking her food from his hand caused a tremor to go through her. She was convinced Hades was going to be the death of her before the night was over.

ABSTINENCE

ABSTINENCE PEERED into the dark room at the lump on the bed. It hadn't budged in a week and it was starting to stink. There wasn't enough AXE in the world to get a woman near him in this state.

She was worried about him starving, but only on the psychic level. Physically, he needed to go on NutriSytem or something because all of his years of overindulgence had hit him like a ton of bricks.

Zeus was fat.

And if he didn't get up and move around, Abstinence was worried he was going to end up like Jabba the Hut, a big slug who couldn't move far enough to catch his own food.

He was so pitiful, she almost felt sorry for what she'd done.

Almost.

It was time he learned some basic object lessons about rewards and punishment—that he didn't automatically get what he wanted simply because he wanted it.

"Zeus?"

"Let me die."

"You're so dramatic. Come on, you need to sit up."

"I can't," he grumbled from beneath the sheets.

"You stink like the back end of a dead skunk." Abstinence turned the light on.

"Turn the light off, I'm hideous!"

Abstinence sighed and rolled her eyes. This was going to be a colossal pain in her ass. "There are only two things hideous about you. Your little temper tantrum and the stench coming from underneath that cover. I'm going to tell you once more to get up and haul your carcass into the shower or I'm going to curse you."

"You already did."

"Oh no, sweets. What I gave you was a gift. This, this will be a curse."

He burrowed deeper into the bed.

"Don't test me," she warned.

Zeus tugged the covers down and Abstinence did her best not to show a reaction. It wasn't that he'd gained weight, because wow, he looked like he'd just opened his mouth under a spigot of sausage gravy and drank until he couldn't move—every day for a hundred years. It was the hollow emptiness in his eyes.

He was starving.

Abstinence found that to be quite the paradox, not to mention ironic.

"Behave and I'll feed you."

"Does this look like it needs to be fed?" He slapped the pile of Jell-O that jiggled in place of his perfect abs.

"Not that, idgit. The other. But not until you get in the shower."

"I don't wanna. I hate this body. I'm not washing it."

"Then you'll never get fed because you stink. Then you'll be fat and *old*."

"How are you going to feed me? No woman will look at me."

"*I* will feed you. Now, don't be contrary. I'm already losing my patience with your petulance. You're a god grown, not a baby to be coddled. Take responsibility for yourself." Abstinence put her hands on her narrow hips.

"You couldn't possibly want this body and if you did, you couldn't have it. You'd die."

"Because you'd crush me? Nah, I'd be fine."

"Won't sex kill you?" He was incredulous.

"We don't have to have sex to have sexual energy to feed you, Zeus." She laughed. For being such an experienced god, he was sure slow to catch on.

"Yeah, but you'd have to want me," Zeus replied in a pitiful tone.

"I do want you, dumbass." Why did he think it was only about how he looked? She didn't know why she wanted the rest of it, self-centered as he was, but she did.

"All you do is insult me."

"Can't seem to help myself," she said merrily.

"You should abstain," he grumbled.

"Looks like you haven't lost your sense of humor with all that whining."

"Why are you doing this?"

"I don't know, honestly. We'll talk about it later, when I can stand to breathe in your presence."

"Good, if you can't stand breathing, maybe that means you won't talk anymore."

"No, I'm going to take your suggestion and *abstain*." She ripped the covers off the bed and flung them to the floor. "Get in that shower right now, Zeus or so help me I'll call Demeter to make it rain in here. You know she'll do it too."

He rose in all of his naked glory to pad to the shower and Abstinence found she wanted to pat his round belly as he went. She kind of liked that he wasn't modern physical perfection any longer. He was real.

Of course they'd have to get some of the weight off, if only because she'd made him sense himself like a mortal and lugging all that baggage around would make him feel like shit. But if the perfect abs and sculpted ass never came back, she'd be okay with that.

Abstinence had been hit with inspiration several days ago in relation to the whole sex issue. She was pretty sure she *could* have sex. Mortals who were pro-abstinence on that front usually waited until marriage or a committed relationship.

All she had to do was be in love with the god she had sex with. That wasn't so bad a gig after all. Now, she didn't know if she loved Zeus, wasn't sure she even wanted to, but it felt good to know her eternity wouldn't be spent in misery.

Abstinence was pleased to notice she was thinking about this job long term as opposed to how long she could hold out. That first real taste of her power and more than that, her purpose, it had been like a drug, but it wasn't an addiction. It fit like a good pair of boots that had already been broken in.

"Do you have anything besides Avalon Organics? Maybe a nice Dead Sea Salt scrub?" he called from the shower.

"Nope, that's it."

"Are you going to join me?"

"I thought you were all unhappy and shy with your new body?"

"You said you'd feed me. I'm hungry."

"I'll feed you after we work out," she called back. Positive reinforcement was her plan of attack.

There was dead silence and then a thud.

She ran into the bathroom. "Oh my gods, what happened? Working out won't kill you, I promise."

"I just dropped the soap."

"Another lesson to be learned." She nodded sagely, even though she knew he couldn't see her. "Never, ever drop the soap."

"Why not?"

A million different scenarios of Zeus dropping the soap skittered through her mind and she debated telling him about it, but decided not to.

"Never mind. Just hurry up."

"So, why would I want to take a shower *before* I work out? That makes no sense."

"Be quiet and scrub."

"One time I let you have the upper hand and now you're all Bossy McBrat. I'm not going to put up with much more of this."

"Whether you like it or not, you don't have much of a choice. If you want to manage this on your own, you go ahead."

"How about you just take your little gift back and we'll call it good."

Abstinence thought on it for a moment. She knew from her time as a psychiatrist that people didn't learn the lessons others wanted them to, they had to be ready to learn them. And maybe Zeus wasn't ready.

"Okay, on one condition."

"Anything."

"Don't go making promises you aren't going to keep, Zeus. Because if you don't keep your promise to me, I'll curse you and you'll suffer such as you never have before."

He pushed back the shower curtain. It was odd seeing the King of the Gods with a duck pattern clutched in his mighty hands. She would have snickered had the situation not been so serious.

"I guess that's fair. What do you want to take this damn thing back?"

"I want you to leave Hera and Hades alone."

"Hell no."

"There's your answer then." The writing was on the wall, why wasn't he reading it? This was a simpler lesson than what she'd hoped her gift would teach him.

"How am I supposed to hold on to my crown if every god of every pantheon knows my wife and brother cuckolded me and I did nothing about it?"

"The same way Hera has since eternity was young."

"It's not the same."

"Oh really?" Abstinence's voice dropped an octave.

"Abi, don't get your feathers ruffled. It is different. You know Bran has been eying my crown for centuries."

"And what would he do with it besides have a bunch of fancy titles after his name and a shiny hat to wear? Hera? Hades would kick his ass into his next incarnation."

"I know, that's the thing. Hades is stronger than me, Abi."

"So what? His dick is probably bigger too. Why do you worry? You didn't want Hera."

"But she was mine."

"Back to that again, are we? You'll never learn." She sighed. "Nevertheless, I want your word you'll leave them alone."

"No."

"Then I guess you're stuck."

"Damn it."

"That was only my first demand, Zeus."

"Double damn. What's the second?"

"Who cares? You wouldn't agree to the first one, so why bother?"

"Fine, I agree. You've got me over a barrel. I guess I'm lucky you didn't ask for something bigger. I'm ready, what's the second thing."

"You go from my temple right now and you never come back."

"What?"

"Do you want your freedom or not? I didn't say any of these were negotiable. They're not."

"What about explainable?"

"No."

"Why not?" He was obviously displeased with her answer, but he was displeased about everything that related to the situation.

"Because I just said they weren't explainable." It was like arguing with a child, or a brick wall that knew how to ask why.

"*Why* aren't they explainable?" he asked again, as if she were the one who didn't understand the question instead of it being him who didn't understand the answer.

"If I went into that, I'd have to go into the reasons I don't want to explain. So, take it or leave it, Zeus."

"I'll leave it."

"You've got to be kidding me."

"Nope. I want to know why more than I want any of those other things right now."

"Why?" she asked tiredly.

"Well, Abilicious, then I'd have to go into reasons I don't want to explain."

Professional cocksucker. Asshole. Bastard.

"Sucks, doesn't it?" he quipped.

Now he thought he had the upper hand? Oh no, not by a

long shot. She could always take all of her toys and go home. Not *this* home, but a new home. The great thing about being Abstinence was that she didn't have a bunch of stuff to move. She could take herself and go whenever she felt like it. Property value be damned.

"It doesn't have to. I'll miss Hera, but I can move."

The curtain jerked open and Zeus stepped out of the shower in all of his round glory, water sluicing off his body and making a great mess on her floor.

"You don't make any sense, Abi. First, you want to help me, you say this is all to help me and now you can't get far enough away from me, but you still offer to feed me with your energy. I don't understand. Make me understand."

She pushed her fingers through her hair in an exasperated motion. "If you don't understand, I can't explain it to you."

"You mean you *won't* explain it to me."

"No, this really is something that if you don't get, you just don't and no one can explain it to you. You're dangerous to me, Zeus."

"Why? I promised not to kiss you again." He looked genuinely confused.

"Because, you great ass, I want you to kiss me."

"Oh."

"And I think I can have sexual relations if I'm in love, but I don't want to love you. You're a bastard. I'm not one of those chicks who are into the fixer-upper types. I don't even usually like the bad boys and for all your blond goodness, football player shoulders and GQ looks, you're bad to the core."

"You must not have thought I was all bad if you decided I was worth all of this lesson learning."

"That's just it, Zeus. You're not ready to learn these lessons."

"I want to be."

"You are so full of Kraken crap, Zeus. It's another line to get into another pair of knickers."

"What if I swore on my godhood not to touch you that way?"

She snorted. "That would suck, as you so eloquently put it."

"What about if I swore not to touch another female as long as you'll have me?"

Abstinence narrowed her eyes. "What about other males? Hera told me about your "special massages"." She made finger quotes in the air.

"Abi, I have to eat."

"Yeah, you're like an addict, only you're addicted to your food. I have enough on my plate to deal with."

He couldn't meet her eyes any longer. "Don't leave me, Abi."

"Co-dependant much?" She realized how harsh it sounded after she'd spoken and Abstinence didn't mean to be cruel, she didn't want to hurt him, but she'd been mistaken to think any sort of interaction with Zeus could be anything but bad for her health.

Sure, he'd shown some moments where it looked like redemption was on the horizon, but she couldn't spend her existence waiting for a moment that might never come. It would be bad for both of them.

"Label me with whatever you want. It doesn't change the fact that you're the only one who's ever thought I was worth this. And you know what? It feels... I don't know how to explain it, but I don't want it to stop."

"You don't want. You do want. You need. What about me, Zeus?"

"I don't know. I figured you got something out of it to keep doing it."

She sighed heavily. "I don't. All I'm going to get is pain."

"Please, Abi. Don't give up on me. I'll bear your curse or blessing; just don't take yourself away from me.

Zeus, the King of the Gods, fell to his knees naked and vulnerable before the fledgling goddess and begged her to stay.

She closed her eyes against the onslaught of emotion rising inside of her. If anything was gluttony, this surely was. His need for her was intoxicating.

"Zeus, promise me about Hera and Hades and I'll stay."
What happened to go away and leave me alone? You idiot.

"Whatever you want, Abi. I promise."

"Get back in the shower. You're naked," she said and tried to break the tension.

"You'll be here when I get out, right?"

"I said I would. I won't leave." Why had she agreed to this? It was madness, pure and simple. Abstinence was sure she'd regret it. Especially when he spoke again.

"You won't regret this, Abi. I swear it."

Of course she would. In her experience, whenever a person promised you wouldn't regret something you'd agreed to against your better judgment, the explosion of the crash and burn was always nuclear.

CHAPTER

TWENTY-ONE

PERSEPHONE

Persephone hadn't seen hide or hair of any of the people who were supposed to be her support system. Her mother was uncharacteristically absent and at first, Persephone had been thrilled. She didn't know what had changed, but the fact Demeter was leaving her to her own devices had her jazzed. Until she needed some motherly guidance and she was nowhere to be found.

Eros wasn't answering his phone either, so she assumed they were together and she couldn't begrudge either of them spending all their time together. They'd both been alone for so long and Eros had loved her mother since she could remember him speaking of such things.

Thanatos wasn't answering his phone and neither was Hades. Was it a conspiracy to take away everyone who meant something to her?

She already knew why Hades was pissed and she knew she deserved it. But Thanatos? Persephone still didn't know what she'd done to make him so angry. She thought she'd been doing what he wanted when she'd offered him her virginity, but he didn't want it.

Why did no one want it? Was there something wrong with her? Persephone had always been told she was beautiful, but maybe they were wrong. Maybe Hades hadn't denied himself because of her maidenly fears but because maybe she was malformed somehow?

The thought almost sent her into another round of tears. No, Thanatos had seemed to want her, but it stung he'd rather jerk off than be with her in that way. It was almost as if he was afraid of her.

But from what Eros has told her, it was women who had such fears and fell in love from intimate contact, not men.

Persephone decided she wanted an answer. Thought she deserved one, really. It was rude to appear in a goddess's bedchamber and then leave. It was her understanding that the "wham and bam" came with a "thank you, ma'am."

She hadn't gotten the bam, so it stood to reason she wasn't due for the thank you either.

And Persephone wasn't going to stand for it. He'd made her cry.

Bullshit.

Persephone was determined to go see him and find out why exactly he wasn't answering his phone. If he didn't want to talk to her, well, too bad. He'd promised to help her and he was going to follow through whether he liked it or not. It was said among the mortals that one couldn't cheat Death. Well, Death was cheating her and that was unacceptable.

She wasn't going to teleport though because she had no idea what she was going to say. Maybe if she took the long way and walked she'd be able to think of something between her temple and his.

Or Nyx's. He stayed there when he was on Olympus. Since his mother was a titan, he governed death not only for the Greek Pantheon but for all of the others as well. It was like Death was a Fortune 500 company and Thanatos was the CEO. He had a board of directors who assisted him and only the really big events required Thanatos in person. The death of a god, for instance. She didn't know why she'd thought of that—feeling morbid she supposed.

Persephone wandered down Ambrosia Lane and the grass grew bright where she walked, the plants perked as if her face were the sun and her breath the rain. She walked slowly so her power touched each and every bloom or vine that reached for it. That gave her a sense of accomplishment. She couldn't bring the Elysian Fields to full bloom on her own like her mother could, but these little bits of nurturing she could share made her happy.

She smiled as she blew a kiss to the ivy that covered the alley wall of Pomegranate Pizza and the Cyclops inside waved to her. They were very kind; she didn't know why they had such a bad reputation. Probably all the human eating they'd done in the early days before they'd been taught better.

Persephone could see Death's pale horse from all the way down the Lane. She still didn't know what she was going to say to him. Maybe just showing up would be enough. She'd show and he'd talk.

The reality of it was more like she'd show and not talk and neither would he. They'd just breathe at each other like a couple of dorks who were too afraid to speak to each other. Which was stupid, Persephone had known Thanatos for all of her life and she'd called him a friend as long as she could remember.

That's what she was going to tell him! He'd said he didn't want to take her virginity because she should love the person she was with. Well, she did love Thanatos because he was her friend. Even though she had limited personal experience, she'd seen firsthand that friends always stayed longer than lovers. What better than to have her first time be with someone who was her friend?

It made perfect sense to Persephone.

A feminine laugh startled her from her reverie and she looked over her shoulder to see Hera and... no. It couldn't be.

But it was. Hades, in all of his dark splendor and he had his arm around Hera. Persephone's brain immediately jumped to all of the reasons he could have his arm around her, why she'd be looking up at him with stars in her eyes and her heart on her lips.

Persephone couldn't breathe, she couldn't walk, she couldn't *be*. The candle of her existence flickered as Hades bent down and kissed Hera with all of the passion he'd held in check when he'd been with Persephone. Hera consumed it eagerly, she was like a fire and his mouth was only kindling.

It was no comfort he didn't love Hera, that his heart had been torn from his chest. It would have been easier to take had he loved her—then Persephone's pain would have had a purpose. This was for nothing. Her love, her plans, every-thing she'd dreamed about was nothing.

She imagined now she knew what he'd felt the day he'd let her go. Nothing could hurt more than this; it was as if her soul was on fire and burning to ash while it was still in her body. Persephone understood how this pain could drive someone to fall into the merciful darkness of oblivion.

Persephone wanted to howl her pain, to scream into the endless sea of the heavens and she didn't want to be in her own skin. If she could have torn it from her bones, she would have. It was sheer agony watching them, but she couldn't look away.

The tears burned down her cheeks like acid and she didn't think anything would ever be as horrible. Until Hades paused and put a hand on Hera's back to still her and he looked up into her gaze where her anguish was bare for him to see.

It was the pity etched on his face that almost did her in. He didn't love Hera, but he didn't love Persephone anymore either. His pity was a sad, faded memory of what his love could have been.

And Hera.

How she wanted to hate her. The need to hate scorched her, but she couldn't summon the emotion itself. Because there was no pity on Hera's face, yet she was sorry for Persephone's pain. Hera had her own demons.

It would be easier if she could hate her, then there'd be a focus, a bullseye for all the despair and pain she felt; someone to blame other than herself.

Hera let go of Hades, almost as if she were nudging him to go to Persephone. Her feet were frozen to the spot, literally. Ice had formed around her feet, it crawled up her legs and swept over her arms and the tears that fell from her eyes became snowflakes. They dusted her lashes, her cheeks and fell softly on her bottom lip. It was now winter in her heart.

"Persephone," he spoke.

"No," she begged.

"You're free, why are you upset? Tell me," he asked kindly as if she were a child.

His kindly concern seemed almost fatherly and it made her sick to her stomach. She wanted to vomit her pain all over him, to make him feel something other than whatever this was. "I didn't want to be free," she managed.

"You'll see, Persephone. In time, you'll understand and thank me for it. I don't understand this, though. I thought you were with Thanatos."

She didn't want to admit she'd only done it to make him jealous, a stupid little game by a stupid little godling. Persephone wondered if her heart was going to crack right out of her chest.

"Oh," he said quietly, as if he knew exactly what she'd done. "You're going to make yourself sick, little one. You have to stop this."

He gathered her against him in a tender hug that was all the more brutal for its softness. Being pressed into his arms, she remembered his kiss, the scent of Bay and Sandalwood washed over her. His sheets smelled the same way.

Now they smelled like Hera. A goddess who'd given him her body completely, a goddess who wasn't afraid to take what she wanted and leave silly little Persephone out in the cold all alone.

"I'm not worth this, Persephone. It was never right between us. Centuries you held your body away from me. Think about this when you've calmed down. Right now, you want me because I'm familiar and your world has shifted."

"You don't know anything about what I want!" she cried.

Persephone's pride demanded she tell him to let go of

her, but she couldn't bear to say the words because it meant he'd never hold her again. That's what he was saying. She clung to him desperately and dug her nails into his back as if that would anchor him there with her.

"Gods, please, Hades. Don't do this to me. Please, please don't..."

"Persephone," he sounded shocked. "I don't want to hurt you."

"You already have and it's okay. I did it to you for centuries."

"Everyone on the Lane can see you, little one. You need to stop this and let go," he said firmly.

"Never," Persephone swore. Letting go of him now was akin to letting go of him in all other aspects too and she wouldn't do it.

He gently pried himself away from her and that was when a frigid wind blew across them both and chilled Persephone to the bone.

"You're turning into your mother," Hades warned.

"It wasn't me," she sniffed.

"No, it wasn't Perserphone." Thanatos said as he materialized. The cold radiated from him like he was made of ice and his black trench coat billowed out behind him like raven's wings. His dark sunglasses were down over his eyes and there was a radiance to him that wasn't bright, it was almost like anti-light. His knee-high cyberpunk boots weren't even touching the lane. He drifted in shadow and the chilled dark.

Persephone knew if he were to raise those glasses she'd see the end of all things in his eyes. She shivered, but didn't move closer to Hades. She felt like a mouse caught in the gaze of a cobra, she was drawn to Thanatos then. If he held out his hand to her, she would have taken it.

All of that icy numbness that radiated from him filled her hollow places and the fountain of pain she'd felt slowed to the trickle of a half-thawed creek in early spring. She wondered if in that moment, his touch would freeze her solid and the idea appealed to her.

Hera joined the gathering. "What's going on?" She put a proprietary hand on Hades and Persephone's ice cracked.

"Persephone would rather die than be without you, Hades."

"You're here to *take* her?" Hera cried.

"Yes," he stated as if his answer didn't matter.

"This is ridiculous," Hades snapped.

"No more ridiculous than you tearing your heart out of your chest," Thanatos answered.

"This is a tantrum by a spoiled godling who didn't get what she wanted," he returned sharply.

"Gently," Hera growled at him.

"Hades, let her come back to you. Or she's going to die," Thanatos said, ever stoic.

"I don't—,"

Thanatos pushed the glasses up on the crown of his head so Hades could see into the long, dark gaze of Death. "For me."

"Of course he will," Hera said before Hades could answer.

The blue electric snap of his power crackled and Hera slapped his arm. "Don't raise your power to me, Hades. You don't have a heart, so you can't be trusted to make the right choice here. Deal with it."

"As my Queen demands," he drawled.

"Damn right," Hera shot back.

This played out in front of Persephone as if she were watching a play instead of living her life. She was numb and cold throughout. She found it ironic and humiliating at the same time it was Hera who'd stood up for her, Hera who had no problem with her going back to Hades. She was so confident in herself and what she had with him that Persephone's presence didn't matter.

"I don't want to go." Persephone wasn't going to go where she wasn't wanted. She'd been so sure he'd want her back, but there was a part of her that asked her why she'd ever think that. She hadn't asked to leave, but she hadn't asked to stay either. How long was he supposed to love her with nothing in return but her selfishness?

"With me?" Thanatos asked quietly as he turned those aurora borealis eyes on her.

"No. With them." Her voice sounded like a rusty hinge. It was a struggle to talk.

"Seph, I won't let you die." With that, Thanatos showed the first irrefutable sign Persephone's death would mean something to him.

"Are you sure, Persephone?" Hera asked kindly. "He doesn't love me, you know. He can't. His heart is in a box like a coffin."

Persephone's lip trembled, but she found the strength to speak. "No, Hera. He doesn't want me. He told me, but I didn't listen. Please can you just go, it hurts to see you. And you're being so nice and I..."

The rest of her ice splintered and that creek that had only given leave to a trickle of pain became a waterfall. She realized that she really did wish Hera well and it stung like a bitch. She didn't find any comfort in the fact he couldn't love Hera. He should love someone.

As another wave of anguish filled her, all of the plants around her died. "Please, go?"

"If you need us," Hera nodded, leaving the rest unsaid as she and Hades left.

Us. One word and it bit deeper than any whip ever could have.

"You're fading, Persephone. You have to choose to live. Choose. Now!" Thanatos demanded.

She didn't want to die. Persephone hurt, she was broken inside, but she didn't want to die. So Persephone didn't understand what he was asking. "I don't know how."

"Look at what you've done." He pointed to the poor plants.

Persephone dug deep inside of herself for a glimmer of joy and found...something. She didn't know what it was, but it was enough to give to the plants she'd abused with her sorrow. They quickly returned to hearty life.

The pain eased. Instead of choking her, it only stabbed her. At least she could breathe.

"Why wouldn't you let me give up?" She was glad he hadn't, one moment of agony didn't make one end eternity, but what did it matter to him?

"Because eternity is a long time to waste on someone who doesn't love."

"And can Death love?"

"That would a horrible thing, would it not? The love of Death. The kiss of Death, to bear his mark and walk in shadow?" Thanatos replied quietly.

"No, not so horrible," Persephone answered honestly.

"What kind of woman would love Death?" Thanatos asked in a careless tone that belied the impact of his words.

Persephone realized then what she'd done wrong that night. Why he acted like he didn't want her. Thanatos loved her. Not as her friend, but he was in love with her. He'd asked Hades to take her. *For me*, he'd said with the kind of quiet intensity that only another master of shadow would understand.

For me. Two words that meant so much more. Take her for me, love her for me, protect her for me, make her live...*for me.*

She hadn't thought there was anything left inside of her to break, but this did it. Something shattered at the revelation. Death asked favor from no creature. He was forever and absolute, but he asked for her.

In a moment of self-pity and suffering, she'd surrendered. She'd craved Death. But another realization struck her like lightning. It hadn't been her own end she'd craved, it had been him: Thanatos. The god, not the office.

She'd needed him desperately; he was the strength that could turn the tide, the immovable object against which the unstoppable force became obsolete.

"I don't know," she answered. "A good one, a bad one, or maybe one who was more human than any goddess would ever admit."

"Don't die, Persephone."

"I'm not going to. I don't want to."

"But you called me; you called Death to your side when you wanted your pain to stop."

"It was you I wanted, Thanatos. Not Death, but you."

"They are the same."

She shook her head in denial. "No, they're not. Death is the timeless mask that's the safety equipment to do your job. Thanatos is the god beneath."

"And what would you have from Thanatos that you don't want from Death?"

"His friendship."

"Aren't you the goth girl's dream?" he sneered. "Death, an old friend come to call, a dark stranger no more?

"Not Death. Thanatos," she corrected gently.

"Does Death have nothing for you?"

"His kiss. It's dark and cold, but it takes away the pain," she confessed.

"And what of Thanatos and his kiss?"

"It incinerates me." The rest of the ice that held her melted and she swayed on her feet.

"What of your love for Hades? How can you want this with me and love him?" He spoke with such derision, but he caught her when she fell. Like she knew he would.

"I don't know," she said as she pressed her cheek against his chest.

NYX

Nyx was less than pleased to see her sad-eyed son dragging Persephone through the front door of her temple. She'd almost rather he'd had the Stolichnaya. A smart ass remark about strays was on the tip of her tongue, but there something about the way he held her—something about the way she nestled against him. It was as if they were both afraid she would break like a defective piece of bone china.

She could rattle that boy's teeth. What the hell was he thinking? Persephone was damaged goods. Not because she'd been shacked up with a god like Hades, he wasn't actually a bad sort, but from all of her drama and godling angst. Thanatos was a god grown and too smart for all of that nonsense. Or so she'd thought.

Nyx sighed and started dragging out the figs. She knew whether he asked for them or not, he'd be needing the fig cakes.

"Thanks, Ma," he mouthed.

She shrugged as if to say *that's what I'm for*.

It gave her a bit of a jolt to see him carrying Persephone upstairs, presumably to his bedroom. Nyx knew he was a god grown—she knew he'd had more than his fair share of women. It comforted her that Persephone didn't look like she could handle a round of bedsport with Death.

She paused—eggs mid whip. Persephone was broken and vulnerable, now would be the perfect time for Thanatos to slide right in. Nyx shook her head at the unintended imagery. That really wasn't the picture she wanted in her head. Great. Now she had something to tell *her* shrink. When she got one. Though it looked like she was on the fast track to needing one.

Nyx put a hand on her stomach and sighed. She was torn between asking Thanatos for all of the sordid details, knowing he'd never tell her otherwise. He'd keep it all bottled up inside like he thought he was a djinn instead of Death. He seemed to appreciate the fact she hadn't asked so far, so Nyx was going to keep going in that vein. One would think after being his mother for an eternity, she'd not have to question her first impulse. It showcased the stark truth that parents were rarely perfect and even given eternity, they still made mistakes.

She finished mixing the batter for the fig cakes and then decided to double it. Persephone wasn't missing any meals and if she was upset, a little comfort eating might make her feel better. Nyx knew would be partaking as well, as soon as she got another shot of that yark-not juice Apollo made.

Unfortunately, Nyx still hadn't told him the news. She kind of didn't want to. She'd been avoiding his calls, but with the way her stomach felt like it was going to get up and walk away without her, she needed some more of that magic brew. Which entailed talking to him.

She tossed the fig cakes in the oven to bake and looked at her phone. For the look she gave it, it might as well have been covered in flying horse crap like her ill-fated knickers. It wasn't the phone's fault she had to use it to call Apollo, so she probably shouldn't smite it. She'd just have to get another one anyway if she did.

Nyx sighed and dialed.

"Looks like I'm out of the doghouse," he said by way of greeting.

"You weren't in the doghouse."

"No? You stood me up and then wouldn't answer my calls. I did something to piss you off."

Why did he sound so fucking cheery? She was sure he wouldn't be later when she dumped this news on him. "Wanna come over?"

"I don't know. Are you going to answer the door? Because let me tell you, I've never had a goddess not open the door when I've come to call. I don't think I care for it," Apollo replied.

"Sorry about that. Things have been what you'd call crazy around here."

"Yeah, I saw that big blow up on the Lane with Persephone and Hades and I saw Thanatos carrying her back to your temple."

"This has absolutely nothing to do with that," she swore.

"Then what does it have to do with?" Apollo asked in a curious tone.

"Can we just talk about that when you get here?" *Oh, do not make me tell you this news on the phone, buddy.*

"Yeah, sure. You're making it sound dire, Nyx. It's not like you're some cheerleader who has to tell the football captain she's pregnant." He laughed.

"Oh, you think that's funny, do you?" Fine. He wanted it that way, he could have it. "It *is* like that."

"Took you long enough."

"What was that?" No, she couldn't have heard him right. Could she?

"I do believe you heard me, Nyx. You were glowing brighter than the sun that morning. I've fathered enough children to know when a goddess is pregnant."

"So, were you just going to let me angst on this all by myself?"

"Hey, I came over. *You* didn't let me in."

"I don't know if I'd let you in now. I can't believe you knew and you just...what if I'd never told you?"

"I didn't have to burn that bridge, did I?" he tossed back.

"I don't know what the hell you're so happy about."

"I'm going to be a father again, Nyx. I'm happy because you made me happy."

"Okay, this is so not the standard fare when the girl gets knocked up on the first date."

"We're gods. And it's not like you don't know me. I didn't pick you up in the bar and take you home for a quick one off. I like you. I want to spend time with you."

"Spending time with me isn't the same as bringing life into the world, Apollo."

"No, it's not. And if we could have waited before we got pregnant, that would have been the best choice. I'm not stupid, I know that. But why are you angry at me because I want to do this with you?"

"I don't know, damn it. But I am."

"Great. Nine months of unprovoked anger," he said with a light laugh.

It was Nyx's turn to laugh. "Oh, honey. Are you sitting

down? Because you want to talk about funny?" She laughed some more. It may have even been a cackle. "It's not nine months."

"Less? I guess that makes sense since you're a titan."

"Wrong again, Apollo. Try nine damn years. Try that one on for size."

Dead silence greeted her on the other end.

"Not so excited now, are you?" she said bitterly.

"I guess that will give us time to establish a solid relationship." His voice was still light.

"Are you kidding me?" What was wrong with him? He was *still* happy. It wasn't logical. He was a male—he had a penis. She knew that for sure. What she didn't know was why he was making these promises. He didn't have to say pretty things to get into her knickers. He'd already been there.

"Not the reaction you wanted? What should I do? Hang up on you? Ask if it's mine? Say it's not? I'm a mature god— you could even say grown. Adult. I knew there was a possibility you could get pregnant when I was between your sweet thighs."

"Have you thought about what we could have made?" she said quietly.

"My daughter if you're throwing up already."

"With Nod, you would have thought our children would have been quiet wispy things. He was the God of Dreams. But I brought forth Sleep and Death. I'm the Goddess of the Night, Apollo. You're the God of the Sun. It would make sense if Dawn wasn't already taken, but she is. As is Twilight. We'd be lucky if she's only the Goddess of Nightmares. And would you really wish that on a small child?"

"Thanatos bears the heaviest weight of all of us and he

turned out fine."

His logic was so... so...*male*. She growled into the phone.

"Look, I'm not dismissing your fears. But no matter what her powers are, she'll be our child, okay? We'll deal with whatever else when it comes. Don't buy trouble," he said in a soothing voice.

She was still pissed. Nyx knew it was illogical and unreasonable. He was being supportive and she was being a bitch. Well, he'd better get used to it. "So, you still want to come over?"

"Have you decided if you're going to open the door?"

Nyx smiled. "I guess."

"I'll see you in a bit. You want the potion don't you?"

Damn it. The whole reason she'd caved and called him and she'd forgotten to ask for it. Did she already have pregnant brain? That didn't usually hit her until year four. She wouldn't trade her children for anything, even this new little being she hadn't met yet, but she despised being pregnant.

"Yeah. I can't eat without it."

"And you waited this long to call me? Nyx, you have to take better care of yourself."

"Rule number one, no nagging."

"Fine. *My* rule number one, take care of yourself."

"Fine." She had the incredibly infantile urge to tell him he wasn't the boss of her.

"There, see? Everything is going to be okay. I'll see you in a little bit." Apollo hung up.

A sharp ringing sound jarred her so she dropped the phone. It clattered to the floor and one of the pieces skittered under the oven. Oven! The cakes. Thank gods for the timer on the oven, or she would have forgotten the damn cakes.

Apollo could get her a new phone. It was his fault she'd dropped this one anyway. She pulled the fig cakes from the over and turned to see her son standing in front of the kitchen island with his mouth hanging open. It almost looked like it was hanging free of muscle and tendon, it sort of wobbled.

"Close your mouth, Thanatos."

Nyx could swear she heard an audible creak as he attempted to close it. "Wait for the cakes to cool off first. I haven't even frosted them yet. Greedy boy."

She knew he wasn't agape at the cakes. He'd probably heard every fricking word she'd said to Apollo. Nyx hadn't planned on telling him yet. He had enough to deal with. It's not like Death didn't have enough on his plate without worrying about her. And she'd be fine.

Apollo had said so.

"I'm going to kill him," he stated finally, when he could get his jaw to work.

"You will do no such thing, Thanatos."

"I will. I am. Right now," he said grimly. He coat began to rustle out behind him as the power of Death infused him.

"Thanatos!" she snapped. "You put that away. I mean it." Nyx indicated the mantle of his power and the cold chill that filled the room. "Haven't I told you not to do that inside? Besides. This is between me and Apollo. You had to know this was a possibility when you set us up. So, if you want to blame anyone, blame yourself."

Nyx was aware that she was tossing out blame like Halloween candy, but she didn't actually mean it. She'd become an expert at manipulating her sons and she didn't do it often, but sometimes, when their power got the better of them during high emotions, she had to so they didn't do something awful. These verbal barbs had gotten to be less of a requirement over the years as her sons had matured and learned to control themselves, but when Thanatos was a baby and he'd get hungry or want attention, everything living within a five mile radius of him dropped dead. She'd only been able to buy the temple on Ambrosia Lane after he'd gone through puberty.

Thinking again about the life inside of her, Nyx knew fear. She was so afraid for her. What kind of life would she have? What would her burdens be?

"You're right, it's my fault. I never should have...I'm sorry, Ma." He looked up at her, his aurora borealis eyes now dark like the abyss.

Nyx crossed around the island and pulled her son to her. He was too tall to tuck his cheek into her shoulder as she had when he was younger, so she put her head on his shoulder and hugged him tightly.

"Listen to me, Thanatos. I'm a goddess grown, a titan. You're older than most of these gods and goddesses running around spawning their own young so I'll not deny this is completely unexpected, but it's not a bad thing. Apollo is your friend. He's a good god, right? He's nothing like Nod. This will be good. Don't you worry about me."

"Ma," he protested.

"Nope. None of that. You've got your own goddess to worry about now, don't you? She's upstairs and her heart's broken over another god. But I'm going to tell you something that should ease your hurt, if only a bit. She called you, didn't she? Her pain called *you*. Not Death, but you. In her greatest time of need, she didn't beg Hades to make it all better. In time, when she realizes her feelings for Hades were of the little godling variety she'll realize what she can have with you is forever and eternal. She'll love you, my son. Be patient with her."

"How do you know, Ma?" He asked and rested his head on hers.

"Because I am the Goddess of the Night, I see all things that transpire beneath the blankets of darkness."

He stiffened. "Oh, you didn't, you know, *look*, did you?"

"I certainly did. Not when you were together of course, but the things Persephone hides in the night, her uncertainty about Hades, her fears of being left alone and how he was the only stable thing she knew... and how she has feelings for you she never had for Hades? Yes, I've seen all of this. I had to know you weren't going to get hurt."

"What if I did get hurt? Would you smite Persephone?"

"Maybe." She pretended to seriously consider it.

"Ma!"

"See? You can go around smiting people because you don't like something they did. Even to someone you love."

"Is this supposed to be a lesson? Because I'm not feeling it."

"I know; it's different when it's your mom."

"Are you saying you love Apollo?"

"No. But I'm saying I like him and in another century or two, it might not be out of the realm of possibility."

"He never stays with anyone that long."

"Good. Then we'll break up before I could do something so stupid."

"You've got an answer for everything, don't you?" Thanatos asked as if this were somehow a revelation.

"Yeah. I'm supposed to. I'm Mom."

"Tell me this, then—,"

"I'm not a Magic Eight ball, Thanatos."

"I didn't even shake you up."

"Fine. What?"

"Persephone will love me. Then what? How can we be

together? I'm Death. I walk in shadow. She's going to be the Goddess of Spring, rebirth. Her power is Life."

Nyx pulled away and cupped her son's cheek. Oh, he was a beautiful boy. Why Persephone hadn't already admitted she was head over ass Nyx would never know. He did tortured almost better than Hades.

"My son." She sighed. "You've bought into your own hype," Nyx said softly.

"What do you mean?"

"I mean that her power may be Life, but you're not polar opposites. You're not even two sides of the same coin like Apollo and I. Look at the mortal world in winter. It seems as if everything is dead and cold, but beneath the ground, life struggles and in the spring it bursts forth. When is birth ever easy? It's hard and ugly, brutal. Yes, the flowers are beautiful. The verdant landscape lovely. But birth and death go hand in hand—often one must die so that another can be born. Even the mortals in the ancient traditions worshipped this cycle, the young stag kills the king stag to take his rightful place and it begins again."

"I've seen her death."

"And does that matter so much when Death holds her close?" She smiled again and patted his cheek. "Go on, she's still upset. Hold your goddess and keep her safe. I'll bring the cakes up after they've cooled." Nyx watched him for a long moment. "So, don't take advantage of her vulnerability. I don't want to walk in on anything."

"Then knock first." He kissed the top of her head and went back up the stairs to his room before she could say anything else.

It was Nyx's turn to stand there with her mouth hanging open on a rusty hinge.

TWENTY-TWO

DEMETER

Darkness crept over her with an old woman's knobby fingers, gnarled shadows clawed and grasped and Demeter's first instinct was to fight, but she realized it was the touch of death. She'd thought Thanatos would come for her, his long coat billowing out behind him and that secret smile he wore like a gentle mask.

But there was no one there, no face to put to the omnipresent shadow. It was heavy like smoke and it filled her lungs; made it impossible to breathe. She was a goddess, breath shouldn't have been vital to her, but she felt the pressure in her chest as if she'd been hit with a wrecking ball. Demeter reached out for Eros, but she couldn't find him.

Oh, gods, he wasn't there!

The place he'd occupied beside her in the bed was cold and empty. He'd been gone for some time. Had he abandoned her to face her fate alone? Not that she didn't deserve

251

it—she knew she did, but she was so afraid. He'd promised to hold her when it was her time. Her heart told her he would have kept that promise, had he known this moment would be the dusk of her life. She wanted to call out to him, but Demeter's fear of dying paralyzed her. So much so when an unseen force knocked her from the bed, she couldn't reach out and find purchase on the sheets or the mattress to keep her body from falling to the ground.

Only, the impact she expected never came. She was caught in a freefall through endless nothing; her stomach flipped and crawled up into her throat—like a dream where one steps off the mountain top and tumbles forever.

This was death? Would her awareness simply blink out as if it had never been when she made impact? Or would this fall be eternal?

Demeter had been to Tartarus, so she knew she hadn't been consigned to eternal torment for her selfishness. Thinking of it, Demeter decided she'd gladly take the eternal torment if she could fix what she'd done to Persephone and tell Eros she loved him.

She wasn't sure if what she felt for him was love, but it was the closest thing that had ever resembled that emotion for her. Demeter didn't take comfort in the knowledge that he knew her heart, or the innermost places of her soul. She needed to tell him, because even though he could see inside of her, he needed to hear it. Words like sugarplums off of her lips.

Yes, like the poem he'd read to her about love-stained kisses and absinthe mist. Demeter wondered if she'd forget in this eternity and that seemed like the biggest crime. She'd take all of her deeds in stark relief, she'd relive each and every horrible thing she'd done from either side of the equation as long as she got these last moments with Eros.

A hot, white nebulous thing blossomed inside of her and with it came the certain knowledge that everything she'd done, while terrible, had moved Persephone exactly where she was supposed to be. She was still learning the lessons that were hers by the threads of Fate, but she would be happy. Despite it all, Persephone would have joy. She would have love. Even though she walked hand in hand with Death, it was where her happily ever after lived and breathed.

Her face was wet with tears and Demeter didn't know if they were of sorrow for wasting the time she'd been given or if it was joy for the bright future her daughter would have with the most unlikely god. She thought maybe it was a little of both. Demeter swore wherever she ended up, she would not drink of Lethe's Stream, the elixir that would steal her memories and her pain. Because it would steal her joy as well. She'd only just felt this palette of emotion and Demeter didn't want to give it up, even if it meant keeping her suffering too.

It was then Demeter surrendered to her twilight, the long shadows that had twisted into a noose eased and she ceased her struggle to take breath that no longer belonged to her. Her last thought was of Eros and the sorrow and guilt she knew he would feel when he returned to find her dead.

Demeter didn't feel as if she were falling any longer, but floating. A warmth lapped at her fingers and toes, it washed over her like she was adrift in an eternal sea. There were stars overhead, millions upon millions sparkling like mischievous winks from a benign being greater than herself —greater than all the gods.

She was still crying, but it was from release. All of the darkness she'd held inside of her was gone. All of the hate and the pain and all she could feel was love. Demeter couldn't quantify it, but she knew in her soul this was real. She'd been touched by something bigger than the universe, but still seemed to fit within the seemingly small confines of her heart.

Demeter was clean, purified somehow. And the tears wouldn't stop. That's when she realized she wasn't in an ocean, it was a sea of tears, what was left to mark the passing of the others before her and Demeter knew with a certainty that she was not alone.

Her hair tangled down in the fronds of the water plants, becoming one with the other greenery and vines. It pulled her down, but she didn't fight, even as the salty tears filled her nose—her mouth. It was fitting she should stay there and Demeter was thankful to know her essence would go on as her fingertips became vines and her legs twined around to thrust deep within a sandy shelf as they became roots.

Just as she'd resigned herself, she was falling again. Demeter hit the floor next to Eros' bed and thunked her head on the edge of the mahogany headboard. She was almost too stunned to notice.

Eros dashed from the bathroom, his toothbrush half hanging out of his mouth. "What happened?"

Demeter tried to pull herself up on the bed, but didn't have much luck. Her limbs were uncoordinated and her body was still numb from her experience. Eros hefted her with ease, toothbrush still at the corner of his mouth and deposited her back in the bed.

With her arm hooked around the back of his neck, her eyes finally focused on his face. "I died, Eros."

He stiffened and the toothbrush fell from its perch to clatter across the floor. "What?"

"It happened. I died." She pressed her lips together to hold back another sob.

"Then how are you here with me?" His hands moved over her and Demeter didn't know if he was checking to see if she was injured or if she was real.

"I don't know." She shook her head. "I can't explain it, but my heart?" She pressed a fist to her chest. "It *hurts*."

"It's okay. You're here with me now. I won't let you go," he swore.

"Eros, it was..." she searched for the word she wanted. "Beautiful."

"Death was beautiful? Like mother like daughter then?" He tried to joke, but she could hear the strain in his voice.

"My heart is so full, it aches with it. Everything you said in your prophecy was true. Love saved me. I don't know how much more time I've been given, but I know it's more than I deserve. And I have to tell you something." She looked up at him, her emerald eyes full of promise.

"Demeter—" he tried to cut her off.

She wouldn't let him. "No. Like I said, I don't know how much more time has been given to me and I don't want to waste it." Demeter kissed him softly before looking into his eyes once again. "Will you live with me and be my love?" she said, quoting Christopher Marlowe back to him as he'd quoted Keats outside her window. "There will I make thee a bed of roses..."

And brought to life by the intensity of her emotion, the room bloomed to life, covered in red roses. They twined around the headboard and footboard, over the windows and the door—in a red carpet of velvet petals across the floor and one lone bloom sparked to life in her hand. Demeter held it out to him carefully, almost as if she were afraid he wouldn't take it.

He accepted the rose from her and held it as if it were the rarest of gems. Eros held it against his chest and it branded itself there—a living embodiment of her love.

Demeter reached out tentative fingers to trace its lines, but his hand covered hers and the love that flowed between them was like a river to the sea and back again. She was reminded of the sea of tears where she found her redemption and she whispered a silent thank you to the universe for all of her bounty.

They made love on their bed of roses and Demeter emerged from the long dark to finally stand in the sun.

CHAPTER
TWENTY-THREE

HERA

"Just what was going on in that head of yours?" Hades finally asked her hours after he'd teleported them back to Tartarus. She knew he'd been waiting for an explanation, but she'd demurred until he had to ask outright.

"What do you mean?" Oh, she knew very well what he meant. He was obviously displeased about being offered up to Persephone like an old handbag she was tired of carrying. Hera hadn't meant it that way, but Persephone's suffering was much like what she'd felt when she first discovered Zeus cheating on her. She had empathy for the godling.

"Hera. Don't play games with me," he warned.

"I couldn't very well let her die, could I?"

"Does her life mean more to you than I do?" Hades asked the question as if he didn't already know the answer and was afraid of it.

"It's not like I was giving you to her like…" The earlier comparison came to mind. "Like last season's Prada."

"Wasn't it?" His glance was sharp like a thousand daggers.

"No. And what do you care about it anyway? You don't have feelings."

"That's where you're wrong, Hera."

"You felt something you didn't like when I offered for that poor heartbroken girl to come to the only place that's felt like her home for the last few centuries? Get over it. You were selfish when you stole her to begin with. Reap what you've sown."

"Doesn't it matter to you that it *hurt* me you could give us up so easily? What about all of your promises, Hera?"

"What about them? I promised you I'd stay and I have. I will. I'm yours, Hades. You think that sad little godling has anything to do with that?"

"Doesn't she?" His jaw was set in a hard line.

"My gods, you are frustrating. You answer every question with another question." She sighed and flopped on the divan.

"Hera, first it's she'll hold her breath until she gets back in my house. Then it's she'll die if she's not in my bed. Then another tantrum until you're gone."

"I thought you loved her," Hera said quietly.

"I loved the idea of her. With my heart no longer in my chest, I can see that now. A little perspective did wonders."

"That doesn't mean it's okay to hurt her or treat her callously."

"You're the only goddess I know who would defend the woman trying to take her man." Hades shook his head.

"And can she take you from me?"

"No."

"Are you sure?" she asked, carefully.

"I said so, didn't I?" he growled, irritated.

"And if we have a fight, are you going to drag me to the surface and install another in my place with no care or concern for what your actions have done to me?"

"Do you *want* me to be with Persephone?"

"I want you to be happy, Hades." *I love you* had been on the tip of her tongue. Gods forbid she should ever say that where he could hear her.

"What if it was being with Persephone?"

"We already had this discussion." His words cut her. What the hell was she doing here? Fuck the fire—she'd jumped out of the frying pan and right into the inferno. This was deeper than she'd ever been into anything. "Nothing's changed."

"I hope for your sake that you haven't fallen in love."

This was the straw that stripped the scales from the dragon. She'd had enough of his self-pity and his fear. Because that's what it was—this aversion to love. It was pure, unadulterated fear.

"And what if I did, Hades? Would it be so horrible?" Hera looked up into his eyes and she refused to be afraid anymore, refused to fear that he would see the truth of her feelings there.

"It would," he said quietly as he nodded. "There would be only pain for you there because I can't love you back."

"Did I ask you for anything but your time and attention? Did I ask you to love me?" Hera asked as if she really required an answer.

"You are now with that hopeful desperation on your face."

"What do you know of it? Nothing," she answered her own question. "You've never loved. You just said that what you felt for Persephone was the love of an idea, not the goddess. So how can you know what it feels like, or what I'm asking you for, or what I can live with?"

"Hera," he began in a low tone that was almost an admonishment.

"Hades," she delivered the rebuke back to him. "Don't presume to know the breadth of a goddess's heart. I don't want anything from you but what you want to give me. I knew you wouldn't love me the day I proposed this partnership. Nothing has changed. We don't even need to have this conversation. You're the one so focused on it."

"Because your pain hurts me," he cried.

"Ah, well then I should stop loving you because of your discomfort?" She rolled her eyes.

"Yes!"

"No. It doesn't work that way. You wanted to have this discussion? Fine. We'll have it. I do love you." He looked stricken at her words, but that didn't stop her. The dam had broken and the tidal wave of her confession couldn't be stopped now. "I love you like the sun loves the sky— content to burn in its arms for eternity. My love is more constant than the stars and when they've shuddered into oblivion, it will still be there—strong in my heart as the day it was born. When the mortal world is nothing but dust and ash and all that makes us sentient has slipped away in the granules of sand through the great hourglass—yes, even then. No matter if you never feel your heart beat again inside your chest, no matter if you never feel anything but lust for me, I will love you."

"Don't say those things." He looked away.

"Why not? You demanded to hear them. So now you will listen." Hera sprang to her feet and grabbed his arm when he would have turned away from her.

"Damn it, Hera. I know I'm your second choice." Hades still wouldn't look at her.

She remembered her promise to the tender heart that had beat for her. Hera had promised she wouldn't hurt him and this had done it, cut him to the core. She took a deep, calming breath. "I chose wrong the first time. I didn't love either one of you then. I was a godling led by my mother's hand. Why does this have to be about the past? Can't it be about us in the here and now?"

"Because it is about the past. It's about punishing Zeus. It's about catching the one that got away and Hera, when you finally see I'm not the catch you made me out to be, all of these things you think you're feeling...they'll crumble to nothing."

"You are everything that you made *yourself* out to be, Hades. I've already told you I don't expect anything from you but honesty and fidelity. Are you telling me you can't deliver?"

"What if I don't want to deliver?"

"Then tell me now and we'll be done with this." Hera steeled herself for whatever answer he would give. She didn't think he'd send her away, but she couldn't believe how callous he'd been with Persephone.

"What happened to the sweet I love yous?" he sneered.

"I said I love you, I didn't say that meant I'd eat your shit sundae with a silver spoon. Love doesn't mean pain."

"There's where you're wrong."

Hera could read the predatory look on his features, he was going to kiss her and he was going to be hard, brutal. He wanted her to tell him to stop. It was the same test from when she'd first come to be with him and she was tired of being tested. She'd already proven herself.

And yet, she wouldn't deny him. She didn't want to.

Hera wanted to be all things to him He was angry, but grudge sex was always good and Hera knew on a primal level he'd never really hurt her physically. In fact, she liked a little hair-pulling.

Hera reached out and threaded her fingers through his hair and yanked him down to her. His kiss was every bit as hard and hungry as she'd expected, but Hades pulled away before she was ready.

"Aren't you going to deny me, Hera? Doesn't this *hurt*?"

"It does hurt, but it's bittersweet. I'll never deny you, Hades. Never," she swore.

That was the source of all of his suffering, being denied. When he was a godling, his mother had preferred Zeus to him, knowing what he'd become. It was ironic that their golden boy had been the one to kill them. Hades had never been given anything—everything he'd possessed he'd been forced to steal.

He'd taken Persephone because he hadn't thought he could have her any other way. And she was too pure, too innocent. It was like he'd seen something in a shop, but didn't have the money to pay for it, so he'd taken it, but he'd never wanted to do anything with it. It was a pretty bauble he wanted to have for the sake of having. He'd coveted her, yes, but he'd never truly loved her.

All of those years of denial hadn't only been for Persephone—they'd been for him too. He hadn't wanted to spoil his prize.

Hera was none of those things. She loved him with the heart of a goddess grown, of a woman. She knew it was almost time to give him her heart, in the literal sense. So he could understand. He'd feel all the things she felt and he'd know her feelings for him were genuine. She wasn't worried about losing any of her devotion to him, or feeling any of the hungry shadows he'd whispered about in dark promise. For Hera loved him with her soul too—with every fiber of her being.

"This means nothing to me, Hera."

"Are you trying to hurt me?"

"No, I'm simply being honest."

"I prefer the hard truth to a pretty lie any day."

It was in that instance that Hera saw the truth for what it was—not the words from his tongue that were like acid, but it was in his eyes. The blue flame had died and it was replaced with the warm chocolate she'd longed to see. He would love her, only he didn't know it yet.

Hera reached up and brushed her knuckles over his cheek. "Don't stop, Hades. Take what's yours."

He growled low in his throat as if the very words she spoke had cut him somehow.

"How can it be mine? I've given you no soft words." His hands were on her hips and he held her flush against him.

"I told you, it's yours. Now. Forever. No soft words in payment, only honesty."

"Why?" he asked again.

He'd already questioned her so many times before. Why, indeed. She'd told him. It was as if he didn't understand the concept. For a smart god, he was being unreasonably obtuse. As if he couldn't fathom her reasons, as if what she said couldn't possibly be true.

She didn't speak the words again; he wasn't ready to hear them. Instead she kissed him tenderly and said with lips all the things she couldn't with her voice.

A sound of desire spiked with the knives of despair was torn from him and Hades grabbed her hair and tilted her face back so he could search her face.

"Deny me."

"No." There was no defiance in her voice, only quiet resolve.

"What if I bent you over this divan and had you right here?"

"You can have me anywhere." She turned from him carefully, his hand still in her hair and she bent over the back of the divan.

Hera was fully clothed, but she'd never felt more naked. His sharp intake of breath indicated he liked it, but what would he do about it? His other hand slid down and cupped the rounded globes of her ass.

"Anywhere? Are you sure about that, Hera?"

"Yes," she promised, with no hesitation. It didn't matter if he was still testing her or not. She was his, body and soul. There was nothing he could ask to do to her that she wouldn't allow. Except treat her as Zeus had, although she was beginning to think even if he did, it wouldn't matter because she loved him. Being apart from him would be more painful than what any of his actions could bring.

But surprisingly, she had faith he wouldn't. She trusted him.

Hera arched in to the caress and braced legs wide apart. "Anything, Hades."

He jerked her leathers down around her thighs and she gasped as the cool air hit her naked skin. She shivered with the chill as well as anticipation. Hades cupped her ass again, but his fingers gravitated up toward her hips and suddenly, she felt the warmth of his breath across her sex.

He'd positioned himself beneath her, between her legs and he kissed her there, his tongue gently pushing at her seam. It shot waves of pleasure through her so sharp, she was thankful to be braced on the divan. His hot tongue was on her clit, flicking hard and fast—just as the sensation built to a fervor, he stopped to thrust inside of her again.

She cried out and pushed against him—her need seemed to please him, to drive him. He focused on her clit again and Hera fisted the woodwork finishing on the back of the divan, her nails marring the soft cherry wood.

Hades entered her with his fingers and tugged lightly on her clit with his teeth while he worked it with his tongue. She tightened her channel around his fingers as her orgasm rocketed through her. Hera was still riding the waves of pleasure, her knees weak when she felt him behind her.

She knew from experience how big his cock was and she stiffened when he pressed himself against her. Did he really mean to take her there? Hera tried to relax as she awaited his next touch.

His long, solid body covered her and he placed a soft kiss at the base of her neck. He grasped her hips and angled them so that she was splayed even wider before him and then he thrust into the wet heat of her slit.

She didn't know whether to be relieved or disappointed, but she couldn't think about it now, not with him inside of her. He filled her and held her angled for maximum penetration.

He thrust into her roughly and his hands moved from her hips to her breasts.

"Don't love me," he whispered raggedly.

"Why?" she managed before she bit down on her lip to fight the sensations he wrought in her.

He slowed his rhythm; kissed her neck again and then brushed his lips against the shell of her ear. "Because then Fate will take you away."

She bucked against him, matching his pace; pleaded

with him to give her more. His confession had made her soar—he needed her for more than this heat between them. Hades' body went rigid, he was about to come.

"I don't love you," he said tenderly as he spilled inside of her.

But he did. She didn't know how, not with his heart in a wooden box, but his words had been a sweet confession. Hera knew it in her soul.

"I don't love you too." Oh, gods, if she were wrong...

He teleported them from behind the divan, to on the divan, and Hera was atop him, her leg thrown across his thigh and he held her with her head on his chest. It was then she saw his scar was gone and she could feel his heart beating beneath her cheek.

"How?" she asked and traced a nail down his sternum.

"I heard it beating thunderously loud when we got back. I went to look and it shot itself into my chest, the bastard. Like one of those face huggers from *Alien*." He was silent for a long moment and Hera was contest simply to be in his arms. "I knew it beat for you," he said more quietly as if he were afraid someone would hear.

"Did it hurt?"

"Worse than prying it out. It tore my scar wide, I could see my ribs. I thought for sure you'd heard it happen."

"Your thirty-four headed shower is kind of loud and you're more than a little bit of a hardass."

He loved her! His heart beat in his chest and it was of its own accord. Hera was almost giddy with the joy that was a starburst inside of her. She splayed her hand over his chest beneath her cheek and she was happy to simply feel its beat.

"I gave you a way out, Hera." His heart was beating

faster now. He was afraid? Or was he angry he felt something for her?

"I don't want a way out."

"Silly goddess."

"Silly god," she corrected. "Don't you know how perfect you are to me? Maybe not the world, but me?"

"You have to stop saying these things, Hera. Fate will—,"

"Fate will nothing!" A woman began to take shape and Hera recognized her voice. It was Thalia.

"Uh," Hera indicated her nakedness.

"I don't care. I'm sick and tired of being blamed for everything that you think is a bad thing. Tell your woman you love her. Right now!" Thalia stomped her foot.

His poor heart was doing an Irish Jig in his chest. He clamped his mouth shut and shook his head in the negative. Even when Thalia narrowed her eyes. He obviously thought it was some kind of test.

"I'm not kidding," she warned and pulled out what looked to be an embroidery sampler. "I will cut your thread..."

"Thalia, I thought you were the Muse of Comedy?"

"I am, but it's my turn to sit in the Fate chair. And isn't Fate supposed to be funny?"

Fate *was* funny like that.

"You know, Hades, I really ought to cut your thread this very minute. Do you have any idea how much work it's been to get you to this very moment? Everything you thought was a shit sundae, to borrow Hera's terminology, was a calculated move on my part to get you here. Now you're telling me you don't trust me? It's bullshit. Unless you don't want Hera?"

"It's okay, Thalia. I don't love him either," she said with a soft smile.

"You two assholes deserve each other. Really. After that long heartfelt confession about the sun in the sky and dying stars and you've been reduced to giggly little middle school games? Ungrateful wretches."

"Oh, no. We're grateful. We're beyond grateful. Thank you, Thalia." When Hades didn't say anything she elbowed him. "Aren't you thankful?"

He still looked like a kid whose mom had asked if he had anything he needed to tell her and his brain was filing through the catalogue of fuck ups and he was deciding what to tell her that would get him in the least trouble if it wasn't the thing she already knew about.

He snapped out of it. "Very thankful."

"Yeah, you better be. You and your brother have been the biggest pain in my ass since I took the job. I'm glad to be done with you. Him, I don't know if I'll ever get there."

"I guess the job is pretty stressful. You never used to speak so harshly."

"Trying to manage spoiled petulant gods will do that to you. Nothing tarnishes a muse faster than being smacked with the banality dick."

Hera giggled. "Sorry. I wasn't difficult was I?"

"Oh no, you even asked for my help, which I was happy to provide. Listen, let's do lunch later this...century, probably is when I'll be free. But I have to run."

"Great. Maybe you'll stop in to Jean Pierre's. It sounds like you need a girl's day."

Thalia sighed, "I do." Then she looked at Hera again. "Sorry about the whole, well, naked."

"It's good. Really. Nothing could spoil this."

"Are you sure?" She raised a brow. "Sorry again. The nature of Fate again."

"See! I knew I shouldn't..." Looks from both women quelled him and he closed his mouth.

Thalia disappeared.

"I'm still not saying it."

"You don't have to."

"I don't want you to say it."

"What?"

"It was weak of me to want to hear it, it's better than ambrosia on your lips. But don't say it."

"Fine. I don't love you. I don't love you. I don't love you. I don't love you. What about that? Can I say that?"

"I don't love you either, Hera. Not until the universe itself goes dark and quiet. Forever."

Who knew saying I don't love you could be so romantic?

"Forever," she echoed.

He was quiet again before he asked, "Stay?"

"Yes."

"For always?"

"Always."

"You don't need any time to yourself to find out who you are?"

"Have you been reading my Cosmo?" She looked up at him.

"Maybe."

"Do you want me to take time away?" After all they'd been through, did he really want her to go gallivanting off on some quest to find herself when what she wanted was right here?

"Never." His reply was fierce and strong. "I don't want you to feel trapped or...I don't want to be the rebound."

"Oh please. Zeus and I may have just gotten divorced,

but our marriage has been dead for centuries. I know who I am. I know what I want and it's 'not loving' you and being with you for all eternity."

"Do you want a proper wedding?" Hades asked softly.

"You didn't ask me to be your wife," she teased.

Oh gods! Did she want the wedding? Hera was getting her happily ever after and suddenly, she was afraid if she closed her hands around it, she'd fuck it up. She hadn't planned on what to do after I love you. Or don't love you, as the case happened to be.

"And I don't have to either. You already said you were mine. Mine involves..." he paused as if he didn't have a good explanation. "Being mine. You can choose the flowers and the cake, but we're doing this."

She'd rather he'd pressed the anal sex issue than demand a wedding. Her mother had taken a century to plan her wedding to Zeus. A CENTURY. Why couldn't they just keep being together the way they were? Shit, if she kept thinking this way, she was going to have to turn in her Chick Card.

"How about something small?" she conceded.

"How about not? Don't you want to be the princess and do the carriage and whatever else women like to have at these things?"

She couldn't believe he was serious. "There's no point in having the whole shebang unless it's a coronation ceremony too."

"Whatever you want, Hera."

Damn. She'd thought that would put him off. It didn't matter, Hera realized. Hades was her forever and she'd deny him nothing. If he wanted her to be a fairy princess in a white dress on their wedding day, she would be. This didn't matter. She didn't need a ceremony to tell her where her heart lay.

"Okay, Hades. I'll wear the dress and we'll have a grand ball."

"Make sure you give me enough time to prepare for war with my brother before you send your invitations. He won't take this coronation thing lightly."

He'd really go through with it. For her. Hera knew she couldn't ask him to do that now. Not over something that didn't matter so much to either of them. "I know you don't want it and you don't want to fight with him. What about if I quit my job and 'stayed home'?" She smiled against his shoulder.

"Abdicate your crown? To who?"

"Abstinence."

"You love being queen." He pushed her hair behind her ear and continued to touch her hair.

"I think I've had enough of it, actually. I've been thinking on it since Abstinence told Zeus that a crown didn't make him who he was. And she was right. I only want to be with you. That's my job now."

"Now and forever," he reiterated as if he still couldn't believe this had happened.

Hera couldn't either, but she wasn't going to question Fate.

TWENTY-FOUR

ABSTINENCE

Her first instinct had proven to be the winning horse right out of the gate. She immediately regretted rescinding her demand that Zeus leave her in peace. He wasn't even trying to make her fail and just looking at him was enough to make her yearn for things she knew could never be hers. He would never truly love her. He might think he did, but Zeus was too selfish to love anyone as deeply or completely as he loved himself. Making love with him without the returned emotion would definitely be indulging herself. It would be fucking, not making love.

Then she'd be back up shit creek with half a paddle and a hole in her boat. Or maybe just a capsized kayak? Either way, it would stink.

Right now, he seemed content to cook with her. Which was just weird. The King of the Gods was in her bare kitchen whipping up lasagna. When he'd asked to cook, she thought for sure he would try to make something in truffle oil, oysters or something else associated with sex. Lasagna pretty tame compared to what she was expecting. For which she was eternally thankful. Oysters made her want to blow chunks. She'd never had them prepared in any way that tasted like anything other than slimy vomit.

He was also humming *La Donna E Mobile*. Damn if that wasn't sexy as hell watching his hands work the dough. Yeah, he even made his own noodles. That made her knees weak and her thighs quiver like nothing else. Worse? Her mouth was watering. She felt like a slobbering bulldog.

She didn't know how well this boded for her previously *slender* figure. Abstinence had been eating like a pig. Well, it was piggery for her. Probably normal for everyone else. Zeus always loaded her plate up like it was for a starving family of seven so she could eat her fill and there would still be more than half left on the plate.

Abstinence wondered how long that could be considered abstaining and if she were cheating Fate. She knew no matter what she thought she was getting away with now, if she were cheating, it would come and take a big bite out of her ass sooner or later.

Truthfully, she hoped she was doing the right thing. Abstinence loved the taste of food, but she wouldn't make herself ill for it. So far, there'd been no repercussions, but that didn't necessarily mean anything. Part of her said she should abstain from ingesting food completely, but he loved to cook and she loved to eat.

It was probably a good thing she'd gotten this gig or she'd be a million pounds and they'd have to roll her out of her house. Or cut out a wall. She licked her lips in anticipation as he dropped the noodles into the boiling pot. Her favorite part of the lasagna was actually the cheese. The more cheese the better. Actually, if there wasn't enough cheese to stop an elephant's heart, she didn't want any. The same with pizza. She especially loved the hard, crusty bits of cheese that crisped on the edges. Yeah, that was nowhere near abstaining because she could eat that stuff with a steam shovel instead of a fork.

Zeus poured another glass of wine and handed this one to her. "So, have you thought any more about what I said?"

Not this again. "We've been over this before. Let's not ruin a nice evening, okay? I like spending this time with you, but if you're going to pressure me, I don't think we can see each other," Abstinence snapped. She knew it had been too good to be true, he would never leave it alone. For self-preservation, Abstinence was going to have to break her promise to him. Every time he asked her, she was a little bit closer to breaking. He almost had her convinced she wouldn't die. He could sell a litter box to a dog.

"Abi, this isn't about sex."

"Everything with you is about sex." She looked at him pointedly.

"I have stayed on my own side of the kitchen all night. Not to mention slaving like a dog over this meal for you."

"If it's not to be mentioned, why mention it?" She raised a brow.

"You argue more than Hera ever did. I don't know why I'm even interested." Zeus tested the noodles and finding them ready, laid them out in the pan.

"I don't either." Abstinence shrugged.

"I just want to fall asleep with you in my arms. Why does that make me the bad guy?" he asked in a sincere tone.

"Stop it!" she cried.

"Stop what?" He seemed genuinely confused.

"This. Acting like you care. That you want something

275

more from me than what you've been told you can't have."
Tears gathered in her eyes, but she'd be damned if she'd cry.

"Abi," he said quietly and leaned across the island to tilt
her face up to his. "I don't want to hurt you. I want to be
with you in whatever ways are allowed to us. I wouldn't
trade all of this for the momentary relief for my cock."

"Why not? You wouldn't have thought twice about
doing it to Hera and you were married to her for eons. Me?
I'm just a new piece of ass on the Lane." Abstinence knew
her words were harsh, but she had to either get through to
him, or make him leave. "Don't try to say you have feelings
for me, because even if you do, this can never work between
us. You have to eat and I won't tolerate infidelity. Shitty of
me, I know, when I can't fill that need. But that's just how I
feel."

"I don't simply *have feelings* for you. I love you."

"You're cruel." The tears slipped down her cheeks one at
a time, even they were not to be indulged in.

He moved around the island and took her into his arms.
"Don't cry. Please don't cry."

She pushed him away. "Don't touch me softly, or say
these things to me. I almost believe you and we both know
how this will end."

"I won't deny there are some challenges, Abi."

"My name is *Merry*."

"Merry," he tested it on his tongue and smiled. "You
know you love me too. Otherwise, you wouldn't have tried
to teach me those lessons."

"You read too much into me doing my job." She turned
away from him, from his warmth and the promise of his
embrace. It was all she could ever have and he was offering
it to her for the taking. Such pretty lies and poison
promises.

"I still felt your desire for me even when I was fat, selfish, and disgusting."

"Because I desire your body doesn't mean I want you as a man." She hated how he brought her dirty secrets to light. Abstinence would rather he didn't know these things, let alone speak of them.

"Good thing too, I'm a god. Not a man."

"You're a sex junkie."

"I am," he admitted as he stepped closer to her and ghosted his fingertips down the side of her cheek. "But I don't want my hit from any other goddess."

"And how long will that last, if I agree? A few pretty days and then I'll cave, I'll ask you to make love to me, because I'll believe everything you say. But you won't make love to me, you'll fuck me and that will be end of both us and me."

Zeus sagged against her with sorrow. "What do I have to do to earn your trust? Give me your gift, Abstinence. Not the one between your thighs, but the kiss of your power again on my brow."

She spun to face him and found herself in his arms, just as she'd feared. They were so strong, so sure and the earnest need in his eyes made her want to believe anything he said to her. His wicked tongue painted pictures of her deepest desires and then told her they were within reach.

He descended as if he were going to kiss her, her eyes fluttered closed and Abstinence knew fear, but she couldn't stop this now if she tried. But moments passed and the deadly brush of his mouth on hers never came. She opened her eyes and his lips were only the breath of a secret away from hers.

Electric lust shot through her and she twined her arms around his neck. His touch at her waist burned through her shirt and scalded her skin. His irises darkened as he sensed her lust and it fed him. The intimacy of the energy exchange was like dumping gasoline on an open flame.

"This is enough for me. I don't need anything else but what's in this space of breath between us. Do you feel it? Can you taste it, Merry?"

Hearing her name, her true name, from his lips was like a forbidden caress. Everything he said, everything he did, it was as if it had all been designed to make her lust. Perhaps it had been a survival tool given to the god at inception.

"This is what I need. Will you give it freely?" he asked her.

She could almost taste the wine on his lips and she wanted him to kiss her now more than she wanted anything else. Even her next breath. Abstinence thought of her sister and her children and the selfish part of her thought that maybe, just maybe, her sister had had enough of the bounty of the universe. Why should it always be Merry who sacrifices? She rose up on tiptoe to close that space, but Zeus retreated as far as she advanced. He held her still.

"No, I won't let you do that. Not until you believe what I feel for you is real."

"Why? I know you didn't simply wake up a new god having learned your lesson."

"Why not?" His golden brows arched in consternation.

"It doesn't work that way."

"Maybe with mortals it doesn't."

"With anyone." Even though she knew better, she still wanted to believe him.

"There was a goddess who cared enough about me to open my eyes to the kind of god I was. I didn't like what I saw when I looked at myself, but I admired what I saw when I looked at you."

"And wanted to have it for your own. You already told me you were trying to get between my *bony* thighs," she drawled.

"It isn't even about that anymore, Merry. I saw your willing sacrifice for those you love, the uphill battle you had with me, but caved not because you didn't want to do it, but because you thought maybe it would do *me* more harm than good. Maybe it would have, but it would have been better for you. But you didn't see it that way. You're like no one I've ever met before."

"Only because you've never cared to really know the people around you. Look at your brother. He's noble and good, but you don't see it."

"I do see it. Now, because you showed me. You make me a better god, Merry. And I find that when you look at me, there's a light in your eyes I've never seen from another. I'd do anything to keep that light shining there. Anything. Even deny myself what I want."

"Are you capable of denying us both for my own good?" Her lips parted in anticipation.

"Yes. I can do anything to keep you safe."

"You say that now. But what about in a hundred years when you've not had intercourse with anything but your hand? Can you really live eternity that way without hating me?" The look of horror on his face told her everything she needed to know. "See, you can't. And I understand."

"I love you. I'll wait to be with you, but if you think in a hundred years you won't believe it by then, maybe that light I thought I saw in your eyes, that belief I felt you had in me for the god I could be, maybe I was mistaken."

He was saying all of the right things, but she was so

afraid. Afraid to really let herself love him, to let herself believe in him and the strength of her power. Abstaining had taught him so much already, unless he was only spewing a line, but his sincerity was sharp like a knife.

Zeus let go of her and finished laying out the lasagna in the pan and shoved it in the oven. She was struck by the mundane nature of the task, but it seemed to be laden with sorrow somehow.

Merry—for she was Merry now and not her office—she hated the pain on his face. She wanted to soothe him, to ease his burden.

"You know, if you cook while having high emotions, the food will taste of them. Nothing I ever made when I was upset ever tasted worth a damn."

He pursed his lips. "It will be fine. Leave it in for an hour. I left more mozzarella and parmesan in the fridge to put on top when it's done."

Zeus walked away.

Wait, what the hell? Where was he going? Was he *leaving*? She'd gotten exactly what she wanted. He was leaving her alone. She knew by the way he'd spoken he wouldn't be back.

The thought of never seeing him in her kitchen again, never laughing with him, or sighing with him over Buffy reruns, or any of the other things they'd come to do together left her with a great, empty chasm in her heart.

She loved the way he held her hand, the way his proximity warmed her to the core and even the way she yearned for him when she knew she couldn't have him. He was leaving and he'd never come back. It was best that she let all of those things be lost to places darker than memory.

And at last, when it was all said and done, she couldn't do it. She couldn't say goodbye.

Merry darted to the door and it was already halfway closed. "Stay!"

For one horrible moment, she didn't think he'd hear her, or if he did, he didn't care. His hand was still on the outside of the doorknob. This was the only time he'd ever used the damn door. "Please."

The door creaked open and Zeus stood in the doorway, his presence filling the entryway. "You don't want me, Merry."

"I do!" she cried and reached for him.

He pulled out of her grasp. "No, you don't. Not like you need to for this to work. You don't trust me and it's not that I mind earning your trust. I've promised I would, it's that you won't let me. You speak in terms of hundreds of years. If you don't trust someone after that long, you never will and that's not fair to either of us. I know I'm a work in progress. As much as it galls me to say it, I've realized I'm not perfect. But if you can't love me the way I love you..." He shrugged and turned to go.

"I'm afraid," she blurted.

"Who isn't? This love shit is scary. I've never told anyone I loved them before. Not even Hera when I asked her to be my wife." He stepped down the stairs. He was still leaving!

"You can stay the night."

"Not good enough."

"You said I taught you things. Maybe you can teach me too," Merry said desperately.

Zeus turned and came back just inside the door. "I'm listening."

"I'm willing to learn to trust you." The words fell off her tongue like lead weights, but after she said them, she wasn't so afraid.

"That's all I was asking for. I know I don't deserve it yet. I hurt you, caused you harm. I don't expect to be immediately forgiven. Only that it's possible."

It seemed Zeus really had learned some sort of lesson, if all of this were real. His words were so pretty, but could it be something that would sustain them? Merry realized then that she didn't need that answer right now and to demand it wasn't fair because it wasn't something either of them could answer. They'd have to jump off that mountain ledge together. He'd jumped already and was tugging on her ankle, but she refused to let go of the rope. That's why it was called "falling in love". One had to let go and fall.

She'd been tripped and pushed, but maybe it would be okay to enjoy the view on the way down. Then she let go with both hands. "I love you."

Merry kissed him with all of the passion she had in her heart.

While later, she'd say she got a little dizzy, it was from the shared intensity of their kiss and not because she was about to die. Although, the lasagna burned and took half her kitchen with it, but they were too busy kissing to notice.

PERSEPHONE

Persephone was cold. She couldn't get warm. Thanatos had plied her with warm fig cakes and wrapped her in down blankets—he'd lit a blaze in the fireplace and given her hot cocoa. Her hands were shaking too violently to hold the mug.

But none of those things offered the heat she craved. She wanted Thanatos to hold her.

She'd always heard Death was cold, his fingers clammy

and kiss frigid and sharp like an icicle dagger. But he was none of those things. His flesh ignited hers with his heat, his hands strong and warm, and his kiss—Sweet Elysium, his kiss was like nothing else she'd ever experienced.

Part of her said this was wrong; she wasn't the only one vulnerable. He was too because he'd made the mistake of loving her. Persephone knew she wasn't worthy of him. She was selfish and vain; she and Hades had been a good match. He'd seen what he'd wanted and he'd taken it, kidnapping her and keeping her from the topside... Yet, somehow, he'd grown. He'd changed.

Then there was the part of her that had only now matured and she ached with the need to be touched. Persephone could see the way Thanatos looked at her, the way his eyes were drawn to the plunging neckline of her Grecian gown, the swells of her breasts as she breathed. He wanted to touch her as badly as she wanted to be touched.

"Still cold, Seph?" He tossed more wood into the fireplace and the flames leapt high.

The way the orange firelight played over his ethereal features entranced her. Almost as if he wasn't Death at all, but the Dawn. And maybe he was. The Dawn was the beginning of things emerging out of the dark.

"I can't get warm. I suppose it's my just desserts for freezing all of Olympus with my emotional vomit." She gave an uncomfortable laugh and shivered.

"You were upset. It was a reasonable reaction. It's not like you killed anyone." Thanatos grinned.

"Thank you," she blurted.

"For what?"

"For everything? For coming when I called you." She bit her lip hesitantly. "For caring about me."

"Seph," he began.

"For asking Hades to take me because you'd rather see me with him than dead of a foolish broken heart. For being patient with me even when what I've done hurts you. For treating me like a goddess instead of a porcelain doll. Everything, Thanatos."

"That's what friends are for."

It sounded as if it had almost killed him to repeat those words to her and oddly enough, it hit her the same way. She didn't like it. "I think we've already crossed the friend line, haven't we? Eros is my friend, my very best friend and he's never had his face in my nether bits." She blushed.

"That's because two virgins don't know what goes where," he teased.

Her face flushed a brighter crimson. "No."

"Well, why hasn't he then?" Thanatos smirked.

"He doesn't make me feel the way you do," she confessed and Persephone felt the tension in the room like a lead weight.

"And how do I make you feel that's so different?" He took off his trench coat and hung it carefully over the back of the chair.

Persephone liked to watch him move, the way the light played on his skin and the sheer grace with which his hard muscles all worked together. She liked the outline of his biceps in his t-shirt, the planes of his broad shoulders and the curve of his back. Persephone loved how his hair looked like moonlight—it was exactly like his mother's, but there was nothing feminine about it on him.

He sat down and tugged off his boots. "You don't know or you don't want to tell me?"

"What? Oh." She'd been utterly distracted simply watching him. "I'm embarrassed to tell you."

"Persephone," he said and made it a point to look at her.

"After a god has been ears deep in your *nether bits* as you've described them, and you've ridden his face like a pony, nothing should ever be a taboo discussion between you. If you don't want to tell me, it's okay."

Persephone blushed so hard she thought her face was going to explode. Memories of that night came flooding back to her and she licked her lips as desire flooded her. Her gaze was immediately drawn to his mouth and all of the delicious things it could do to her. She realized she was staring and the long moment that was all the heavier for the silence. She took a shaky breath, as if something so banal could ever wipe out the flame of white-hot desire for him. But she had to say this, lust or no, embarrassed or no. He deserved to hear it.

"I never saw you until you kissed me. What I mean is I never really *looked* at you."

He waited patiently for her continue, no judgment on his face and no other emotion either. He was Death in that moment and yet he was not. It was a curious melding and she was intrigued. Most gods would already be wound up by what she'd said, done listening with a retort on their tongues. Not Thanatos. He listened to her—heard what she had to say before he started thinking of his own reply. She imagined he'd been a solemn little boy and wondered what he'd been like then. Nyx had kept him away from the other godlings until he was old enough to control his power. He must have been so alone. The thought twisted her heart.

"But when you kissed me, it wasn't supposed to be something real."

"What do you mean by real?" he asked evenly. Still, there was no judgment on his face, no reaction to her but wanting the meaning beneath her words before he responded.

Persephone looked into the crackling flames of the fire, watching them dance instead of looking at him. It had been easier to speak of such things when she'd been close to orgasm and the stark, blunt force of her words had been used as a tool. This was a baring of her heart and her soul, of her deepest desires. Ones she'd only now come to face.

"It wasn't supposed to make my skin feel like it was on fire. It wasn't supposed to keep burning after you'd stopped. The memory of it wasn't supposed to live in a whisper and haunt me with fantasies of all the other things that could happen between us." She forced herself to look at him so he could see the truth of it in her eyes. "If you wanted them."

This time, it was Thanatos who couldn't look at her. With his elbows propped on his knees, he leaned in to the bowl of his hands before he pushed his hand through his hair. "Gods, Persephone. You scare the shit out of me."

His reaction wasn't what she'd expected. "I don't understand. Tell me what I'm doing wrong," she pleaded. Should she not have told him how he made her feel?

He focused on her. "You're offering me almost everything I want, Persephone."

"Almost? Where have I fallen short?" She didn't ask this as a precursor to an argument, she wanted to know what he thought was lacking and if she could fix it, she would. Persephone wanted to please him.

"You don't love me, Seph. You're in love with Hades." He spoke as if this were an irrefutable fact.

"What happened to simply taking what I offered?" she asked quietly.

"Because I'm not that kind of god anymore." He shrugged as if this revelation had only hit him in the last few moments. "I used to be, but I want someone I can bring home to my mother. I want my own godlings. I want a family, a life. Tail is easy to score—even tail as lovely as yours."

"How do you know I don't want those things?" she questioned, ignoring the slap to her feminine charms, and biting down on the core of what he'd said.

"You don't want them with *me*." He leaned back in the chair, so sure of the truth in his words.

The way he said it tore at her. As if there were no way she could possibly want a future with him. Images of what their godlings would look like slammed into her hard and fast. She wondered what it would feel like to be round with his young and her power sang at the thought of bringing forth life. She'd never thought of this with Hades, it had never occurred to her. But the idea of that part of Thanatos growing inside of her filled her with joy.

"You never asked me. How do you know? You and Hades both keep making choices for me. I can choose what I want for myself."

"Obviously, you can't be trusted," he said lightly, an attempt to ease the tension. "You chose to go back to Hades because you loved him. Now, you're playing at wanting a relationship with me while your heart is full of another god. You don't know what you want. Have you tried being alone? Living with yourself?"

"I'm not playing at anything. I've lived with myself for a long time, Thanatos. And I do love Hades, I always will. Love, true and honest love, it doesn't ever leave you. If you love someone, it stays with you for all the days of your life. But that doesn't mean I don't have feelings for you."

"I call bullshit, Persephone." His face was a mask of stone.

"What do you mean?" She didn't understand. He didn't believe her?

"Only hours ago you were ready to die—,"

"No!" she cut him off. He didn't understand at all. "I wasn't. I called Death because I wanted *you*. I wasn't going anywhere. I hurt, yes. And I still do. But when I'm in your arms, the whole universe falls away and there's nothing but me and you. Isn't that a place to start?"

He moved to the bed and took her hand gently. "And when you tire of me and realize I'm no replacement for Hades, what then, Seph? You leave me broken and begging for some surcease of sorrow?"

"You speak so eloquently of suffering." It was hard to keep the condemnation out of her voice, but she didn't want to fight with him, she wanted him to understand what she was feeling. The truth of what it was and the truth of what it would be.

"I know her well."

"Not your own you don't. You've inured yourself to the grief of the world. Is that why you're so afraid of having any of your own?" Persephone asked while she twined her fingers through his to take the sting out of her words.

"I'm not afraid, I'm pragmatic." He looked defeated.

"Sometimes, they're one and the same. Look at the mortals' lives. It would be pragmatic for them to never love because you are always there, Thanatos. You take everyone. To love for them is to lose and to suffer. Yet, they continue to do it without reservation. You asked me what I would do if I only had one day left to live—,"

"I said a week."

"Whatever. Don't try to change the subject. If I knew my time was limited, you'd asked me what I would do. I'm ready to answer you." A feeling of warmth welled inside of her like a hot spring and her hands finally stopped shaking. "I would spend it with you, Thanatos."

"You say that now." He didn't speak coldly, but there was no warmth in his words either.

"Yes, I do. But you look for the truth of it. Death and all things that are his belong to you too. So look at me, use your power and look into me and see the truth of it." She took his other hand and opened herself to the harsh gaze of Death.

And he looked.

The power of Death fell over him in a black shroud and the fire dwindled to nothing—the last ember frozen in his presence. The vast abyss of the dark filled his eyes and the anti-light radiated from him as the winter of all living things filled the room. He stared into her and looked for the end of her eternity.

"Persephone." His voice had changed; it reverberated through her and settled into the hollow places in her bones. "Peer back in to the arctic dark and speak again of things warm and sacred."

If she'd been a lesser creature, that voice would have shattered her bones from the inside out instead of creeping over them in a dark caress. Her skin would have turned to papyrus and the rest of her body would have met its decay in a swift embrace, but she was not a lesser creature. Persephone was the next Goddess of Spring. Life pulsed through her sure and strong. She hadn't let go of his hands, but she gripped them tighter. Persephone stared back into the dark as he'd demanded, but she didn't fear the things hiding in the shadows, or wonder what was looking back at her. She knew what was looking at her and it was the god she...*loved*.

How could she have fallen in love with him? Persephone knew she could love him, a god like Thanatos was easy to love, but her heart had been so full of Hades. Maybe he was right, maybe she just afraid to be alone and she'd convinced herself to love him. She didn't want to be alone.

No, that wasn't correct. She didn't want to be alone without *him*. Without Thanatos. Without Death. *This* being before her, this incarnation of the end of all things, she loved him too—accepted him for what he was. He was so utterly beautiful in all his forms.

Eros had told her a heart chooses not where it loves. He'd also told her that it was possible to love more than person at once, possible to be *in love* with more than person at once as long she loved them both more than herself.

And she did love them both more than herself, but she wasn't in love with both of them.

In that moment as she drifted into shadow with her heart and soul open to his view and her own, she realized her love for Hades hadn't been what she thought it was. It was her dependence on him as a protector and he'd known it. Seeing him with Hera had shattered the foundations of her world—of what she believed was safe. He'd forced her to stand on her own.

Something she could do now, with or without Thanatos. She wasn't falling into his arms to hope he'd catch her and hold her up. She wanted to hold him up too. She wanted to be the one he presented to his mother, the one with whom he shared his burdens and the one who made the world burn away when he was in her arms.

"Yes, Thanatos. If I could choose where I would take my last breath, it would be with you." She spoke clearly, with the surety of a goddess who would do anything for the god she loved.

He leaned in closer to her and she knew he was going to kiss her. Persephone wanted his mouth on hers no matter if his lips were the great and terrible scimitar of Death, or if he were simply Thanatos.

His kiss was hot and hungry, an incongruity with his chilled demeanor and icy appearance. She surrendered to his embrace. Her gown slid off her shoulders and bared her to him; the material bunched in his fists.

There was a flutter of fear of the unknown, but not enough to tell him to stop. Persephone wanted this with him, only him. She'd been stupid to think she could let him touch her so intimately and it wouldn't mean anything more to either of them—further, she'd been stupid to think she wanted it that way.

Persephone pushed her hands beneath his shirt, her palms explored his hard body and she delighted in each touch; every ripple of muscle and new spanse of heated flesh beneath her fingertips.

His lips were a reverent tribute on the hollow of her throat and he cupped her breast as he bent to taste the pink bud of her nipple. She cried out when he took her into his hot mouth.

"Would you be loved by Death?"

"Yes," she said, breathless.

He runched her dress around her waist and she didn't hesitate to reach between them to the waist of his black fatigues. She pushed them down his hips. When he lay naked between her thighs, his cock poised at her entrance, the chill left the room and Death's power faded back inside the god on top of her. He smoothed his hand over her brow and studied her with tenderness for a long moment.

"I wasn't going to ask you, I hate how it sounds. But I have to know, are you sure you want this? With me?" His tone promised there would be no recriminations, no anger if she said no. "I want forever, Seph."

This time, she could answer the question. She didn't need him to take away her culpability, to push her beyond the edges of desire and take what he wanted so she could blame him for it later. Persephone wasn't afraid. This was what she wanted and she was going to take it.

She wrapped her legs around his waist and ghosted her thumb over his bottom lip and then pulled him down to her. "Yes, Thanatos. We'll belong to each other forever." Persephone brushed her lips over his. "Yes," she said again.

Arching up to meet his thrust as he pushed into her, Persephone was surprised there was only a little pain. A brief burn that was over as quickly as it had sparked. At first it was a foreign feeling, another's body inside of her own, but then it was perfect. Their bodies working in tandem to bring each other to the height of pleasure.

He froze when he sank fully inside of her and groaned softly, it was obviously a kind of pain to hold his body still. Persephone instinctively rolled her hips against him and urged him on. Thanatos moved experimentally, his length and breadth stretched her almost beyond endurance, but the more he touched her, weaving his spell of desire, the more she wanted. Even now, with his cock inside her, she couldn't get close enough to him.

Persephone clung to his shoulders and he braced her bottom with his forearm and tilted the angle of her hips so he penetrated deep. She cried out and threw her head back as he hit the core of her. He answered her cry with one of pure male satisfaction.

"Please," she begged, but she wasn't sure what she was begging for. This didn't feel anything like the times when she'd brought herself off, or when his mouth had been on her clit and made her scream. This was something different; if Persephone didn't find the edge soon she'd shatter.

But then she shattered anyway.

It felt like she was breaking apart, but he was making her whole again. Then the bliss hit, different than the other times, but just as good. He took her mouth to silence her cries and they rode the waves of ecstasy together.

As they crashed back down to Olympus, Persephone was struck again by how right this was between them. For better or worse, she belonged to Thanatos forever.

"I love you," she whispered into his ear.

He propped himself up on his elbow and looked down at her with so much tenderness it made her ache. "You're just saying that because I'm good between the sheets."

Her jaw dropped, but snapped shut when Thanatos gave her a wry grin and kissed her forehead. "I love you too, Persephone."

"How much do you love me?" she asked, giving him a secret smile of her own.

"Oh, here's the catch, huh?" He laughed. "What is it you want, goddess of my heart?"

"Can we do that again?" she asked shyly.

He proceeded to show her just how many times they could, in fact, do that again.

CHAPTER
TWENTY-FIVE

NYX

Nyx's temple shook as if the Furies themselves were rattling the foundation.

It wasn't because she'd woken up fat, although she had. Her ankles were roughly the size of grapefruits and her breasts—they'd always been nice—but they'd ballooned into prize-winning watermelons. And her ass, that didn't even bear thinking about. It probably looked like two pumpkins that had been welded together. But no, none of these were why her temple rattled.

Neither was it because she felt like she was going to hurl, even though Nyx was sure she was going to blow Technicolor chunks all over the place like a sick mash-up of *The Exorcist* and *Design on a Dime*. It wasn't even because her...whatever he was—Apollo—was sleeping soundly on the couch while she fussed, faunched, and made a general ruckus.

It was because for all intents and purposes, Nyx was in labor.

A situation she found to be completely untenable because her gestation should have been nine years. The irony of it smacked her in the face like a wet newspaper. She'd been bitching about being pregnant for so long and now, she wasn't going to be.

So much for she and Apollo "getting to know each other" before they became parents. What the hell were they going to do? No, better yet, what was she going to do? She hadn't even chosen a goddess to attend the birth.

Another pain ripped through her and Nyx had to grab the rail on the stairs to catch her breath. Nyx, the Goddess of Night and badass titan was ready to cry. She hadn't even had a chance to read *What to Expect When You're Expecting*. Supposedly, there were even drugs that made the pain go away. She wasn't even going to get to try those.

Her stomach heaved to one side and then dropped suddenly.

"Oh shit," she whispered.

"Huh, what's...oh my gods. Nyx?" Apollo said as he blinked stupidly.

"Yeah, so much for getting to know each other, huh?"

"I thought you said—"

"I know what I said!" she snapped.

"What do you want me to do? Have you chosen a goddess to help you?" Apollo leapt into action, literally. He was immediately in front of her, his hand making soothing circles on her back and he was talking softly in her ear.

He was obviously a pro.

Asshole.

Nyx sighed. She knew logically he wasn't an asshole for having fathered children before this one. He wasn't even an asshole for fathering this one. She'd lain down with him of her own free will. He was being supportive and trying to comfort her. She had no reason to be angry with him. Nyx was usually very logical, but at this moment, she felt positively certifiable and logic could take a flying fuck at a rolling Cyclops.

She'd wanted to ask Athena, but it didn't seem appropriate given the recent nature of their interactions. She didn't know what to do. Nyx wanted this to all go away, she wanted it to be handled for her and she wanted the pain to stop.

"How about I call Artemis? Childbirth is among her powers."

Sweet Tartarus and Hell on a barge. Artemis was too dizzy to help her do anything. Another stabbing pain ravaged her and fluid gushed from between her thighs. Nyx found herself nodding along before she knew what she was doing.

"Artemis!" he called.

"Brother, I hear and I—shit," Artemis exclaimed as she manifested. "Oh, this is nice. What the hell? Why didn't you tell me?"

"This is a recent development."

"We thought we had nine years," Nyx groaned.

Artemis put a hand on Nyx's extended belly and she smiled. "She's so strong." Then Artemis frowned. "She's a titan."

"What?" Nyx and Apollo said at the same time.

"That's why she grew so quickly. She will have dominion over Nothing."

"I don't understand," Nyx managed as she grabbed her midsection again and Apollo led her to the couch.

"She is an anti-god. Her realm will be the Abyss, the nowhere and nothing that exists in darkness of the outer reaches of the mind of gods and men. Nightmares and the things there that are rotted and fetid. I'm sorry."

"Why are you sorry?" Apollo asked.

Nyx answered for her. "She won't help Ephialtes be born."

"You *will*," Apollo said in a dangerous tone.

"I won't, brother. I can't." Artemis shook her head. "She could destroy us all. Imagine living in an eternal nightmare because you didn't feed her on time or her diaper is wet. Think of all the horrors she could make real on only her whim. I just can't."

"This is my daughter. Your niece."

Tears slipped down Artemis' cheeks. "I know. And it breaks my heart." She made a gesture before she disappeared and Nyx's labor pains stopped and so did the shaking of the temple.

"What has she done?" Apollo demanded when he saw Nyx's body go slack with defeat.

"She stopped my labor."

"Will she die?" Apollo asked in a strained voice, the fear written on his face.

"Yes." Nyx felt despair tighten around her heart.

"Her name, I didn't know you'd chosen," Apollo whispered.

"I didn't either until then. She knows who she is. She must have whispered it to me." Nyx rubbed her belly again and then she looked at Apollo with renewed purpose. "I'm not letting my baby die. I've managed Death, I can do Nightmares too."

"*We* can." Apollo took her hand. "Tell me how."

"Your son is the God of Medicine. Call him." Nyx sent soothing thoughts to the new life inside of her. She promised her many things, if only she'd hold on. Her little

Ephie. Nyx was flooded by the warmth of love and implicit trust that came from her. No child who could feel those pure feelings would willfully or wantonly unleash all of that darkness. Ephie was going to be a gatekeeper, like Hades. Exposed to the dark, able to command it, but not evil.

"And Thanatos."

"How about we see if he shows up on his own?" she said softly. If things went poorly, he would be there, called by his duty. She loved her son dearly, but prayed she wouldn't see him during the ordeal.

"I want our family, Nyx." His golden skin had gone ashen and pale.

"I do too."

Then Nyx screamed and darkness descended like a plague over Olympus. All of the light was gone, not even the spark of a candle could be seen. Nothing, but the soft glow that haloed Apollo—the manifestation of his power.

"Nyx?" he questioned.

But she barely heard him. All she was aware of was the pain. Nyx felt as if she'd been slammed into an iron maiden, sharp spikes pierced her everywhere. She could feel Ephie's will to live and Nyx fed it with her own power. After all, where did Nightmares rest, but in the arms of the Night?

She rallied her strength, called her power. When even the dark, unnamable things cast their own shadow in the pitch she'd wrought like a shroud—Nyx willed her child to come forth. Artemis had cursed her to prevent natural labor, but she could do nothing about unnatural things.

Nyx knew if she had to demand this infant tear her apart to get out, she'd do it. She would have laughed at herself had she not felt like that was exactly what Ephie was doing. Only weeks ago, she'd been sure she didn't even want a child and now, she'd give up her life to make sure this one took her first breath.

If she lived through this, she and Apollo were going to have to discuss birth control. If he was serious about commitment, he could damn well get a vasectomy. Suddenly, that didn't matter. The knowledge came to her there would be no more after Ephie, thanks to Artemis' curse.

Damn her. Nyx didn't want more children, but she disliked having the choice taken from her. She understood why Artemis had done what she did, but Nyx was pretty sure as soon as Ephie was born, she was going to smite the bitch. Where did she, a goddess, get off making that kind of choice for a titan? How dare she, this godling's godling, think to use her power against Nyx.

Her rage boiled and erupted from her in thick tendrils of black tar that smothered everything in its wake. It poured from her mouth, her eyes and her fingertips as Night was brought to down to bear on the world of immortals.

The pain she'd felt was a distant memory as he power coursed through her and she became one with the darkness. Existence fell away like a dream when crushed beneath the weight of shadow.

There were twin beams of light that seemed to be immune to her strength and she smote them with the eternal dark where Death was born. The lights flickered like fireflies and the bleak abyss choked them into silence, but then blazed to brilliant light.

One became the pure silvery benediction of the moon smiling down upon her brow, her pale fingers easing the bloodlust and madness. The other became the pure fire of the sun whose warm light didn't burn, but kissed her tenderly—held her gently.

The omniscient dark dwindled back to the source inside of Nyx and she realized it wasn't the sun and moon at all, but Apollo and Artemis.

The Goddess of the Moon and the Hunt was smiling down at her lovingly, her hands cool and soothing like the water of a pure spring over her forehead.

"Are you back with us, Nyx?" Artemis asked kindly, her hands still working their magic.

"What happened? Why did you come back" Nyx demanded.

"I never left. Your child dying was what you feared most. A close second was that no one would be here to help you. Perfectly natural fears for a mother, but your fear for her was so strong that Ephie's power manifested," Artemis answered.

"What have I done?" Feeling came back to Nyx's fingers and she realized Apollo was still holding her hand.

"Nothing we couldn't withstand. We're fine, love. One more push and our daughter will be here. One more," Apollo urged gently.

Nyx didn't know what was real and what wasn't. She was afraid and the darkness came again, wrapped itself around her like armor. Apollo didn't even flinch. Perhaps whatever she'd done hadn't been so bad.

Lightning and thunder struck just as Nyx pushed Ephie into the world. The child was strangely silent and Nyx feared the worst.

"Let me see her!" she demanded.

"What in the name of Tartarus have you done!" Zeus thundered from the doorway.

Nyx looked up to see the King of Gods standing alone with his fury, charred handprints burned into place around his neck where someone or something had tried to strangle him. But she couldn't care about that. All that mattered was Ephie.

Artemis was still smiling. She handed the strangely silent baby to Nyx who took her eagerly and put her to her breast. The child latched on and drank, looking up into her mother's eyes as she did.

Nyx felt a surge of love and she counted Ephie's fingers and toes to make sure she only had ten of each—no tentacles, no hooves. The baby's hair was dark and downy, already down to her shoulders. Her bright eyes were the gray of a sky before a storm. Her skin was pale and almost silver, just like Hypnos and Thanatos had been. Only where their fingernails were a dark shade of blue, Ephie's were gold. She was beautiful.

"I'm still waiting for an answer," Zeus thundered.

"She had a baby, Dad. Duh, what's it look like?" Artemis snorted, but then grinned. "I'm an Auntie!" She looked thoughtful before adding, "Again."

"You slept with my *son*?" Zeus thundered.

"Don't tell me you..." Apollo started, but trailed off. He couldn't find the words to finish.

Nyx raised a brow. "Listen here, buddy. I just pushed out a bowling ball through something the size of a lemon and you want to make an issue about who I've slept with?" she growled.

"No. NO! I'd never do that." Apollo shook his head adamantly. Because he knew what was good for him. Even though the look on his face said he was displeased by this development.

"She's Hera's best friend. Of course she didn't sleep with Dad. Another *duh*." She looked at Nyx. "Did they both have a bowl of stupid for breakfast today instead of ambrosia?"

"I don't know, but it's making me *angry*," Nyx warned.

"And obviously, we won't like you when you're angry." Artemis grinned.

"So you weren't trying to kill me?" Zeus asked, unsure of what had just happened.

"If I were trying to kill you, you'd be dead," Nyx answered honestly. And right then, the idea had merit. He'd made it a point to kill titans and Ephie was a titan. She bared her teeth involuntarily.

"Then explain this!" He pointed to the marks around his neck.

"You're still breathing aren't you?" she growled.

Zeus raised a thunderbolt, but Apollo and Artemis both stepped in front of her.

"Would you really smite my mate and my daughter?" Apollo asked in a measured tone, all the more dangerous for the calm veneer it cast over violent waters.

"I won't tolerate this kind of disrespect. Not from my own children." He raised the thunderbolt higher.

Ephie wailed and the darkness returned with more force than anything Nyx had conjured. She crooned to the baby and soothed her.

"Your fears call her power, Dad. You fear we've rebelled against you and we have. It's what children do. Get over it." Artemis shrugged. She took Ephie from Nyx and shoved her at Zeus. He almost tripped trying to get away from her. "She's a baby, not a cootie. Come here and hold your grand-daughter."

Zeus wouldn't have, but Abstinence poked her head in the door behind him. "What are you doing over—is that a baby? Oh my goodness!"

"You might as well come in too," Nyx said as she had

Apollo fluff the pillows behind her on the couch. Fuck. Her couch was ruined.

"Do you mean to tell me that's your granddaughter and you're not going to hold her? You ass." Abstinence shoved him unmercifully toward the squalling bundle.

"She doesn't like me," Zeus said.

"No one likes you. Hold her!" Abstinence demanded.

This was the first Nyx had seen of the new goddess and she had to say, she liked what she saw.

"You like me," Zeus said with his trademarked smirk.

"Not right now I don't." She held up her hand. "Don't even start. I don't care if Nyx did try to choke you. She was in labor. She gets a free pass."

"Fine." Zeus was sullen, but the look on his face changed when he realized the titan had been shoved into his arms. He held her carefully, as if she were some specimen of bug he hadn't seen before.

Nyx was hit with another vision, and she didn't know if it was real or not, but it was of Ephie bouncing on Zeus' knee in a room with black and purple tulle. She cooed happily while cramming the tip of a thunderbolt in her mouth while he bounced her.

So it came as no surprise to Nyx when he cradled her close and smiled. Ephie stopped crying.

"You'd think you'd never held a baby before," Apollo said sharply.

"I haven't. Most of my children weren't born like this. They weren't babies," Zeus whispered. "I think I like these things."

"Don't get too used to them. You're not having any off of this goddess," Abstinence was quick to add while she handed the baby back to Nyx.

Zeus gave her a look that said they would certainly see about that.

"Come on now, let's leave them alone." She dragged the King of the Gods out of the temple behind her.

"She's really something," Artemis stated.

"She is, indeed. I'm still not telling him she's a titan. Not until she's old enough to defend herself," Nyx said.

"Good. I don't want him to know," Apollo said. "Can I see my daughter now?" He gathered Ephie to him.

"I'm going to go too." Artemis turned to leave and that was when Nyx saw the same burned lines around her neck that Zeus had.

"Artemis!" Nyx cried. "Did I do that?"

"Oh." She blushed and put her hand to her neck. "It's nothing. It will heal. Battle scars from bringing my niece into the world. I'm proud of them."

"I'm sorry," Nyx said. Those words felt inadequate to express everything she was feeling, but dizzy Artemis wasn't so dizzy after all. She seemed to know. Artemis bent to embrace her.

"I meant it when I said it's okay. I'd be angry too if I thought someone was trying to keep my child from being born. Let me be Goddessmother with Hera, and we'll call it good." She grinned.

Nyx was humbled. "I'd be honored for you to be Goddessmother. Ephie couldn't ask for better." She felt herself get teary. "Damn."

"I know. I love you too, Nyx." Artemis winked and disappeared.

"Did I hurt you as well?" she asked when Apollo slipped in behind her on the couch and put Ephie into her arms.

"All that matters is that Ephie was born. That must have been some nightmare."

"I thought Artemis said she wouldn't help and she cursed my labor to stop so Ephie would die."

"She'd never do that."

"She cried about it, but she did it." Nyx wasn't going to cry, she refused. "It wasn't all bad, though."

"No?" he asked quietly and waited for her to continue.

"You said you wanted our family."

"That part was real. When you passed out, Artemis told me to talk to you. I do want our family, Nyx. If you'll have me."

"Was that something like a proposal?"

"As close as I could come without you kicking me," he replied.

"I wouldn't kick you." She laughed.

"Don't lie. You didn't even want to call our first and only date a date."

"Why did it have to be a date?" Nyx still didn't understand why he was so obsessed with labeling things.

"Why not?"

She snorted and snuggled against him. "Look where we are now."

"I wouldn't want to be anywhere else." He kissed the top of her head.

In that moment, she knew she didn't want to be anywhere else either. One date hadn't killed her, but she was never going on another one. She got it perfect the first time.

"Me either," she answered so quietly she didn't know if he'd heard her.

"Thank you for our daughter, Nyx. She's beautiful."

"You helped." She didn't know what else to say. *You're welcome* sounded incredibly pompous, like she miracled her there all by herself.

"I didn't do anything important. I didn't do anything a million other males couldn't do. But you, you brought life and love out of darkness. You're amazing."

"Quit that, I already said I'd have you. You don't have to sweet talk me."

"I mean every damn word," Apollo swore.

"I kind of love you," Nyx said on a sigh. As soon as it was out of her mouth, she wondered if she could shove it back inside, but it was like a Jack-in-the-Box. The bitch was out; there was no shoving it back anywhere.

"I kind of love you, too." He kissed her cheek tenderly.

Nyx's exhaustion overtook her and she dropped off to a sweet slumber not in Avoidance Nyx fashion, but sharing this quiet peace with the new additions to her family.

TWENTY-SIX

The Wedding and Happily Ever After

T he bride wore black.

Yet it was a joyous occasion. She was radiant from where she stood at the altar, her hand linked with that of her dark prince. The diamond on her finger sparkled and burned with the life of a star the Lord of the Underworld had persuaded to reside in the diamond for Hera's pleasure—an eternal burn that signified the love that burned eternal in his heart.

The groom wore purple velvet at the bride's request. Black riding pants and his knee-high Hessians like a proper fantasy hero. His raven hair still fell over his brow in the way of surly young men, but the hard lines etched in his face were gone and if the young goddesses of Olympus had found him handsome through his suffering, his appeal doubled with the wry smile that curved his sensual mouth. But that special smile, it was only for Hera. His eyes sought nothing but her, his hands nothing but her skin, and his kisses only for her lips.

The wedding wasn't the biggest surprise to the guests. It was the god who gave the bride away. Hera's father had passed into oblivion many eons past and she had no brothers or other family to take the ceremonial role in giving her keeping to another. Yet, it was fitting for Zeus to give her hand in marriage to his brother.

He stood tall and proud as he walked his ex-wife down the aisle. Zeus had nothing but warmth in his eyes for the goddess who had once belonged to him and he had nothing but goodwill in his heart when he placed Hera's hand in Hades' and stated for all present company to hear, that he did in fact, give this goddess to be married.

After the ceremony, Persephone found Hades. No words were spoken between them, but so much had been said. She hugged him tight the way a little girl would her father and the smile he had for her was the same. It had been with that little girl's heart she'd loved him, and while he dwelled in his own place in her woman's heart, her woman's love was only for Thanatos. Her smile said all the things she'd never be able to articulate the same way her splayed fingers over her rounded belly expressed the joy and peace she'd found with Death. Although, Hades already knew how happy she was, he'd given her away at her wedding.

Demeter and Eros weren't in attendance, although Aphrodite had performed the ceremony and given the couple her blessing. They were on their own honeymoon.

Nyx and Apollo were there, Hypnos had come for nanny duty. He cheated, whenever Ephie became upset, he'd put her to sleep until he could hand her off to Zeus. She liked chewing on the thunderbolts. They tickled. Apollo kept pushing her to set a date, but Nyx was still determined no one could quantify their relationship but them. Until Apollo told her that was how he wanted to quantify it and Nyx didn't have any other argument. Hera had done it again after her first marriage had been a failure, so maybe there was hope for Nyx. With a god like Apollo, she was sure there would be. She loved him more than breath, after all.

As for Abstinence and Zeus, well, neither of them had quite decided who was wearing the toga in that partnership. Everyone expected another wedding, she was now Queen of the Gods and her place was beside her King. Or so Zeus was fond of telling her.

And Fate decided that everyone lived Happily Ever After —whether they wanted to or not.

About the Author

Saranna De Wylde has always been fascinated by things better left in the dark. She wrote her first story after watching The Exorcist at a slumber party. Since then, she's published horror, romance and narrative nonfiction. Like all writers, Saranna has held a variety of jobs, from operations supervisor for an airline, to an assistant for a call girl, to a corrections officer. But like Hemingway said, "Once writing has become your major vice and greatest pleasure, only death can stop it." So she traded in her cuffs for a full-time keyboard. She loves to hear from her readers.

Keep up with releases, events and access to special content by signing up the Saranna DeWylde newsletter here: www.corvuscoraxbooks.com

Also by Saranna DeWylde

Desperate Housewives of Avalon

Desperate Housewives of Olympus: Ares

Other Series:

Margie Majors: Middle-Aged Vampire Slayer

10 Days

Fairy Godmothers Inc.

The Woolven Secret

Saranna also writes as Sara Arden, Sara Wylde, Sara Lunsford, and Sara Ravencroft.